Also by Frances McNamara

ℭℨ

The Emily Cabot Mysteries

Death at the Fair

Death at Hull House

DEATH
AT
PULLMAN

Frances McNamara

ALLIUM PRESS OF CHICAGO

Allium Press of Chicago
www.alliumpress.com

This is a work of fiction. Descriptions and
portrayals of real people, events, organizations, or
establishments are intended to provide background
for the story and are used fictitiously. Other
characters and situations are drawn from the
author's imagination and are not intended to be real.

Book/cover design and map by E. C. Victorson

Front cover image (bottom): adapted from
"The Chicago Strikes" by Frederic Remington
Harper's Weekly Magazine, July 21, 1894
Title page image: "The Strikers' Relief Headquarters
in Kensington" from *The Pullman Strike*
by Rev. William H. Carwardine, 1894

ISBN: 978-0-9840676-9-5

To my friend and editor

Emily Victorson

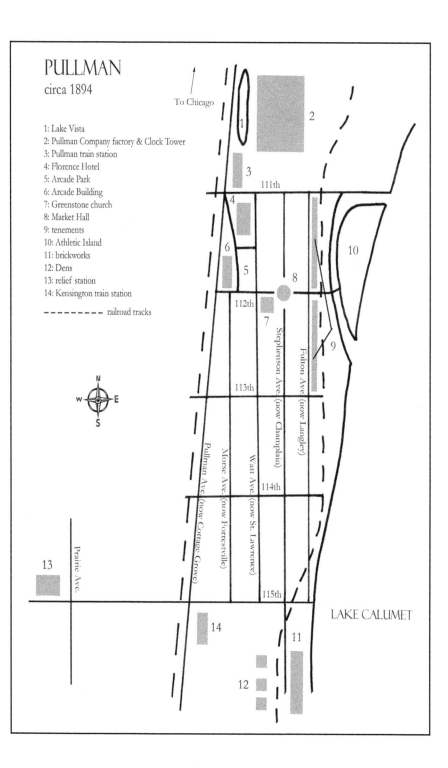

Death at Pullman

⊄

PROLOGUE

The mind tries to refuse such a sight, tries to deny it. A young man, tall and thin in frayed overalls and undershirt, shouldn't be so still, with his feet swaying an arm's length away and at the level of your face like that. I could see the worn soles and broken laces of his scuffed work boots, and above them, his bony hands with dirt ground into their creases and around his broken fingernails. Freckles stood out on his white face and his eyes were closed. One side of his head was encrusted with dried blood matted into his thick brown hair. Surely, he was too young to die—he was no older than me! Was this what we would all come to in such violent times? Was this how it ended—with the body of a poor young man swinging at the end of a rope?

ONE

I once heard a lecture given by a well-known naturalist at the University of Chicago. He described how a species of snake sheds its skin, slithering out and leaving behind a cracked and drying carcass of itself. How liberating it must feel to be free of that. I imagine the reptile emerges scratched and sore but is soon healed by the touch of the wet grass and mud. I think when we are young—as I was at the time of these events—the growth we experience is just this sort of harsh shedding. But, like the reptile, we are destined to repeat the experience—always thinking we have at last grown into our final transformation when, in fact, we are only beginning another cycle.

I came to Chicago from Boston in 1892, to be a graduate student in sociology—the year the University of Chicago opened its doors. I had exposed a murderer—albeit too late to save two victims. I had been expelled from the university, was exiled to a settlement house, and worked among the tenements of the city. There I learned the truth about my own father's death and some other truths about myself. I was at my mother's bedside when she died, and I had rejected both a fellowship and a marriage proposal. I was scheduled to return to the university in the fall, but on my own terms. Meanwhile, I had found a new home at Hull House, the famous settlement house on the west side of Chicago.

So it was on that fine spring morning in 1894 that I found myself in the town of Pullman, south of Chicago. There was the small matter of a disagreement between the owner of the Pullman Palace Car Company and the workers. The Civic Federation, a group of reformers who regularly supported progressive solutions to problems in the city, had decided to investigate the situation.

They invited my mentor, Jane Addams, to assist and she brought me along. It was exactly the type of action that made work at Hull House so much more satisfactory than the mere study of urban problems that was undertaken at the university. We did not plan to write a report. On the contrary, we wanted to recommend a fair and equitable solution. We wanted to reopen the doors of the factory and put the people back to work. But there was a rather good-looking young man who wanted to stop us. I didn't think much of his chances.

"Really, Miss Addams, I cannot consent to this deviation from the plan. A very fine luncheon has been prepared for the committee and it is waiting. Please, join us inside." Mr. William Jennings, a representative of the Pullman Company, stood ramrod straight in his dark suit with an enamel American flag pinned to the lapel. He had already taken us on a thorough tour of the Pullman factory that morning. We saw shops where they built the cars, repaired any problems, and decorated the interiors, down to the curtains in the windows. Our guide explained that once a Pullman car was completed, it was delivered to one of the country's railroad lines, where it was hooked up to their existing stock. The palace cars were all passenger vehicles, and luxurious ones at that. They were owned and maintained by the Pullman Company and only leased to the various railroads.

Mr. Jennings was tall, with a military bearing, and I thought his height and broad shoulders must have given him an advantage over most adversaries. But the opponent he faced now was not impressed by his air of authority.

Jane Addams was petite beside him, looking up into his face. She was probably only a few years older than Mr. Jennings, but she was as immovable as a block of granite and as imperturbable as a brick wall. She had established her settlement house in the belief that "we can do no good cut off from the more than half of mankind that must struggle to survive" and I sometimes thought that Joan of Arc must have been very like her. She was determined to follow her path no matter what obstacles the world put in her way. Poor Mr. Jennings was really no match for her, but he didn't know that yet.

"Thank you very much, Mr. Jennings, but Miss Cabot and I have an appointment with a Mr. MacGregor from the strike committee. We are very grateful for your information concerning the position of the company with regard to the strike. Now we would like to hear from the other side."

The man's face reddened perceptibly. "Miss Addams, I really cannot permit this. It is much too dangerous. I cannot ensure your safety in the circumstances and Mr. Pullman would never forgive me if you were to come to any harm. I really must insist."

It was a standoff. Jane Addams completely ignored the man's protests. She sailed through the low gate towards the street and I followed. The poor man appeared somewhat exasperated. After all, what could he do? Despite the fact that nearby there was a crowd of other men in suits, also wearing flags on their lapels, milling about, Mr. Jennings could hardly call on them to restrain us. He was at a distinct disadvantage. But, before the conflict came to a head, Mr. Louis Safer, a prominent banker who was also from the Civic Federation, followed us out through the fence and turned back to the Pullman assistant manager.

"If that is your concern, I will accompany the ladies and see that they come to no harm." He was a stout man in his sixties with a full white beard.

Jennings hesitated. I could see an angry red line on his neck above the stiff white collar but I doubted he would try to order the older man to stay. Instead, he tried to persuade him. "We have a very fine cook at the Florence, Mr. Safer. I'm sure you will regret missing her soup. You won't get anything nearly as good from them, you know."

The banker considered the young man from under bushy white eyebrows. "From what I hear, we will get very little, Mr. Jennings. The state of the food supply down here is one of the situations we were sent to investigate. According to the papers, your people are near starvation. No, sir, I can afford to pass on your fine soup today." He patted his bulging stomach. "Thank you kindly. We will rejoin you later. We know where the office is." He turned to us. "Come, ladies, let us find our friends the workers."

Mr. Jennings had no choice but to turn away smartly and lead the rest of the group up the stairs, across the wide veranda, and into the Florence Hotel, named for George Pullman's favorite daughter. They followed him, a dozen or so other members of the Civic Federation, like sheep, I thought. But I got a whiff of roasted meat then and my empty stomach almost made me regret our parting.

When I volunteered to help Miss Addams with the investigation, I had never before visited the famous factory town. When George Pullman erected his factory to build and service his railway cars, he had also constructed a whole town where his workers could live away from the dirt and crime of the working neighborhoods of the city. During the World's Columbian Exposition the previous year, visitors from all over the world had taken a day from their sightseeing to travel to the model town and admire the many improvements in living conditions it offered. As we walked through the well-tended lawns and neat brick buildings I couldn't help but be impressed with how favorably it all compared to the rickety wooden tenements of Chicago's West Side. How much better off the children of our neighborhood would have been in such a well-kept place, I thought. Pullman was such an improvement over the living conditions in the slums and tenements that its failure was unthinkable. Yet conditions had led the workers to strike. It was hard to imagine how such good intentions could culminate in such a catastrophe. I wanted to know why they had. I was sure there was a way to correct the situation. Walking through the model town only made me more determined, for I admired the idea behind it even more after seeing it.

The three of us turned back to the view of the carefully tended greens and gardens facing the hotel. To our north the massive buildings of the factory stood empty. While we had toured there in the morning, the works were shuttered by the workers' strike and management's immediate response in the form of a lockout. In front of the works we could see the small artificial Lake Vista surrounded by a park. Now we turned to the east to head into the town itself. When we reached the main street, we were met by a smallish middle-aged man who swept off a woolen cap to greet us solemnly.

"Miss Addams? I am Ian MacGregor and I chair the grievance committee for the local chapters of the American Railway Union. I am also president of Local 210. There are nineteen locals represented in Pullman. And on behalf of all of them I want to thank you for agreeing to meet with us."

I was very curious to meet this man since he was the first person from the railroad union who had ever contacted us. He was a very solid little man who seemed planted wherever he stood. Balding, with a lined face and dark, leathery skin, he had stringy muscles that stood out well defined in his neck and forearms. I knew he was a skilled metalworker responsible for a team of men who worked on building the structures of the Pullman cars. He spoke slowly with frequent halts, as if to meditate before committing his thoughts to complete sentences. A cautious and conscientious man, he was as far from the popular image of a fiery union agitator as could be imagined.

Miss Addams introduced me and Mr. Safer, then Mr. MacGregor gravely asked us to follow him to his home. He walked slowly, answering questions from Miss Addams about the town. Mr. Safer and I walked behind, as Mr. MacGregor explained that the larger houses facing the tree-lined street were rented to the company officers and that the very large building to our right, beyond a little park, was the Arcade containing shops, a bank, and the library. It was a very stratified society, with the managers in the north and the houses becoming smaller and meaner as you travelled south. Still, the lawns and buildings were trim and well maintained. It reflected an ordered society where people could live in very pleasant surroundings even if only the wealthier members could afford the fees to use the library or attend the little theater. At least they would have something to aspire to. I admired the physical beauty of the place. How could people not do better than in the dirty city by living in this place? I could see how—with a little moderation and compromise—this could be the best place in the world. The very attractiveness of the town made me determined, right there and then, that the problem of this strike must be resolved quickly. I knew from experience that this was just the sort of thing that Hull House reformers could help to accomplish. And, with the hubris of the inexperienced, I convinced myself that our object would be easily accomplished. It seemed so obvious.

Mr. MacGregor was responding to our admiration of a fine big church constructed of a curious green stone as we turned a corner to head east. "Aye, it's a fine building, but it went unused for some years as the rent was too high."

"Good lord, Pullman charges high rents for the Lord's house?" Mr. Safer was scandalized.

Mr. MacGregor stopped, as was his way, and considered the structure across the street as he prepared a further statement. "The Presbyterians eventually rented it. For I believe they bargained down the price. But it's closed now for the time being."

"Closed?" Jane Addams was surprised. "Surely in times of trouble the congregation seeks solace in prayer?"

Mr. MacGregor spent a further moment preparing his response. "The Reverend Oggel spoke against the strike from the pulpit. People were not favorably impressed. Soon after that, the Reverend left on vacation. There's no news on when he plans to return." We stopped for a moment, Miss Addams shaking her head and Mr. Safer raising a hairy eyebrow at this information. But MacGregor merely turned and led us on to the next corner. I knew

Miss Addams would be appalled by the clergyman's desertion of his flock in their time of need, so I expected her to comment on that, but she was the one who turned the conversation down an entirely different route with her next question.

"The company provides a hospital, doesn't it?"

This caused Mr. MacGregor to halt again to consider his response. Finally, it came. "Aye. But it's not easy to get to see the doctor. It's there for the company. So when a man is hurt he goes, and before the doctor will see him he must talk to the lawyer. The lawyer has a paper with a design of the human body and he notes on it where the man is injured and then the man must sign a paper, you see, before the doctor will see him. But it is closed now because of the lockout, you see. And we've no medical care for the moment."

I heard Miss Addams cluck with annoyance at that, but she walked along, listening as our guide led us down the street, pointing out the Market Hall where all of the meat and vegetables—raised on the Pullman Company farm three miles south—were sold. It was called "Sewage Farm" because waste collected from the homes was turned into fertilizer at a company plant and used to fertilize the fields. Mr. MacGregor reported that prices were higher than in the neighboring town of Kensington. But I was impressed that the market was such a very clean and attractive place. Modern dwellings with open arches over the sidewalks formed a circle around the hall. North, to our left, we could look up a tree-lined street to the main gate and clock tower of the factory. It was a great improvement over the views we had left behind in the neighborhood of Hull House. It made me wonder why in the world would workers lucky enough to live here ever want to strike. I kept my thoughts to myself, however. Presumably that was the question we were here to investigate.

After we all had admired the view, Mr. MacGregor led us south again, to an area where the housing was less impressive, but still well kept. They were small row houses in yellow brick.

Two blocks down, a quiet crowd of men stood in front of what turned out to be Mr. MacGregor's doorstep. They were quiet because they were being harangued by an Amazon of a woman with red hair, who was wearing a dress of midnight blue taffeta. Her back was to us.

TWO

T his sight brought our Mr. MacGregor to a halt as he moved back and forth on his feet, ruminating his next action. Meanwhile the woman's voice rang out and a feather jiggled on the tiny hat perched on her flamboyantly colored hair.

"And sure it's a fine thing for all of you to be making a show of it and talking to the papers and making your lists of grievances. Grievances. I'll show you grievances. It's in the face of my little brother and sister here." She gestured and I noticed the little girl hiding behind her, clinging to her bustle, and the little boy at her other side that she thrust forward with a strong left hand in the small of his back. Both children were barefoot and looked dirty. "What about them? How will they live? How will they eat, while you go on with your speeches? It's a fine mess you've made. And how will you get out of it, then? Will you tell me that? It's pride it is, and you know what that comes before. You think he'll listen, sitting in his big fine mansion on Prairie Avenue? Do you? Do you think he's going without his own dinner then? He's laughing at you, you bunch of chumps. He doesn't have to do a thing, just sit there and let you starve. You're fools, you are. All of you." The little feather was trembling with the woman's fury as she stopped for a break.

Mr. MacGregor attempted to get her attention by clearing his throat but when that made no impression he quickly called out, "Gracie." His voice collided with hers as she took up her harangue again. The call was loud enough so that she swung around as if to defend herself from a rear attack and the sight of us stopped her, at least temporarily.

Before she could start up again, Mr. MacGregor stepped forward. "Gracie, we have visitors. Miss Addams, Miss Cabot, and Mr. Safer have come from the Civic Federation that has offered to arbitrate." He turned back towards us. "Mrs. Foley grew up here. She lives in the city now, so I assume she's come for a visit."

The woman had frozen at the sight of us, her eyes narrowed in a frown of suspicion. She was tall, buxom, and big boned, probably about my own age of twenty-four. The delicate embroidery and velvet insets of her dress appeared to be far too fine for a workman's daughter, yet it was perfectly modest. The fact that the cut and bustle were slightly out of fashion suggested that she might be in service and had received a cast-off from her mistress.

It was obvious that Mr. MacGregor hoped to silence her with his introductions, but she was having none of it. "Ian MacGregor, you should be ashamed of yourself. Come for a visit indeed. I've come to bring food so they don't starve out here." She held up a large basket and I could see the little boy in front of her held another one. "How do you expect them to live now that you've all shut the place down? And you've got Brian and Joe in it. You know they're all the little ones have. Who's going to feed them when the boys are blacklisted, then? Will you?"

But then MacGregor put an end to it. He was a small man and seemed smaller with her looming over him, but he suddenly stamped a foot. "Gracie Foley, stop it, woman." He glared at her. "You know perfectly well your father Sean O'Malley, if he were alive today, would be a stalwart supporter of our cause. His sons can do no less. You don't live here. You don't work here any longer. In the name of your dead father, who was my friend for all these many years, I tell you now to leave off. Be gone with you. Go about your business and leave us to ours."

Gracie Foley appeared to shrink back at this blast from the little man. I thought she looked hurt. Somehow the invocation of her father silenced her and she grabbed the little girl's hand and pushed rudely through the crowd without a word more.

Meanwhile, Mr. MacGregor stood for a moment with his eyes closed, as if recovering from a blow, but before the chatter could begin he opened his eyes and ran them over the group of men who stood before his house.

"And these are the representatives of the locals," he told us formally. Then he proceeded to introduce each one, naming the number and type of local he represented. There was one woman, I noticed, but I soon lost track and wondered how I would ever remember all those names when it came to addressing them later. To my relief, it soon became clear that they would not be joining us for the meal. Mr. MacGregor dismissed them, apologizing but assuring us that they each had duties to attend to. I saw a knowing look pass between Miss Addams and Mr. Safer and realized that, unlike the company representative, Mr. Jennings, these workers probably did not have the resources to feed a large number of people. It occurred to me that even the addition of Mr. Safer to our meal was probably a strain. We mounted the steps and were led into the dining room of Mr. MacGregor's house where a tureen of soup, a loaf of bread, some cheese, and a pot of weak tea were served to us by a pretty young girl with a braid of shiny blonde hair coiled around her head.

She was introduced as MacGregor's daughter, Fiona, who worked in a department of the Pullman factory where they made draperies and linens for the cars. She looked about sixteen years old with blue eyes, delicate bones, and a small turned-up nose. She wore a dress in a flowery print and an apron gaily decorated with needlework. I felt guilty when she excused herself after laying out the meal for us. I couldn't help wondering if she was absenting herself because there wasn't enough food to go around. But when I opened my mouth to protest I received a firm nudge under the table from Miss Addams and I remembered how she had explained that commenting on any perceived lack on such an occasion was always taken as an insult. I held my tongue as Fiona left us and I heard a door close somewhere in the background.

I think I managed to hide my own ravenous appetite as I forced myself to savor each spoonful of the soup and bite of the bread. The meager meal did more to convince us of the seriousness of the food situation than any of the talk that followed. I don't think MacGregor planned it that way, and that was all the more reason the point was brought home sharply to the three of us who would return to the city and remember this meal later, as we dined on plates of food that would be heaping in comparison.

The dining room was at the back of the house and two windows were open wide, overlooking the tiny yard and alley. There was a slight breeze in the warm air and I could hear the shiver of leaves in a tree and the twittering calls of birds. It all seemed so peaceful compared to the noise and dirt and hurry around Hull House at this time of day.

Mr. MacGregor apologized for the outburst from Gracie Foley that we had witnessed. He explained that her father, who had worked for Pullman since the beginning, had died the previous spring and her two brothers were left supporting two younger children. She herself left when she married and she was now a widow and a laundress in the city. I thought that explained her attire but there was something else about her history not spoken, something that made him uneasy. Apparently he had been a longtime friend and comrade of her father's.

When we had consumed our portions and refused additional helpings, Mr. MacGregor rose and went to the next room, returning with two other men who joined us in a cup of the weak and lukewarm tea.

One, introduced as Mr. Leonard Stark, was a middle-aged man, like MacGregor. But he was thicker around the waist and looked softer and less muscular than the metalworker. He had brown hair cut very short and a large moustache and thick eyebrows. It soon became clear that he was MacGregor's right-hand man for running errands and carrying messages.

The second man was younger, in his thirties I guessed. He

had a swarthy complexion, a thatch of very dark hair with one piece that frequently fell down onto his forehead, heavy sideburns, and large brown eyes fringed with long lashes. Of medium height but with muscular shoulders and arms, his calloused hands were large and he frequently used them to emphasize what he was saying. From the very first, there was about him a sense of vigor that evoked a raw masculinity. It was not that he was threatening, but he seemed to hold a reserve of energy in his springy walk and ease of motion. He gave the impression that he was like a cat poised ready to jump. He was not at all like the men of my previous acquaintance—my father, my brother, or the men at the university.

Mr. MacGregor introduced him as Mr. Raoul LeClerc and explained that he was a representative of the American Railway Union, or ARU, and its leader, Mr. Eugene Debs. I noticed Mr. Safer fumble with his napkin and push his chair back from the table at this introduction. There was a lot of suspicion about that new labor union and the ambitions of Mr. Debs and the other organizers. Memories of the Haymarket bombing during a labor protest eight years before were still vivid and there was an embedded fear that labor agitators were determined to wreak havoc at the least provocation. Miss Addams acknowledged the introductions but then briskly brought the conversation back around to the Pullman situation, stating frankly that it was that local situation alone, and the hope of finding a peaceful solution to it, that had brought the delegates from the Civic Federation down to the company town. I saw Mr. Safer raise his eyebrows in surprise when she went on to ask the ARU representative to excuse us while we continued our discussions in private with Mr. MacGregor. I could tell that Miss Addams was not impressed by the charisma of LeClerc. I saw him flush slightly but he bowed his head politely and assured Mr. MacGregor that he understood the need for discretion. He asserted that the desire of the ARU was only to see a just conclusion to the strike. He left graciously but

MacGregor had to invent an errand to get rid of Mr. Stark, who appeared to be oblivious to Miss Addams's request for privacy and determined to remain until actually ordered away.

Having cleared the decks, as it were, there followed an intense discussion between MacGregor and Miss Addams of the particulars of the situation to which Mr. Safer and I mainly provided an audience. During the morning tour Miss Addams had asked some pointed questions of the company representatives, so pointed that someone unfamiliar with her methods, such as Mr. Safer, might have judged her to be prejudiced in favor of the workers. But no one would think that now, listening to her catechize Mr. MacGregor with equal force concerning the company's claims. I saw Mr. Safer sit back and listen and I could tell his respect for my mentor was growing.

Mr. MacGregor explained that, fine as the surroundings of the town of Pullman might seem, people couldn't afford to live there. But it was worse than that, much worse. The people down here were falling deeply into debt as their salaries were lowered, while rents were kept at the same levels. The company itself was sending them into an impossible spiral of self-destruction.

He told us that when the Pullman works were originally opened, the company built a rail line from the city and freely allowed workers to use it. Once the town was built, however, workers were expected to live there and the cost of the train fare became prohibitive. All buildings in the town were owned by the company and subject to the rules laid down by them. Rents were high compared to nearby towns and while supposedly you could choose to live anywhere, in practice those who did not live in Pullman were more likely to suffer when there were layoffs.

The previous year brought an economic recession to the whole country. At Pullman this had amounted to a slash in the workers' wages. MacGregor himself had been making thirty cents an hour a year before. By the time the strike began his pay was cut to twenty and one-half cents per hour, which amounted to one dollar and fifty-one cents a day. Meanwhile, the rent for his house had been, and remained at, seventeen dollars a month and he was charged seventy-one cents a month for water. He told us the company made a profit of thirty-two thousand dollars on water and I heard Mr. Safer's chair scrape against the floor. The charge for gas was more than MacGregor could afford so he just did without it. I imagined the little house must be very cold and dark in the winter months and shivered at the thought. He told us most workers had experienced a reduction of twenty-five to fifty percent of their pay. Only managers had not received any pay cuts and rents had remained the same for all of them.

The manner in which rent was collected was even more disturbing. Mr. MacGregor explained that paychecks were issued by the Pullman Bank in the Arcade Building. At one time the company had withheld rent and given a check for only what was left over. When this was ruled illegal by a court challenge the bank began to issue two checks, one for rent owed and the other for the balance. They would then pressure the worker to sign over the rent check. With rents so high and the cut in wages it was only too easy to get behind. He told us stories of workers who had been pressured into endorsing the rent checks and then were left with less than a dollar to live on until the next payday.

Despite these pitiful and all too believable stories, Miss Addams was relentless in presenting the company's claims. Wasn't it true that the company suffered from a reduction in the number of orders? Wasn't it preferable for the company to reduce the wages but continue employment for more people as opposed to downright layoffs? Wasn't it in the interest of the workers for the company to continue in a strong financial position?

"Of course, we all of us want the company to prosper," MacGregor burst out at last. "We don't want to bring it down and it's not possible to believe that Mr. Pullman—who designed such a fine town for his workers—would not want the best for them."

I heard Mr. Safer moving restlessly beside me but I was

mesmerized by the story I was hearing. MacGregor went on. "But it's not working. We cannot pay the same rent when the wages go down. I think, I truly believe, Miss Addams, that if we the workingmen could only talk directly to Mr. Pullman, could lay our case before him, then together we could find a solution. But the managers, like that Mr. Jennings, they won't let us near him. So that's the root of it. That's what's behind it all, forming unions and all. To talk to Mr. Pullman directly, you see.

"Let me tell you what happened. We formed a grievance committee to talk—and only to talk. But we met with the managers, not Pullman, you see. Now, we made it a condition that none of the leaders who went to the talk could be punished for speaking out like. Well, we only got to talk to Jennings, and Wicke, and some others, not Mr. Pullman like we asked. And less than a week later three of the members of the grievance committee were fired. Even so, we might not have done it but that we heard there would be a lockout. Miss Addams, one of the worst things, the very worst thing, is the way some of them, like that Jennings, they make spies of us, of our own brothers. They knew what we planned ahead of time, they spread rumors and fear. I tell you, if it weren't for the spies planted by Jennings and his lot, there might not have been a strike at all."

"So, you would be willing to compromise. If we can set up a meeting with Mr. Pullman himself, you would participate?"

A light gleamed in Mr. MacGregor's eyes. "Oh, miss, if you could arrange that it would be the answer to all our prayers. We believe, we know, that those who have been representing the man cannot have been telling him the truth. If only we can make the case to the man himself, and not to his managers, he has to listen."

I heard Mr. Safer cough, preparatory to injecting a statement here, I am sure, when suddenly we heard screams. They tore through the pleasant peace of the afternoon and we all froze in response. They came from a distance, but they did not stop. They went on and on.

"What is it? What is happening? I must go, I must . . . " our host said. Then, with uncharacteristic haste he leapt up, knocking his chair against the wall, and rushed from the room.

We followed him down a dark stairway through the little back garden and alley and out into the street. Soon we were beyond the town, on muddy flats, racing towards a large shed with wide-open doors on both sides. Beyond it, all I could see was Lake Calumet spread out to the horizon.

The screams rose and fell with stutters and then a rippling scream of terror and disbelief. We rushed into the open shed to find Fiona crumpled on the ground, hands to her face, staring above her at a man's corpse as it swung from the rafters in a gentle breeze. Around his neck was a rope holding a board on which was scrawled the word "SPY".

THREE

MacGregor knelt down to put his arms around his daughter, who quickly buried her face in his shoulder, sobbing. At least the screams had stopped. The rest of us halted, inevitably staring up at the body hanging there. I couldn't help but be conscious of others who had heard the screams and come rushing in through the wide-open doors. They, too, stopped to stare, stunned by the sight.

"We must get him down." Jane Addams stepped forward, breaking the stunned silence and finally awakening me and the other people who had barely entered the building.

"Over there." Mr. MacGregor waved to some of the men, including Raoul LeClerc. "Let him down from there." I saw that he was sending them to the opposite wall and looking up, I could see that the rope from which the poor man hung went through a pulley system that led across the rafters and down the wall to a cleat. It must have been used to lift heavy items.

Meanwhile, Mr. MacGregor motioned to Mr. Stark with his left hand, as he continued to hold his daughter to his chest. "Lennie, go to the Florence. Tell them what's happened and tell them to get the police. Slowly now," he called to the men feeding the rope to lower the body.

Miss Addams came and took Fiona from him, saying that she would take the girl back to the house. I helped Mr. MacGregor catch the body as it was lowered slowly and we laid it out on the ground as gently as we could. The crowd of people—men, women and children—had begun to inch closer when suddenly they parted and Mr. MacGregor looked up. "Joe, we don't know what happened. We only just found him."

I looked up from the face of the dead man and had the shock of thinking I saw him alive again. I realized it must be the man's brother, but before I could say anything he was shoved aside and Mrs. Gracie Foley stood in front of us. "What is going on now, then?" she began, but then she recognized the corpse. "Oh, no. Oh, Brian." She sank down, pushing us out of her way to take the dead man by the shoulders as if to shake him awake. "Brian? Brian, luv. Oh, my lord, oh God. Jesus, Mary, and Joseph. Oh, no, Brian, oh no."

She let him sink back to the floor and her hand caressed his face, pushing away his hair. You could see that he had been struck on the head and the left side of his face was crusted with dried blood. Her fingers found the rope then and I saw her eyes grow wide as she felt around his neck and looked up to where it went into the rafters. I heard a gasp as she looked down and saw the sign that hung around his neck.

"You, you, you murderers, all of you," she screamed, as she turned back to the crowd.

"Now, Gracie, we don't know what happened here," MacGregor began but she cut him off.

"You bloody murderers. What did you do to him?" She slapped away Ian MacGregor's hand and began to try to loosen the rope. Kneeling there beside her, I saw it was not the type of hangman's noose seen in illustrations but just an ordinary knot. She had to fight with it in her fury but it was soon released. She tossed the end away, pulled the rope holding the sign over the dead man's head, and, rising up on her knees, threw it as far as she could.

I could feel the crowd stirring angrily, just as she cursed them again, "You pack of dirty murderers!" But then her head dropped and she sobbed, addressing the corpse. "Oh, Brian, dearie, how could this happen. And what is to become of us? Oh, Brian."

At her sobs, I sensed all the anger and antagonism of the surrounding crowd disappear in a single exhalation. A couple of the women moved forward in a sympathetic posture but, just then, there was a disturbance from the doorway.

"Move aside, now, move aside. Get out of the way, if you please. We have the police with us. Move aside." These commands came from Mr. Jennings. Two uniformed policemen, swinging clubs in a menacing way, preceded him and the people in the crowd parted for their advance, although they moved only as far as was absolutely necessary, then stood looking on with sullen faces. I was reminded of the tension the strike caused between the two groups as Jennings strode forward, impatiently followed by two men in suits and a half dozen more grim-looking policemen.

"MacGregor, what's going on here?" Mr. Jennings demanded.

Ian MacGregor stood up to face them. "It's Brian O'Malley, sir. We found him hanging here. He's dead, sir. That's why I sent Lennie Stark to get you."

"I see. Well, what happened? Did he do it himself, then? Is this the result of your strike, MacGregor? The man got so desperate he hung himself, is that it?"

There was a murmur of protest from the crowd and the policemen turned towards the sound, swinging their clubs and catching them in their hands with a slap. They surrounded the company managers as if to protect them. Mr. MacGregor moved uneasily and I thought of the sign that had been around the dead man's neck. He didn't want to mention it. The air was trembling with anticipation already. "We don't know what happened. We only just came and found him."

"Yes, well, move away. Move away. Let us see." He put an arm out to push the smaller man out of his way, stepping forward with a frown on his handsome face. "I hold you responsible, MacGregor. You and the other agitators. This is what happens. We'll have no violence here, I tell you. Any violence will be met with an iron fist. It won't be tolerated. Miss Cabot, what are you doing here? I warned you the situation was dangerous. I must ask you to leave, for your own good. Who's this? If it isn't Gracie O'Malley. I thought you left Pullman, Gracie. Thrown out by your father, wasn't it? What are you doing here?"

"Here, now, it's her brother was killed," Mr. MacGregor told him.

"Well, I'm very sorry, but you'd better step away and let the police handle this." He spoke to Gracie's back as she was still kneeling over her brother.

"Really, Mr. Jennings," I began, but Gracie stood up and turned around slowly to face the assistant manager of the factory. She was nearly as tall as he was and she looked him in the eye. I could see she was quivering slightly with rage.

"It's Mrs. Foley to you, Mr. Jennings. This is my brother and he's been murdered. Murdered. Do you hear? This is my brother's body and I will be taking it home for a proper wake and burial and I'm not asking your permission. So you can step out of the way yourself. Joe, you get a few of the lads and carry him back to the house now." She stood eye to eye with Jennings and I stood up to move out of the way as Joe O'Malley and three other young men picked up the dead body. Jennings set his jaw and his face flushed with anger, but Ian MacGregor placed his short form between the two angry people.

"Let them go, Mr. Jennings. Let her take the poor boy home for burying. It's been a shock to all of us. I can tell you what we saw when we found him."

I saw Jennings draw his gaze away from Gracie Foley's insolent stare and glance down at the small man, then around at the crowd of angry people.

"Oh, for heavens sake, Mr. Jennings," I pleaded. "Let them have him."

He frowned but nodded stiffly to a policeman standing in their way. "Let them go."

The small, sorry procession marched out with Gracie Foley following, back rigid and face frozen, as if carved in stone. The crowd made way for them and watched in silence as they went out the shed doors.

Jennings shook himself and looked around. "We'll need to talk to some of you at the police station," he announced. "MacGregor, Stark, Connelly, Deriva, that one." He pointed at Raoul LeClerc and one of the officers took him by the shoulder. It was obvious that he was picking out the men who were known organizers of the strike or who were connected to the unions. There was a murmur of protest from the crowd and I was suddenly aware that now there were several hundred people, mostly men, gathered in and around this big shed and there were only eight in Jennings's party. But Jennings continued to harangue them as if unaware that he was outnumbered. "The rest of you, go home. Go now, or you'll be arrested."

There was an angry roar at this threat and suddenly the way to the door was blocked with bodies. Jennings got riled at that and shouted, "Out of the way, you."

There might have been blows exchanged but Mr. MacGregor stepped forward. "Do as he says, men. Go on home. We're not being arrested. We are only going with them to tell them what we know about what happened to Brian O'Malley, and if any of you know anything you should come forward. There's been enough violence today. Go and make sure his family has what they need. We'll return soon and we'll meet in the usual place. There will be no trouble here now."

With that, he led the way through the crowd, followed by the other union men and the police, who had to scurry to keep up with them. Jennings lingered to speak to me and Mr. Safer.

"Where is Miss Addams? Is she all right?"

"Yes. Mr. MacGregor's daughter found the dead man. She was very upset and Miss Addams took her away, back to their home," I told him. "I trust Mr. MacGregor will be all right. He will be, won't he, Mr. Jennings?"

He scowled at me. "I warned you it wasn't safe here, Miss Cabot. I really must insist that you and Miss Addams leave on the next available train. I have already sent the rest of your delegation home. Things seem to have settled down here for the moment but there's no telling when more violence will break out. I simply cannot be responsible for your safety."

"But you will let him go, won't you? Mr. MacGregor, I mean?"

"Really, Miss Cabot. That is not up to me. That is a police matter now."

I didn't comment on how the police appeared to respond to his commands. I did not want to leave without making sure Mr. MacGregor would be treated fairly. "But Mr. MacGregor could not have been involved in what happened to that man. He was with us all afternoon, wasn't he, Mr. Safer? We heard Fiona scream and followed him here. The man was already dead, hanging from that rope with that sign around his neck," I told him, pointing to where the board fell when Gracie flung it away. "But Mr. MacGregor was with us every moment since we left you."

"That is quite true," Mr. Safer confirmed. "He cannot have been involved."

Jennings bent to retrieve the sign and stood staring at it with a puzzled look on his face. Then he looked up, following the line of the rope to the pulley and across the ceiling and down to where it had been fastened to the wall. He put the sign under his arm and turned to us. "I really must get you out of here as soon as possible. I will arrange for a special carriage."

"That will not be necessary," Mr. Safer told him. "I came in my own carriage. If you will have it sent to MacGregor's house we can retrieve Miss Addams and I will take the ladies back to the city."

"Yes, sir. I will do that immediately. That would be very kind of you. I'm sorry your mission has been a failure. But maybe now you will understand what we mean when we tell you this is a very dangerous and vicious group of agitators we are facing here and there is nothing we can do but stand firm against them and their influence." He turned smartly then and strode out the door.

FOUR

y racing heartbeat had slowed down to the rhythm of the clip-clop of the horse's hooves by the time Mr. Safer's carriage carried us back to the heart of the city. But we were not returning to Hull House just yet. We had discussed the situation thoroughly on the return trip and concluded that—even though our attempt to mediate had so far failed—the situation was so desperate that an appeal directly to Mr. George Pullman himself must at least be attempted. We were all agreed that any reasonable person must understand the inequity of the situation in which the same company that found itself in the position of reducing its workers' salaries would not, at the same time, reduce the rent those workers paid back to the company. Not to do so was ludicrous and could not be defended. The situation we found in Pullman was bad and would soon get much worse. Food was scarce and medical attention was nonexistent. But we had sensed clearly that the striking workers were shocked by the violent death of Brian O'Malley. Mr. Pullman had only to offer even a slight reduction in rent and everyone concerned would be relieved to see the end to this strike. We felt sure that he would be as appalled as we were by the violent turn of events and that he must want to seize this opportunity to put it all behind both himself and his workers.

Miss Addams and I, at least, were convinced that Mr. Pullman would welcome this opportunity to end the strike. I noticed that Mr. Safer did not directly contradict us, but he appeared to have a much less optimistic expectation of how Pullman would react to the news. Nonetheless, the banker firmly agreed that the next step must be to approach the man directly.

So it was that we found ourselves trotting along Prairie Avenue on the near south side of the city. Here Pullman's mansion stood alongside the huge new homes of people such as Marshall Field and John Glessner. I was curious to see the home of the inventor of the Pullman Palace Cars.

When my father was alive, we took Pullman cars a number of times to visit an aunt in Albany. I remembered how amazed we had been to walk into a decorated drawing room with red plush chairs, chandeliers, and varnished wood siding. The ceilings were painted like those of a French chateau and curtains hung in the windows. But most clever and curious had been the way the room was transformed at night into tiers of sleeping berths separated by hangings. My brother and I had our own little room that way. The dining car was even more lavish, with delicate china and cut glass decanters. Never would any other train trip measure up after that and I often remembered that comfort when I later travelled west in less luxurious compartments. The Palace Cars had introduced a standard of comfort to travel that changed the way people thought about long trips. It was George Pullman who recognized that desire in the public and exploited it.

As we slowed to turn, I glimpsed the striking stone house of my friends, John and Fannie Glessner, just across from the drive of the Pullman mansion. Mr. Safer assured us that as an old friend, or at least familiar acquaintance, of George Pullman he felt no compunction about arriving without an appointment on an errand of such importance.

Mr. Safer was recognized and greeted by a dignified butler who led us into a drawing room to wait while he went to see if Mr. Pullman would see us. It was only a short while before we were joined by the man himself.

"Louis, how are you? This is a surprise." Pullman heartily shook Mr. Safer's hand and the banker introduced us, apologizing for the intrusion and briefly explaining our errand. At this, the millionaire's expression turned sour.

He was a man of large frame with short graying hair, dark eyebrows, and a spade-shaped brush of white beard on his chin. He looked displeased when he heard what we had come for and cut off the explanations by abruptly turning and leading us to his study. We followed him across the broad foyer to a book-lined room where he took his place behind a massive mahogany desk, gesturing to chairs facing him. When we were seated he leaned back in his armchair, regarding us with a grim expression. I noticed Mr. Safer was already shaking his head with disappointment but Miss Addams took up the argument.

"Mr. Pullman, we have just returned from a visit to your company town. As part of a committee of the Civic Federation we were asked to attempt to arbitrate the dispute between you and your workers, which has led to this strike and lockout. We have news of a most terrible tragedy there."

"If you refer to the man found hung in the brick shed, I have been informed," he interrupted. "Mr. Wickes, the plant manager, telephoned me. I can only say I am not surprised by further evidence of violent methods used by these union agitators in their attempts to intimidate and dictate to the working men. I hold Mr. Debs and his union responsible. Such violence was unheard of before they made their unwelcome appearance."

"Exactly who is responsible is not yet known and must be left to the police," Miss Addams told him. "But it is clear that all of the people are terribly shocked by this act. We have come to encourage you to take advantage of this horrible tragedy by bringing this strike to an end. Having spent the afternoon speaking with a representative of the strike committee we are very confident that it would be possible in this hour of grief to fulfill our mission and to arbitrate a just agreement that will end this strike. We are sure that a minor adjustment to lower the rents during this time of economic distress is all it would take to get the workers to agree to return to the works by next week at the latest."

"There is nothing to arbitrate," Pullman pronounced from

across his vast desk, without moving a muscle, beyond the stiff up and down of his jaw to form the words.

"But, Mr. Pullman, surely you see that they cannot live so. Their demand is for an increase in pay by a third which would return it to the levels of one year ago, but after hearing them out we are convinced that they would settle for a reduction in rent which is comparable to the reduction in wages they have experienced."

"I will tell you, Miss Addams, what I have told them. A year ago the works employed some five thousand eight hundred. Due to the general economic depression contracts were down and it was necessary to lay off many men. By November of last year there were only two thousand on the payroll. In order to employ as many men as possible it has been necessary to bid on contracts at a rate much lower than we have ever done before. And this was done only with a view towards providing employment for as many as possible. To do this we bid for contracts at a loss, even eliminating use of capital and machinery costs from the estimates. By doing so we have managed to keep four thousand three hundred on the payroll although it has had to be done at a lower rate. Even so—as I have offered to show them in the books—the current contract for Long Island cars is being done at a loss of twelve dollars a car." He carefully straightened several items on his desk before he continued. "Furthermore, we have expended an additional one hundred and sixty thousand dollars on improvements to the town itself since last August, which would have been spread over several years were it not for the desire to provide employment."

"Yes, but Mr. Pullman, the rents have remained what they were a year ago. With less work at a lower pay scale you must see that the people are inevitably falling into debt. They cannot pay the rents."

"These are hard economic times, Miss Addams, as Mr. Safer, a banker, can tell you. The Pullman Loan and Savings showed over four hundred and eighty thousand dollars in workers' savings at this time last year. By November that had fallen to three hundred and twenty-four thousand but since then it has been rising slightly, which shows an overall improvement in situation for them."

"But, sir, the individual situations are quite dire. I have seen evidence of an elderly woman facing eviction and a man with eight children who, after paying back rent, was left with two dollars to feed them. The report is that on average there is only eight cents per meal available. Don't you see? You must lower the rents, sir."

"Excuse me, madam, I must do nothing of the sort. The capital invested in the building of the town is being repaid via the rents. The investment was very heavy and the return on that investment is currently below four percent. No reduction is possible."

At this, the banker, Mr. Safer, spoke up. "You must extend the return over a longer term and lower it. Good God, man, the company paid dividends this year higher than any comparable company in the country."

This criticism caused Pullman's dark eyebrows to lower and a pronounced frown to appear on the millionaire industrialist's face. "That is no business of yours, sir. It is my company. It bears my name. It will be run according to my orders and no others. I tell you there is nothing to arbitrate. We took contracts at a loss in order to keep the men employed. We would better have closed the shops for the winter and lost no money that way. We will lose nothing by this and, as in the strike of eighty-six, they will soon come to their senses. At that time they stayed out ten days before they voluntarily returned to their places. This time they will have to wait until we reopen the works. Then Mr. Debs will see what will happen."

I stared at him, appalled. So that was his plan. He wanted them to starve. Then, when they were most desperate, he would reopen the works and see how many of them would stay faithful to their pledge to strike and how many would return on the same conditions, having gained nothing but debt. It was diabolical.

"But, Mr. Pullman," I couldn't help asking, "surely you will lose money by leaving unfinished the work for which you have already signed contracts."

"We will lose nothing. There are strike clauses in all of the contracts. The company will lose nothing by this."

I was dumbfounded. I had no idea such things existed.

Jane Addams took up the fight. "Mr. Pullman, it is clear that you have every right and duty to preserve the company which you have worked so hard to build. But what of the people? Surely they are *your* people under *your* care. We all admire the town you built for your workers. We have thought it the best, the most exemplary, plan for a modern industry. Surely you do not want to see the people of your model town in such dire straits. The children are hungry."

He sat up in his chair, his shoulders twitching like a bear bothered by a wasp. "You are mistaken, madam, if you think the town of Pullman was at any time planned as an exercise in philanthropy. It was not. It was, and remains, a business proposition. The town of Pullman was built for productivity and it must produce. In building it far from the noise and dirt of the city it was my intention not only to increase productivity by providing healthful surroundings, but to prevent the infiltration of these foreign agitators with their unions and demonstrations. I will not have it, Miss Addams." His fist came down on the desk. "I will not be dictated to by the likes of Debs and his union. It is absurd for the Pullman workers to even be included in a railway union. The Pullman works are not a railway. It is only by a technicality, and because the company owns the line from the city to the town, that they dare to unionize here. I will not have it."

Mr. Safer answered this. "But they are part of the American Railway Union, George, whether it's by a technicality or not. And a lot of people are worried about what could happen. Don't you see there is a lot of sympathy for them out there? It makes no sense that you cut the wages but leave the rents up. That is creating a huge amount of sympathy for the strike. And if it goes on there is fear that there may be a boycott of the Pullman cars. There is talk of railway men refusing to hook up the palace cars. What will happen then?"

"That is not my problem, Louis. The railroads contract for the use of the cars and the roads will bear the expense if they do not get them hooked up."

"You'll make no friends of the others if you go on in this stubborn fashion, George." Mr. Safer shook his head.

"I am not in business to make friends, Safer. I am in business to make money. The Pullman Company will not suffer from this strike."

"You mean not financially, Mr. Pullman," Miss Addams said. "But the Pullman workers are suffering. Very badly."

"Enough, madam. Even my own children—my lazy, good-for-nothing, spendthrift sons and my ignorant younger daughter—dare to criticize. Only Florence, my eldest, knows enough to leave this to me. I will do no more. The workmen can distance themselves from those dangerous union agitators and return to reason, or they can make it on their own. They are criminals, Debs and his men. You will see."

It was clear the interview was over, with frustration on both sides, but as we rose to leave I couldn't help asking one more question. "Mr. Pullman, does the company really employ men to spy on their fellow workers?"

The millionaire rose to his feet impatiently and marched us to the door while he talked. "You have no idea of the type of men we are up against, young woman. Don't you know what happened at Haymarket? They are dangerous. There is every reason to believe they will attempt sabotage. We have received information that there is a plot to blow up the clock tower in the administration building. You ask me, do we plant spies at their meetings? I tell you we will do everything necessary to preserve the Pullman factory works. Now, good evening."

With that he closed the wide-paneled door of his library in my face, leaving the still dignified, if slightly startled, butler to lead us to the front entrance.

I felt a burning in my chest as I followed the others. It was incredible to me that this man could be so heartless. He did not have one ounce of feeling for the worried, hungry people I had met in Pullman that morning. They were nothing to him, not even faces. They were amounts beside a dollar sign in the ledgers of the Pullman Loan and Savings, that was all. I was disgusted as we drove away from the stone mansion where the portly industrialist was no doubt sitting down to an elegant supper with his recalcitrant younger children and his obsequious eldest daughter. I could not understand how Florence Pullman could ratify her father's inflated opinion of himself and his all-knowingness.

In my youthful ignorance I did not understand the type of man George Pullman was. I did not believe he meant what he said. It took me a long time to learn to understand the ideologues of wealth. Like religious zealots, they meant exactly what they said. They believed very firmly that there was a set of rules for profit that must be followed with all of the rigorousness of a ritual. Not to follow the rules that would lead to the optimum profit was to risk apostasy. Most of us, even those with a comfortable mode of living, were made uncomfortable by the misfortunes of others. Not so for Mr. Pullman and his ilk. They had a view of the world as distorted as a mirror in a funhouse and, by their view, all the world was right only if maximum profit was sustained. But I did not yet have enough experience of the world to understand that, on the warm April day that I met Mr. George Pullman.

I gritted my teeth. He was wrong and Mr. MacGregor and the rest of the workers could prove him wrong by staying together. I didn't believe him when he claimed the company would not be hurt by the strike. I thought Mr. Safer's question had indicated that the railroad clients of Pullman Company were already unhappy with his actions. If he wouldn't listen to the workers, he would have to listen to those who purchased his cars. I believed the workers could win this. They could teach that arrogant man a lesson. But they would need help, a lot of help from people like Miss Addams, and Mr. Safer, and from Debs, and the American Railway Union. It would be a tough fight but I knew I wanted to be in it and to see them win. They had to.

At Hull House that night we called an emergency meeting in the residents' dining room. In those familiar surroundings where we had made plans to fight city aldermen and a smallpox epidemic in the past, now we planned to help the people of Pullman. It was decided that I would go down to set up a relief station and wagons would follow, bringing food and other supplies. A temporary clinic would be set up as well. Miss Addams and the others would go out to the drawing rooms of Prairie Avenue and elsewhere to raise funds for the effort.

I had a difficult time getting to sleep that night. My mind was full of arguments I should have used to convince George Pullman and his manager, Mr. Jennings. I was terribly worried about the fate of Mr. MacGregor and the others, although Miss Addams had contacted the mayor about the situation with the police. I practiced arguments to explain how they could not have been involved in the death and why they must be released. Not only Mr. MacGregor, but Mr. LeClerc and the others, must be released. After a fitful sleep I rose with these arguments and worries still playing in my head. I had counter arguments prepared for every possible situation except for one. During my ruminations I had not contemplated or rehearsed what I would say when faced with a man whose proposal of marriage I had refused the very last time I saw him.

FIVE

He saw me before I had time to avoid him, or even to prepare myself. It was in the great open space of Twelfth Street Station where I was headed for Track Four to take the train to Pullman. Head down, I weaved through the early morning crowds while rehearsing the arguments for why Mr. MacGregor and Mr. LeClerc must be released. I was terribly afraid the police would keep them in jail and when I finally looked up, there he was, right beside my train.

"Stephen, what are you doing here?"

"I will be accompanying you to Pullman, Miss Cabot." Of course, the formality of address was proper but it made me wince.

"I thought you were at the university." After my refusal of his marriage proposal, I naïvely thought that Stephen would continue his clinic duties in the Hull House neighborhood, and that we would still work side-by-side. I had tried to show how polite and mature I could be in the circumstances but, the morning after I turned him down, he left the Hull House men's quarters to return to his research at the University of Chicago. No one else found this at all surprising, since for months he had divided his time between work in the laboratory and time on the West Side training visiting nurses. No one else knew of his proposal and my refusal. Only I had been shocked by his removal to Hyde Park and only I had to hide my reaction.

"I was visiting in the city when Miss Addams contacted me last night. But I thought you were too devoted to your studies to be distracted by something so mundane?" He was being supercilious. I had refused his offer on the grounds that I would not be allowed to take up an offered lectureship at the University if I were married.

"My university position begins in the fall, meanwhile I accompanied Miss Addams to Pullman yesterday and I was chosen to set up the relief station there." I felt myself becoming warm. I was conscious of the heavy black serge dress and jacket I wore, still deep in mourning after the death of my mother the previous spring. The fabric seemed to get heavier as the weather grew warmer, and only increased my irritation. "Doctor, I must protest. I am quite capable of doing this by myself. Thank you very much, but I need neither your help nor your protection. You are mistaken if you think that my youth or lack of experience mean that I require your assistance—I do not." A dozen years my senior, it irked me that the doctor had only proposed to me out of pity. I was orphaned and lacking in means when my mother passed away. He had assumed, mistakenly, that I could not survive without his protection. I was determined to prove him wrong.

"You are mistaken, Miss Cabot. I would not presume to attempt to assist you in any way whatsoever, aware as I am of your distaste for any help from me. However, the case for the people of Pullman is not the same. Presumably they would not disdain well-meaning assistance, and unless you have recently received sufficient medical training to be capable of establishing a clinic, my assistance is required and was requested by Miss Addams. Unless you feel that you must set that up as well? By yourself? Without assistance?"

My face burned. Talking to him when he was in this mood was like trying to find my way out of a maze. I kept turning down blind alleys and having to trace my way back from a dead end. "Of course, Miss Addams would not have known of our situation when she consulted you," I began. He could have refused or recommended someone else. He must have known I had not told anyone of his proposal and my refusal.

"Our situation? You mean the fact that you refused an offer of marriage from me? Surely, Miss Cabot, you would not be so selfish as to deprive the people of Pullman of medical care merely to save yourself a mild embarrassment? Do you want me to leave, then?"

"No, of course not." Before I could explain myself there was a call from behind me.

"Emily!"

"Alden, what are you doing here?"

"I'm here for the story." He pulled out a notebook, waving it in my face and taking out a pencil, which he tucked behind his ear. "You'll be happy to hear I have succeeded in finding a job—reporter, for the *Sentinel.*"

After my mother's death two months before, my brother Alden had also moved from the men's dormitory at Hull House. It was after his recuperation from a gunshot wound that he had returned from his time in Boston. My friend Clara Shea had nursed him during his recovery. He had nearly died earlier that spring and he was all the family I had left. So it was a relief to see him whole and filled with the energy that drove him, even if I knew he would use it to tease and provoke me, as he always did. He had decided to return to Chicago and I knew he had been seeking employment.

"Oh, Alden, that's wonderful—I guess." So, it seemed that he had settled in Chicago. Now, with both of our parents dead, there was no longer a home for us in Boston.

"No guess about it. I'll be a three-day wonder, especially when I get the big story. *Death in Pullman: Hull House Comes to the Rescue.*"

"But how did you know?"

"Him," he gestured, with a tip of his head.

I looked up and saw Stephen watching us. I was perturbed—had he told my brother about the marriage proposal? If so, I would never hear the end of it. But Alden seemed unaware and it was a topic he would never leave alone, if he knew of my refusal.

"Come on. We can talk on board. It's leaving." Alden grabbed the satchel Dr. Chapman had been carrying in his good left hand and jumped up the steps of the railway car. I followed with the doctor helping me as best he could. His right arm had been injured during a smallpox epidemic on the West Side. While he was administering vaccinations in a sweatshop, a hysterical little tailor let loose with a shotgun, shattering the doctor's arm.

I settled into a window seat while Alden swung the satchel up to the overhead rack and sat down opposite me. I made room for the doctor but he rather pointedly slid into the seat beside my brother. From that vantage point, I could not avoid his gaze. I gritted my teeth and willed myself to keep from squirming. It was two of them against my one.

As the train pulled away, I quickly told them all about our trip to Pullman the day before, the discovery of the dead man, and our visit to the Pullman mansion.

"He wants them to suffer. He wants them to feel the pinch, to feel hunger. Then, he will reopen the works and try to get some of them to give up on the strike. He wants to break them that way and will never make a single concession. He can't be allowed to get away with it. We must help them so that they can hold out as long as it takes. Even if he reopens the factory, they can't go back."

"Many will go back, if he reopens," the doctor warned me. "If a man must watch his family go hungry because he cannot feed them, how can you expect him not to go back to a job that will stave off the hunger, even if only for a while? That is a very difficult thing to ask a man to do, to watch his family starve."

"But that is why we must provide relief. We have flour, and sugar, and salt coming down today and there will be more tomorrow. Miss Addams will speak for them and get aid. They must stay together or they will never get Pullman to give in to anything."

"You may find them reluctant to take aid." The doctor was intent on being perverse with me. "Working people hate to be forced to take charity. They are more proud than the millionaires of Prairie Avenue of the few hard-earned comforts in their homes, because they provide them themselves. They will hate the idea of taking charity, you'll see. Faced with the choice of taking charity from you, or low wages from Pullman, they will be hard put not to return to work."

"But they must stick together. That is what the union is for. They are part of the American Railway Union."

"That's Debs's new union," Alden contributed. "It's huge. They say it's only a technicality that the Pullman workers are in it, but if the rest of the union decides to refuse to hook up the Pullman Palace Cars, that could have a huge impact. It's all over the country. But what about this man that died, Em? I heard he was a spy. That's not saying much for the solidarity of the Pullman workers if they have company spies and then they execute them."

"Alden, you've no cause to say that. The man was found in a huge shed that's part of the Pullman factory complex. He was hung from the rafters with a sign with the word 'spy' painted on it and hung around his neck. But I don't believe Mr. MacGregor—who's the leader of the strike committee—knew anything about it. The company man, Jennings, came with the police and took away Mr. MacGregor, even though we told them he was with us all afternoon and could not have been involved. The police are under the influence of the company. They were at Jennings's beck and call. We were terribly concerned about Mr. MacGregor and the others being treated fairly, but Mr. Safer and Miss Addams contacted the mayor and got him to assign Detective Whitbread to the investigation. He's to meet us down there."

"Hah, the mayor lives in Pullman, did you know that?" my brother asked. "Mayor Hopkins worked there at one time but he has no love for Pullman. He got out by investing in a grocery in the next town. He supports the strikers. But no doubt Pullman has his own supporters in the local precinct, despite City Hall. Well, you know it'll be all right with Whitey on it." I had worked with Detective Whitbread while compiling statistics on crime for a study at the university. We all came to know him as a man of complete integrity, immune from the political forces that too often influenced justice in the city.

Dr. Chapman had another word of caution. "You are in sympathy with the workers, Miss Cabot. But you know Whitbread will go after the truth of what happened. If the strikers did kill the man, because he was discovered to be a spy for the company, Whitbread will expose them."

"I asked Mr. Pullman if they really used spies. He as good as said they did. He said there is a plot to blow up one of the buildings. But I cannot believe that Mr. MacGregor would do anything—or allow any of the men to do anything—of that kind. He has them organized to patrol the outside of the factory to make sure there is no sabotage. Wait until you meet him. You'll see." I felt that I knew more than the two men about what was happening at Pullman. They had not seen what I had seen. They had not heard the workers' complaints, and they had not seen the dead man hanging from the rafters, or helped to lower his empty body to the ground. They had not seen the policemen threaten the crowd and protect the managers. And, most importantly, they had not heard the stubborn selfish words of the man who could put an end to all of it—George Pullman.

The train was pulling to a stop at the neat brick building that was the Pullman depot. On the platform, I could see the tall figure of Detective Whitbread in his wool suit and bowler hat, beside the squat figure of Mr. MacGregor. I was enormously relieved that the union leader had been released. So much for all of the arguments I had spent such time and care concocting. I should have had confidence in Detective Whitbread. He would not let innocent men stay behind bars.

As we followed Alden out of the car, Dr. Chapman added a word of advice. "You may find that your brother and the other men of the press are your best allies, Emily. There's little the strikers will be able to do to influence a man like Pullman, but the press may be able to at least tell their story to the world." It was another warning from him. He had no confidence in my ability to handle any situation and I found it galling. I brushed past him and stepped down to the platform.

SIX

Detective Whitbread was anxious to hurry us on our way as soon as we left the train, but Mr. MacGregor stood his ground and insisted on speaking his thanks.
"Miss Cabot, we are very grateful to you and Miss Addams. The food that is being sent will be greatly appreciated and we were glad to have the detective arrange for the release of the men taken yesterday."

"Yes, yes," Detective Whitbread interrupted. "They don't have any idea what they are doing down here about a murder investigation. The mayor has asked me to handle it and it will be done to everybody's satisfaction. But now we must get down to the Dens. They have allowed the family to take the body away without a proper examination and if we don't hurry they'll have it in the ground before we can see it. Dr. Chapman, what luck you've come along. I need your services, if you will. I have a carriage. Quickly now. And, Mr. Cabot, I'm glad to see you've recovered. Come along. I'll need you to give me a report, Miss Cabot, as well. Everyone in, please, there's no time to waste."

He hurried us around the side of the building to a large open carriage he had commandeered from the Pullman stables. As we got in and started moving, I was once again impressed by the breadth of the town itself.

Meanwhile, Mr. MacGregor appeared somewhat concerned about our errand. He explained that we were going to the O'Malley home where Brian O'Malley was being waked preparatory to a funeral at the Holy Rosary Church in the nearby town of Kensington. The O'Malleys occupied one of the brickyard cottages that were known as the "Dens" and he tried to prepare us for the visit.

"They've fallen on hard times, the O'Malleys have, since the father, Sean, died last year. Brian was a carpenter and got work in the repair shops sometimes. But Joe, he could only get work in the brickyards. And they had to move to the Dens. Gracie will be there—Mrs. Foley that you met yesterday, she that was Gracie O'Malley." He stopped and thought about that for a while.

"She should not have been allowed to take the body away without a proper examination by a doctor," Detective Whitbread told him. "It was entirely improper."

Remembering the tension of the scene in the shed, I thought it would have been a mistake to try to stop Mrs. Foley, but I did not try to explain. Mr. MacGregor's brow was creased with worry.

"Perhaps I should tell you a little of Mrs. Foley's story." He moved uncomfortably but, after looking at the skeptical expression on Whitbread's long face, he decided to continue. "Gracie is the oldest of the family. She was always forward. Outspoken, you might say. Her mother died when the littlest one in the family was born. Gracie and the two older boys—Brian and Joe—helped raise the young'uns. Her father got Gracie a job in the laundry here, but she thought she was treated unfairly and it's not her way to keep quiet. Her father told her to keep her peace, but she wouldn't, and when she spoke up she was laid off.

"Well, she had been seeing one of lads that worked in the brickyard with Joe. Brendan Foley, he was. He was a drinker and lazy, but he talked big and he impressed the women. Well, he got laid off himself, no surprise, but then Sean found out that Gracie was with child. I think they must have planned to marry, but when Brendan got laid off he moved into the city and they had nothing to live on to get married. But Sean, he was furious. He threw Gracie out and she had to go to the city. Well, I think they got married then, but Sean still refused to talk to her and he forbade the others to keep in touch with her at all. And Brian supported his da and wouldn't let her come to visit at all, even after she was married to Brendan and they lost the child and all." He sighed.

"Sean was a good man but a hard one. When he got hurt in an accident—a packing crate fell on him—he wouldn't let them send for her, and Brian supported him again that time. I don't suppose he knew he would die of it. But he did. And at the funeral Brian still wouldn't let the others even talk to her. It was terrible to watch. She was there, you see, but far away from the grave when they put him in it. And by then I heard Brendan Foley had got himself killed in a barroom. Gracie had gotten work as a laundress, though, and she stayed in the city."

We were all quiet as the carriage took us away from the last of the brick row houses and towards the mud flats. The shed where the body was found was off to our left and Lake Calumet beyond. Ahead of us we could see four rows of wooden shanties. These were like nothing in the rest of the clean and tidy brick town. Even those of us used to the rickety wooden tenements crowded into the slums of the West Side were appalled by these buildings that looked barely habitable. It was unusually quiet as we approached. I could see a wagon holding a wooden coffin standing beside one of the last of the shanties. Between the sounds of the hoof beats and jangling harnesses of our carriage we could hear the mournful wailing sound of pipe music floating across the mud.

"That'll be Joe, the younger brother," Mr. MacGregor told us. "Uilleann pipes he plays. That's a mournful sound, then. He used to play for the dances in the Market Hall before, when his father was alive." The little man shook his head and we all listened as we pulled to a stop before the last structure. There were people standing quietly in the yard, spilling over into the next shack, and others around a lean-to on the side that I judged must be the kitchen, such as it was.

As the music stopped, Detective Whitbread climbed down.

"Mr. MacGregor, Dr. Chapman, if you will."

Dr. Chapman stepped down, then reached back to take his satchel from Alden. Mr. MacGregor followed, seeming reluctant.

I decided to join them as they went up the two small steps into the gloom of the interior. People moved out of the way with curious looks. It was obvious that there was little room inside, however, and most were paying their respects, then moving to the yard of the next house. As people came out, the men slipped surreptitiously around the side of the building to the group by the lean-to.

Inside it was dark, except for two banks of candles at the head and foot of a table where the body of Brian O'Malley was laid out, covered by what looked like a linen tablecloth up to his chin. I was startled to see Fiona MacGregor sitting beside the dead man on a low stool. Her father was also surprised and I saw her look up at him with fear in her eyes. Then she stood and quickly pushed past me out of the room. As her father turned to watch her go, Gracie Foley rose up from the gloom of the corner.

"Ian MacGregor, it's a great nerve you have coming to pay your respects. He wasn't good enough for you and your precious daughter in life, was our Brian? But you'll weep for him in death, is that it? We've no use for your crocodile tears here. Be gone." There was great scorn in her voice and I saw tears in the eyes of the little man as he looked at the white face of the dead boy. I thought he was too choked with tears to answer her taunts. Or perhaps he had been rendered immovable by the words of the woman. Looming up from behind the corpse, with the candles lighting her face from below, I could almost believe Gracie Foley was some kind of witch.

"You are Mrs. Foley?" Detective Whitbread broke the spell in his usual mundane way. "I am Detective Henry Whitbread. I am investigating your brother's death. I'm very sorry for your loss, madam, but we must look at your brother's body before you can take it away for interment."

This was a very uncharacteristic attempt on Detective Whitbread's part to soften, and apologize for, the intrusions necessary in his job. Gracie Foley was not acquainted with my policeman friend, however, and when she moved her concentrated gaze from poor Mr. MacGregor to the detective there was sharp animosity in her eyes.

"You will do no such thing. You'll not touch him. You, who work for the company and the great and greedy Mr. George Pullman, you'll not put your hands on him. Have you no shame? Is it not enough you've killed him? Him who was the only support for the children? You killed our father at your works and now you've killed our brother. Can you not leave him be, so that we can mourn him in peace?" She was breathing fast, her face red with anger, and she took two steps to put herself between Whitbread and the dead man.

"Calm yourself, madam. We mean no disrespect. On the contrary, we are here to see that justice is done. We are in no way connected to the Pullman Company. I am a detective of the Chicago Police Department sent to investigate the circumstances of your brother's death. This is Dr. Chapman, a medical doctor. If you will just give us a few moments alone with the body, we will discover what we can from it and be on our way."

She laughed. It was a harsh sound, a bitter response. "You are from the police? And you say you are not connected to the company? Hah! You dare to say you are not in his pay? You dare to speak of justice? What do you know of justice? What justice is there in Pullman? What justice is it that the children go hungry? What justice is it that their father is taken away from them? What justice is it that they are forced to live in a shack like this? What justice is it that men like him," she pointed at MacGregor, "with their strikes and their causes can murder their brother and bring us to starvation?"

MacGregor blinked, then turned and left the room, pushing past me. I was concerned that the woman was on the brink of hysteria, but it was a controlled rage. She planted herself between the table and Detective Whitbread, bending forward from the waist to spit her words into his face. Whitbread was not an emotional man himself. He relied upon fact and logic and was relentless in pursuit of them, with perfect disregard for extraneous influences. His greatest point of pride was his integrity and I had seen him risk job and livelihood in defense of his reputation. He was not about to have it impugned. He cocked his head.

"I repeat, madam. We are here in the pursuit of justice. We have not been dispatched by the Pullman Company, Mr. MacGregor and his strike committee, or anyone else. We represent only the people of the city of Chicago, who demand that a deed such as the murder of your brother be investigated and the perpetrator brought to justice. This is our errand, nothing else. To accomplish it, we will have to view your brother's body to determine the true cause of death. You can assist us, or you can attempt to hinder us, in which case I will have the unwelcome duty of putting you under arrest."

He returned her concentrated glare coolly and I had no doubt he would arrest her and brave the anger of the crowd that was gathering in the yard behind my back.

"Mrs. Foley," Dr. Chapman intervened. "I am Stephen Chapman. I'm a doctor and I have come to Pullman at the request of Miss Jane Addams to provide medical care to those who need it during this strike. I can vouch for Detective Whitbread. He is not in the pay of George Pullman, or Mr. MacGregor, or anyone else. It is Mayor Hopkins who has asked Detective Whitbread to investigate in order to ensure that everything is done to find whoever did this to your brother. Please let us examine his body. It will not take long and then you can take him to the church. If you like, we can ask your priest to come in while we do the examination. Would that help?"

Whitbread turned to frown at the doctor, releasing his gaze from the deadlock with Gracie Foley. She watched them with narrowed eyes. "Dr. Chapman, we have work to get on with. We cannot be waiting for a priest."

"Whitbread, if we must wait for a priest we will. I will not do the examination without the consent of Mrs. Foley, so unless you want to find another medical man, you will wait."

As they continued to argue, Gracie Foley's eyes fell on mine. "He really does not work for Mr. Pullman, Mrs. Foley. He refuses to be influenced by anyone. He will find the truth."

Somehow the bickering that had broken out between the two men managed to drain the rage out of Gracie Foley. I thought she recognized in it something about the male character that she could trust more than any show of force. Suddenly, she stepped away from the table. At that the men stopped talking. Before Whitbread could question her move, Dr. Chapman stepped to the table and began to gently fold back the sheet draping the body. The man was clothed in a threadbare jacket and pants that the doctor began to remove. When Mrs. Foley pushed her way out the door, wiping tears from her cheeks, I followed, hoping to allow them privacy. I stood beside her outside as she sniffed back her tears. Mr. MacGregor had moved off by himself on the mud flats and he looked away towards Lake Calumet. Gracie glared at his figure.

"He has a nerve coming, him and his daughter. Brian wasn't good enough for her. 'Twas that he was Catholic. Ian MacGregor claimed a great friendship with my father but when Brian and Fiona wanted to marry they both of them—MacGregor and my father—stepped in the way. They forbade it. On the grounds of religion. That was a Christian act, now wasn't it?"

I could think of no response. I didn't like to leave her side. She radiated an intense anger, yet she drew my sympathy like a wounded animal might. Her glare had not left Ian MacGregor's figure and, as if he felt it—though he was turned away—I saw him head across the mud flats to the large, long shed where we had found Brian O'Malley the day before. I saw Gracie finally remove her gaze from him and my eyes followed to where a gleaming horse and buggy were trotting up the dirt road. She nodded towards it and looked me in the eye.

"But I no longer care for the church or anyone else. Mr. Mooney is not Catholic but he has asked me to marry him and I will. Mr. Mooney is not a union man and Mr. Mooney is not a creature of Pullman." With that she left me to step towards the buggy that drew to a halt. It was a short, fussy man who carefully set the reins and whip and climbed down to greet Gracie Foley. He wore a bowler hat and a slick black suit with stripes and shiny patent leather boots. From where I stood, I thought he looked at least as old as Mr. MacGregor and his height was such that his eyes barely reached Gracie's shoulder. But he took her hand and bowed over it and reached up into the carriage for a large bunch of lilies that he placed in her arms. When he followed her as she headed back to the shack I saw him nod to the men with the wagon bearing the wooden coffin and I thought perhaps it would be with his assistance that Brian O'Malley was decently buried that day.

I was relieved to see Detective Whitbread and the doctor exiting the house before Gracie returned. And I was impressed to see Mr. Mooney introduce himself and listen with deliberation as they explained their errand. It seemed to me it was only with his express dismissal that they turned away and joined me.

"Mr. MacGregor has already walked to the shed," I told the doctor as he joined me. Whitbread was instructing the driver of our carriage where to meet us. I looked around for Alden and saw him standing with a group of men near the back by the lean-to. I made a move towards him, but Dr. Chapman put a hand on my arm.

"I should leave him."

"But, the way he's behaving, I'm afraid he'll give offense." It seemed to me that he and the other men were standing around talking and laughing. I was afraid of what Gracie Foley would say if she caught them at it. "What will Mrs. Foley think?"

"It's a custom," Dr. Chapman told me, taking my arm and leading me after the detective, who had begun his long-legged trek across the mud to the shed. "The men gather and tell stories about the dead man. They even pass around a jug." He hung on to me as I squirmed around to look. "It's a rite of passing. The women ignore it, as they ignore much they don't approve of in their men."

With a sigh I gave up on my brother and concentrated on getting to the shed. Gracie Foley's bitter history was on my mind as I trudged along beside the man I had chosen not to marry. For Gracie, like so many women, marrying Mr. Mooney was a feat and she paraded him as an accomplishment she was proud of. My own younger sister, Rose, had done no less when she announced her engagement to the son of an important banking family in Boston. My move to Chicago to study at the university had allowed me to avoid such an accomplishment. But it had not been achieved easily and my own actions had exiled me. Faced with an opportunity to return to those studies on my own terms, or to accept the protection of the doctor, I had refused to be sheltered. It was not an accomplishment in my eyes, it was a defeat—or it would have been for me.

I took a final look back at the decrepit shack, and the impeccable livery of Mr. Mooney that would take Gracie Foley away from it all, then turned firmly forward to enter the building where her brother had been killed. Earlier, Mr. MacGregor explained to me that the shed was used to dry the bricks that were made from the mud of the surrounding area.

We found Detective Whitbread in consultation with Mr. MacGregor, hearing his version of the scene the day before. He climbed around examining the ropes and pulleys, then took me through my own description of what I had seen, stopping me again and again to describe the corpse in a way that made me shudder as I remembered details. Finally, he drew the doctor over to a sort of metal shelf where there were a number of tools laid out. I waited, getting chilled in the breeze that blew through the open doors on both sides. I looked away from Pullman, out east towards the lake. I had no desire to explore the two wings of the building that were packed high with mud bricks drying in the shelter. At last the two men joined me. Detective Whitbread appeared to be very pleased with himself and he was rubbing his hands together.

"So, you agree then? That must have been what happened?"

"Yes. It can have been no other way."

"What?" I asked. "What did you find out?"

Whitbread hastened to be the one to expound on the topic. "Based on the examination of the body, and confirmed by examination of the site, we can state with certainty the cause of death."

"But how can that be in question?" I asked. "We know the cause of death, he was hung." I shivered as soon as I said it. I could picture the body still hanging there as it had been the day before.

"On the contrary, Miss Cabot, any such assumption would be totally inaccurate. What we have established, beyond a doubt, is that the man did *not* die of hanging. He was dead before his body was hung."

SEVEN

I remembered the matted hair and brown crusts of blood on the head of the dead man. Standing in the drafty shed with a breeze from Lake Calumet passing through one wide doorway and then out the other, it was as if I could still see the work boots hanging there. "But, I saw him hanging!"

"Yes, but he did not *die* by hanging," Detective Whitbread strode back to the bench and pointed at the corner. "There was a struggle and Brian O'Malley hit his temple here."

He returned to the middle of the shed and examined the rope that hung slack from the pulley above. But why would someone hang the man if he was already dead? It made no sense.

"When you arrived, Miss Cabot, the body was hanging from this pulley, is that correct?"

"Yes, that's correct," I answered the detective reluctantly.

"And there was a sign hung around his neck, you said?" Whitbread peered into the shadows of the shed. "Where is it?"

I could see it in my mind. It had been a board, a piece of a packing case with the letters streaking as the wet paint dripped down. The word "spy" was scrawled on it.

"Mr. Jennings took it away with him," I told him.

"It should not have been permitted. Ah, here." Whitbread moved back to the bench. "Here is the paint. It was black, was it? Well, he did not bother to reseal the tin. It has dried up. And this stick was used, an indication of haste, since he did not bother to find a paintbrush. The sign was to label the dead man as a spy, then. Meant as a warning to others."

It was an ugly thought. If there was a fight and the man had hit his head, why not get help, or even leave him and run away?

How, and why, someone could paint the sign and put it around his neck, then hoist the body into the air, was impossible to imagine. Yet he had been here yesterday, swaying in the breeze, like some kind of a deadly warning.

"I cannot believe Brian was a spy for the company," Mr. MacGregor protested. "He was a good man, a carpenter. He joined his local but he only went along like the rest. There was some talk about spies, but it was nothing but rumor. We had not decided to walk out, not finally. It was provisional, you see. There was a plan in case it looked like the company would lock us out. We were only going to call them out if the company moved. There was confusion that day and suddenly the word went around to go and we went, but later it was said that someone had told the managers about the plan and they had made it look like they were planning to shut down, to force us to go out. But it was confusion. Everyone was on edge. They laid off three of the committee even though they promised they wouldn't." He shook his head with regret. "I fear we won't ever know exactly what happened, but it was bound to come sooner or later."

"But some of the men thought there was a spy or spies who informed the company about the plans?" Whitbread asked.

MacGregor looked him in the eye. "The company has always had informers they pay to find out what the union men are planning. They have money to pay them and it is hard for a poor man to pass up the temptation sometimes."

"And the others resented the traitor in their midst?"

"Certainly. But I cannot believe it was Brian. He did not know the details any more than another and he had no money from such a deal. You saw his sister. She came down to bring food, being as the little ones were hungry. He would not have let them go hungry if he had money in his pocket, no matter where it came from. And he would not have wanted to beg from his sister. He was a proud man, like his father before him."

"Perhaps he knew it was worth his life to expose the treachery and kept it hidden," the detective told him. "Or perhaps the man or men who killed him made a mistake. Desperate, angry men will turn on the nearest prey, MacGregor, and your men are desperate, are they not?"

"None of them would do this," MacGregor protested. "They none of them would kill a man for that."

"But someone has, Mr. MacGregor. Someone has." Under his stern gaze the little union man's head bowed and his feet shuffled on the floor. There was nothing he could say to refute this. The detective straightened up his lanky body. "Well, I must go and retrieve the evidence from that company man. Who is it again?"

"Mr. William Jennings," I told him. "You'll find him at the Florence Hotel. I met him yesterday when I was here with Miss Addams and the committee from the Civic Federation."

"Good. We'll go there next. The carriage is waiting."

But Mr. MacGregor hung back as Whitbread turned away. "If you please, sir. We are most grateful for the assistance that Miss Cabot and Dr. Chapman are bringing from people in the city. There are some who are waiting for it. I must go now to attend to them and let them know when help will arrive. And, then, I would not be welcome at the Florence. The company has made it a kind of headquarters, if you see what I mean, and they would not like me there any more than we would want one of them at our meetings." He stood solidly, waiting for his point to be acknowledged.

Dr. Chapman turned to the detective. "MacGregor is right. I've come to tend to the medical needs of the striking men and women and since, as he says, there are some waiting, I must go and see them now." MacGregor nodded in vigorous agreement. "And Miss Cabot must find a place for the supplies that will arrive this afternoon. Have you found some place in the town where we may set up the relief station and clinic, Mr. MacGregor?"

"Not in the town itself, doctor, for we don't want to be obliged to the company. But just over the tracks in Kensington we've been offered the use of the top floors over a grocery. It belongs to Mayor Hopkins and his partner and they have kindly given us a meeting room and offices. We should go and get you settled. There'll be some waiting who are sick and would be grateful for your help."

"You see, Detective? We must part company, you to pursue your investigation, and the rest of us to do what we were sent here to do."

"But the supplies will not be down until later," I interjected. "I could come to the hotel, if you like, and find Mr. Jennings for you. I won't be needed until later." It was not as if Detective Whitbread would have any trouble finding anyone he wanted to question, but I was uneasy about what the company man would say. I knew Whitbread to be incorruptible but, all the same, I wanted to be able to hear and refute anything the manager might say against the striking workers. They couldn't defend themselves, but I was an outside observer and I had met the cold and stubborn man they were up against. I knew they needed as much help and as many advocates as possible to stand up to the blows that man was prepared to level at them. The doctor frowned and shook his head at me but, in the end, he did not object.

By the time we had traversed the mud flats back to the carriage it was agreed that I would stop at the hotel with Whitbread while Mr. MacGregor and the doctor went on to the Kensington strike headquarters. Alden was nowhere to be seen, but none of us thought he needed looking after. He was like a cat that always lands on its feet and he would find his way to us when he was ready.

I could not help but be impressed again by the beauty and charm of the neat little row houses, wide tree-lined streets, and pretty flowerbeds of the town as we trotted back through it. It was such a perfect environment for people to live happily. What a terrible shame that it had come to the point where the inhabitants were divided into those who were sick and hungry and those who were so stubbornly dominant and yet living in fear of their striking neighbors. They could live in harmony—I was sure of it, even if they were not.

The carriage stopped at the west door of the hotel, and then quickly turned away as I followed Detective Whitbread up the wide steps and across the spacious veranda. We moved out of the bright spring sunshine into the darkness of the interior, where the sweet, sharp scent of pipe smoke hit my nostrils before my eyes became accustomed to the gloom. The lobby boasted a very high ceiling and was paneled in dark wood, with rectangular windows set high up on the front wall. To my left, the detective had stepped up to an L-shaped marble counter, behind which a man wearing a trim suit and sporting a pince-nez regarded me over the policeman's shoulder. He did not look welcoming, but Whitbread took out his badge and displayed it under the man's nose.

"I am Detective Henry Whitbread from the Chicago police. This is Miss Cabot. We are looking for a Mr. William Jennings, if you please."

The man at the desk did not seem at all pleased about this request and frowned. To my right, tall pocket doors stood open into a smoking parlor where one man looked up from his newspaper in alarm. Men's voices and the click of billiard balls came from one direction, while the muffled sounds of glassware and crockery could be heard from what must be the dining room. It was obvious, from the reaction I was getting, that we had entered through the men's entrance and women were not allowed in this section. This was the type of distinction Detective Whitbread hardly ever acknowledged, certainly not when he was pursuing a case. The frowning clerk at the counter was just about to object to my presence when Mr. Jennings came out of the smoking room, pulling on his jacket and looking around alertly.

"Hello, did I hear my name? Ah, Miss Cabot, how do you do? And you, sir, can I help you?"

"Detective Whitbread, Chicago police. I need to interview you concerning the events of yesterday. Can we go someplace private?"

"Yes, of course." Jennings looked doubtfully over the detective's shoulder at the still frowning clerk. He opened his mouth with a suggestion, then changed his mind, glancing at me and then back to the clerk. "I know. I was just about to go in to dinner. You'll join me, won't you? Both of you?" He stepped over to offer me his elbow. "You never got to try our soup yesterday, Miss Cabot. You really must. Would you mind, Detective? It's on the company, of course. This way." He ushered me down a corridor and we came to the north door where there was a ladies' parlor on the left and the entrance to the dining room on the right. I could almost hear a sigh of relief behind us as my feminine presence was ejected from that very masculine realm. The world could return to normal for them.

The smells of roasting meat and baked bread filled the room and made me feel hungry, as an apron-clad waiter led us to a round table by a window. We had returned late to Hull House the previous night and fed on cold meats as we made our plans. I found the thought of a warm meal very tempting. But I thought guiltily of the others who had gone on to wait for the supplies. We knew that food was in short supply for the striking workers and it seemed like a traitorous thing to do to sit here and eat well while they were waiting for a wagonload of basic foodstuffs. But a bowl of steaming, green-pea soup dotted with large chunks of red ham was almost immediately put before me. It smelled delicious. Both men dipped their spoons and tasted the hot brew, but I wet my lips and was undecided. How could I fill my stomach when so many were going hungry?

"I have returned, Mr. Jennings, to organize a relief station for the workers. During our trip yesterday it came to our attention that many of the men are hard-pressed to feed their families."

That stopped the next spoonful from reaching the assistant manager's mouth, but Detective Whitbread ate on methodically. He usually had a dictum for any circumstance in life and I could imagine the present one would be to sip your soup while it's hot. But William Jennings was more sensitive to my implied disapproval.

"That could be easily righted, Miss Cabot, if they would stop this strike and return to work. It is not those of us in the company who have brought this on them. They have brought it on themselves and only they can right it by leaving off from this hasty and unwise action and returning to their jobs while there are still positions there for them."

Meanwhile, Detective Whitbread had made his way down to the bottom of his bowl and wiped his moustache with his napkin. "It is quite nourishing, Miss Cabot, please eat. Mr. Jennings, I understand that yesterday you removed a signboard that had been around the neck of the man who was killed. That was unfortunate. The local constabulary should not have allowed it. I must ask that you return it to me."

Jennings flushed at this. If he expected deference from Whitbread, based on treating him to dinner, he had much to learn about my policeman friend. I hid a smile by dipping into a spoonful of the soup. It was delicious and whether it was from hunger or the realization that the men could not get on with their meal until I had finished my bowl, I quickly worked my way to the bottom as Whitbread interrogated Mr. Jennings.

"It is in the office. I will take you there immediately after our meal," he told Whitbread. "I didn't want it to disappear. By the time I got there it had already been removed from the dead man. We will do all we can to assist your investigation, of course. I'm not sure why Mayor Hopkins felt you needed to be brought down from the city, but we will cooperate."

"I should certainly hope so, sir. A man has been murdered and it is the duty of every citizen to cooperate fully, in order that we may find and arrest his killer. Were you acquainted with the deceased, Mr. Brian O'Malley?"

"I did make a statement last night that was taken down at the station, you know."

"I have read your statement, but I have been assigned to the investigation and I must ask you to answer additional questions."

At that moment our soup plates were whisked away to be replaced by steaming plates of roast beef with mashed potatoes in a rich brown gravy and small green peas on the side. Having eaten the soup I felt no more compunction about tasting the meal, but I paid close attention to the two men as I ate.

"Of course, of course, Detective, we are most eager to have this settled and the miscreant brought to justice. It is a terrible thing and it demonstrates how very dangerous these labor agitators can be. It is just this sort of violence that we have feared from the first. Once it begins there's no telling where it will end. We depend on you as the local authorities to protect us from this violence and to prevent it from spreading. That's why the local police took in those men last night. We must keep this from spreading or we will all be in danger."

"Mr. Jennings, it is the duty of the police to protect all of the people, whether they be on the side of the company or the strikers. That is not at issue. Please answer the question. Were you acquainted with the dead man?" Having posed the question, Whitbread took up his knife and fork to attack his meat. Jennings reached across to the breadbasket and took a roll that he proceeded to tear apart.

"There are more than three thousand men employed in the works and I am in the legal department, so I certainly do not know them all. But I knew of the family. The father died last year and had been a long-time employee." His eyes slid across at me and back to the policeman. He was remembering that I had been in the shed the day before. "I recognized his sister when I arrived. There was some trouble between her and the rest of the family that was widely known. She argued with her father and brothers and left the town a couple of years ago."

I swallowed the mouthful of meat I was chewing. How very ungallant of Mr. Jennings. It sounded like he was trying to implicate Gracie Foley in her brother's death.

But Detective Whitbread was not to be deflected from the subject at hand. "Someone seems to have thought Brian O'Malley was a company spy. Was he, Mr. Jennings?"

The assistant manager had taken up his knife and fork but now put them down to respond. "I don't know if you realize how very dangerous these agitators can be, Detective. If you think their plans are limited to peaceful protest, you are naïve. Oh, MacGregor and the others will say that they tell the men to stay away, or even that they organize them to patrol the perimeters, claiming they want to prevent sabotage. But in secret they have other plans, plans for violence. We know there are plans to destroy some of the buildings, but we're not sure which ones. We think they may want to damage the clock tower in the center of the administration building, as a symbol. They might even be planning to blow it up. We have every right to try to protect the company's property. We have the duty to do so. We are only helping you and the other local authorities whose job it is to protect us."

"So you *do* plant spies among the men?" I accused him.

He flushed. "Not every man agrees with the tactics of the strikers, Miss Cabot. Some of them are not happy that they are deprived of their wages because the union organizers command a strike. Some of them want to see the strikers defeated, but they're intimidated. They can't say so. If there are some who are willing to help us to prevent the violence that others plan to perpetrate in their name, why should you blame them? If by so doing they can get enough to feed their families, do you not sympathize with them?" he asked, pointing with his knife to my own laden plate. It made me put down my utensils, feeling guilty at eating so heartily when I had come down to help keep the workers from starving. And it made me angry.

"You and Mr. Pullman just want to break them," I objected. "The only thing they have is solidarity. By staying together they can force you to rectify an impossible situation and it's the only means they have. So you try to corrupt them and grow a canker from within by planting spies among them. It is despicable."

Detective Whitbread intervened. "Miss Cabot, we are not here to discuss the strike, if you please. That must be settled elsewhere. We are here to find out the truth of what happened to Mr. O'Malley. Now, Mr. Jennings, I ask you again, was Brian O'Malley working for you as an informant about the strikers' plans, or for any other matter?"

Jennings put his head down and worked viciously away at his meat with his knife. He answered through clenched teeth. "Yes. He told us there were rumors of a plot to blow up the clock tower. He was trying to find out more about it."

"Rumors," I huffed.

"Quiet, Miss Cabot, if you please. Did you pay Mr. O'Malley?"

"Yes. He was paid fifty dollars and promised more when he had further information."

I stopped eating, and sat there steaming, but held my tongue. I could only imagine that, once a man with a family to feed had sacrificed his principles enough to inform on his comrades, the temptation to provide more information and receive more money, even if he had to make it up, would be hard to resist. It seemed a particularly insidious and evil practice to get men to spy on their fellow men. I was disgusted.

There was a strained silence as Detective Whitbread considered this information while he finished off his meal. Finally, Jennings set down his utensils. Like me, he seemed to have lost his appetite.

"Whitbread, you must see what this means. O'Malley must have been getting close to the plot. To protect it they killed him.

That means they plan to go through with it. We must demand that you do everything in your power to thwart them. It is the duty of the authorities to protect the company property. How will it look for the police department and Mayor Hopkins—who openly sympathizes with the strikers—if they succeed in blowing up the works? You must arrest the leaders immediately. If this conspiracy is carried out, you will bear part of the blame."

Detective Whitbread calmly wiped his mouth with his napkin, leaving it on the table and waving away the coffee that was offered by our waiter.

"It is the duty of the city to protect all of its citizens, Mr. Jennings, and we will do so to the best of our ability. But that does not justify widespread arrest and detention without cause. As you know, that would be wholly illegal. Nor would it solve your problem. Arrest of the wrong persons would only exacerbate the situation, sir. We must uncover the truth and apprehend the real culprits. To that end, I will leave you after retrieving that sign—which bit of evidence should never have been removed from the scene of the crime."

Jennings rose stiffly and led us to a small office where he produced the sign. Then Whitbread marched us out through the front door again, ignoring the disapproving glances from the desk clerk. The carriage was waiting to take us to join MacGregor, Dr. Chapman, and the others at the Kensington strike headquarters.

"Do you think it's true that Brian O'Malley was spying for them?" I asked, as we clip-clopped away from the neatly tended lawns and flowerbeds of Pullman and into the dirtier and more crowded brick buildings of the next town.

"It seems quite possible in the circumstances. Quite likely, really. There are probably a few well-paid spies of the company who have infiltrated the strikers' organization." I knew he was right and it depressed me. "But I must say there is a question to be answered about where the money went," he continued. "If Brian O'Malley earned fifty dollars from the company, where is it? And why did he send for Mrs. Foley if he had that to fall back on? From what we have heard, he would have hated to have to ask her for help. In fact I could understand how the thought of needing to appeal to her after such treatment might even drive him to work for the company as a spy. But if he did so, why appeal to her? And what brought her down here, shunned as she was by her family, if not such an appeal?"

EIGHT

The headquarters for the strikers was a much less impressive building than the Florence Hotel. A few minutes away, it was beyond the limits of the company town. It seemed a bad omen that it was down a street where saloons occupied every other storefront. I knew that George Pullman had forbidden sales of alcohol within the limits of the town of Pullman, except at the hotel where high prices kept the workingmen from temptation. It seemed a sorry comment on how fragile the neat order of the town really was that these rows of saloons had crept up to the very edges as if lying in wait to ensnare the men if they stepped over the town line. It made me more exasperated than ever to think that all the good things about the model community were being put at risk by this dispute. If only George Pullman would lower the rents to ensure the men could continue to live within the limits of the town, where they could be safe from all of this. I knew he and others would only point to these establishments and ask why there was money to spend here if rents were too high, and they would score that point.

The carriage stopped in front of the S & H Grocery building, where the upper floors had been offered for the use of the strikers. We were directed up the stairs to a large meeting room where we found Mr. MacGregor and his men setting up folding wooden chairs and benches. Detective Whitbread demanded his attention, but he ignored the detective to speak to me.

"We have a meeting later . . . we're just setting up now. The offices are on the next two floors, miss. The doctor is using one of them and there are rooms for the supplies on the top floor, when they come." He looked anxious.

"They will come, Mr. MacGregor. It will take some time as they are driving two wagons," I assured him.

"I must ask you some questions, MacGregor," Detective Whitbread insisted, and the smaller man led us to the front of the room where there was a raised platform set up for a speaker. He seemed distracted.

"We've been told by Mr. Jennings that Brian O'Malley was providing information to the company." MacGregor shook his head sorrowfully. "Yes," Whitbread insisted, "so it would seem. Mr. Jennings also alleges that Mr. O'Malley told them of a plot to blow up the clock tower and he was pursuing details of this plot when he was killed. I must ask you, Mr. MacGregor, whether you are aware of any such conspiracy and I must warn you that anyone attempting such a thing will pay a heavy price."

"No, no, Detective Whitbread. The men would never do such a thing, I promise you. Never. We know the company would like nothing better than to accuse us of such violence. It is for that very reason that we have organized the men to patrol the perimeter of the works. Here, look here." He led us to a wall near the door where a sheet was posted listing names and times. "These are the patrols. We're watching the works to prevent any such thing. We know they'd like to be able to accuse us of sabotage but we won't allow it. The men have been told repeatedly to stay away from the works unless they're on these patrols." He slapped the page. "And they've agreed to stay away from the saloons as well. We know the company wants to make us look like a drunken mob. But we won't let them."

Detective Whitbread eyed the list, frowning. "That sounds very good, Mr. MacGregor, but I warn you again. Violence of any kind will not be tolerated. If any of the men, whether under your orders or not, cause damage to the Pullman property, they will be apprehended and punished. There is reason to believe that Brian O'Malley had information about such a plot and it led to his death. We will find the truth about this, MacGregor,

I promise you and if you have been concealing it or protecting hot heads, woe be unto you."

"We have not. We have not. We have no desire to interfere with the works. In fact, quite the opposite. We look for other ways to influence the company. We have Mr. Debs coming to speak to the men. Don't be alarmed. He is as anxious as we are to gain sympathy for our plight. We want to tell the world of the injustice of the situation. We know that to damage the works would only harm our cause. We look to the world for sympathy. The most vigorous action contemplated would be to convince the railway men to refuse to hook up the Pullman cars until we have justice. That is all, I assure you."

"For your own sake, I hope it is true. But I must speak to anyone who might have seen Mr. O'Malley yesterday before he died."

"Yes, yes." MacGregor waved over Mr. Stark, who had stopped setting up chairs and was watching us. "Lennie, this is Detective Whitbread. He's looking for men who might have seen Brian yesterday. Take him around. I'll take Miss Cabot up to the offices so she can see where we plan to store the supplies and where the clinic has been set up."

As I followed him across the room I couldn't help feeling that he was anxious to escape the detective's questions. We went up the stairway to a narrow corridor where there were a dozen or so people, men and women, milling about with anxious frowns on their faces. As we walked through them I heard Mr. MacGregor whisper, "Later, it's coming," and I realized they were waiting for the promised supplies. They were hungry themselves, had hungry families at home, and had been waiting all day for the supplies to arrive. MacGregor opened the door into one of the offices, apologizing as he did so. "The businesses over here in Kensington have been good about extending credit, but people are worried about the amount of debt they are building. They will be very grateful for anything Miss Addams can provide."

"I'm sure the wagons will be down soon, Mr. MacGregor. Their wait will not be in vain," I assured him as we entered the office.

It was a fair-sized room with windows overlooking the street. Mr. MacGregor explained that they had set up the clinic here. The wooden desk had been pushed to the side and behind it Dr. Chapman sat, looking worn out. There was a soiled sheet of brown paper with a half-eaten cheese sandwich at his elbow as if he had pushed it away, too tired to eat. He was facing Fiona MacGregor, who sat on a wooden chair placed in front of the desk. A cot had been set up in the middle of the room and several more chairs were pushed back around the walls. Taking it all in, I focused on the girl again and saw there were tears in her eyes that she brushed away quickly at the sight of her father. I thought the lines of the doctor's face smoothed a little as we entered, as if we brought him some relief and it made me wonder what they had been discussing. I waved a hand to prevent him from standing at my entrance. It struck me at that moment that he would much rather have been on a stool in his laboratory in Hyde Park. I forgot the awkwardness that stood between us.

"Oh, Stephen," I blurted out, "we talked to Mr. Jennings and he is claiming that Brian O'Malley knew about a plot to blow up the clock tower. He thinks he found out something and was killed for that." Too late I remembered Fiona's love for the dead man. She shivered a little in her seat and I regretted speaking so bluntly.

"I cannot believe such a thing," Mr. MacGregor piped up. "I do not believe any of the men are so desperate and I cannot believe Brian would spy for them. Whatever I thought of him, he was a good boy and he would not betray us." He shot a worried look at his daughter's back, but her head, with the shiny braid so tightly wound around it, was bent. Dr. Chapman sighed.

"Fiona has been very helpful in seeing to those who came for treatment," he told MacGregor. "I must thank her very much. There is a danger of malaria here, and there may be some tuberculosis. We must not allow any of them to go hungry, it will only make them weak and easy prey to the diseases."

"The supplies have not arrived yet," I told him. "They should be here any time now. But I am very worried about the investigation. I don't believe Jennings when he says Brian O'Malley was a company spy. Jennings can vilify the poor man any way he chooses and it cannot be denied from beyond the grave."

Stephen looked down at his hands, rubbing his fingers on the edges of the brown paper. "Perhaps he would not deny it, Emily. What makes you so sure the man was not taking money from the company if they say it was so?" I saw Fiona put a hand to her forehead as if to shade her eyes. It was unlike the doctor to be so unkind.

"But it is unfair," I insisted. "There is no proof. Only Jennings's say so. Mr. MacGregor says O'Malley would not do it and he knew the man."

The doctor glanced at the bowed head of the girl sitting across from him. "We cannot know what any man may do in a desperate situation. He may not know himself until the time comes. It is only when he is tested that he knows, so you would be wrong to assume you know what he would do. I have no doubt there are things about the dead man that are unknown to Mr. MacGregor."

I opened my mouth, but this insistent disagreement was so unexpected, I didn't know what to say. I didn't have an argument to hand. I blushed to remember our meeting in the train station that morning. Perhaps it was only to irk me that he was being so contrary. It was so unfair and so unlike the doctor, who was usually kind.

He locked his gaze with mine, but when he spoke it was only to say, "I believe your wagons have arrived."

A cry of joy from Mr. MacGregor, who dashed to the window, confirmed this and I hurried downstairs with him to recruit helpers and begin the unloading. It took more than an hour, with MacGregor supervising below and Fiona and I directing the stacking and unpacking of the sacks and boxes on the third floor. We convinced those who were waiting to help with this and I was glad to see their expressions of relief as they realized their wait had not been in vain and that they would really take home at least some of the food that they needed.

It was hard work carrying all of the goods up three flights but the men had their own system and switched off so there were often new faces. It must have been a relief to them to have a definite assignment. They weren't used to the idleness that went with the strike. It occurred to me that Mr. MacGregor must be hard pressed to set up things like the patrols to keep them busy. It let me see for the first time how overwhelming the actual physical strength was of the large number of men involved. Their gruff, shambling presence quickly filled up the two storerooms. I found myself ordering them around in a loud voice just to maintain some order among all the men and boxes. They took it in good stead, though, and even seemed amused by me.

The last boxes were brought in and heaved onto the top of a stack, followed by my empty-handed brother, Alden, who surveyed the result with a critical eye. But I forestalled any helpful suggestions from that quarter with one baleful glance. I was exhausted at that point and perched on top of a crate as I entered the final lines in my ledger book with a pencil, so as not to be encumbered by a bottle of ink.

"What did you find out?" I asked. The last time I had seen my brother, he was in the crowd of mourners at Brian O'Malley's wake.

"About Brian? They don't think he was a spy, anyhow. There is a general belief that the company hired men from Pinkerton and planted them as spies some time ago. It's only a rumor, but I heard it again and again. No one could point to any proof, but there's a lot of suspicion that someone leaked the plans for the walkout. If it's Pinkerton men, like they believe, then O'Malley's out. His family's been here forever. But I'm afraid they just want it to be some unknown hireling of Pullman's. They don't want to believe it's one of their own. On the other hand, Brian O'Malley was truly desperate. Neither he nor his brother Joe were working full-time, even before the strike. And they were having trouble feeding the younger ones, Pat and Lilly." He shook his head. "It's really bleak, Emily. I've never seen anything like it. But with his sister—Mrs. Foley—feelings were very bitter there. So bitter they say he never would have accepted help from her, not even food for the little ones."

"Alden, if no one believes Brian O'Malley was a spy, who do they think killed him?"

He shrugged. "For them, any bad in the world must come from the company. The company is the enemy and they blame the company men for everything."

"But that doesn't make sense."

"Don't worry, Emily. Whitbread will figure it out. He always does."

Remembering my meal at the Florence Hotel, I couldn't help worrying about how the investigation was going.

"The company representative claims there was a plot to blow up the clock tower and Brian O'Malley was killed trying to find out about it," I told my brother. "They are insisting the police investigate the threat. Mr. Jennings wanted Whitbread to arrest Mr. MacGregor and the others. He said if anything happens they'll hold the police to blame for letting those men go. Pullman and the company have so much power, Alden. They would even threaten the mayor. I don't know how ordinary men like the strikers would ever be able to stand against them." I was slumped on the crate, hugging my ledger book. It felt good to have my feet swinging loose with no weight on them. I was tired.

"Ah, but you forget the numbers of men and women who are actually in the union. There's a big contingent of shop-girls in this, you know, and even then, they're not alone. Do you know who's downstairs on the second floor this very minute?"

I looked at him feeling stupid with fatigue. His blue eyes glittered with excitement. "You don't know, do you? Honestly,

Emily, you have such a limited viewpoint. You hone in on one single thing like unloading those wagons and you completely miss everything around you. Why, in the two hours that you have been stacking boxes, the street out front has filled up with . . . it must be a thousand people. Don't you know what they're here for?"

"Alden, Miss Addams trusted *me* to come down and organize the relief station. She is out trying to get donations. But I am the one who needs to deal with them. That's what I came for and that's what I have been doing." I was indignant. It was true that I had concentrated on the task at hand, to the exclusion of anything else. There had been people to assign, contents to be sorted out, and inventory to be recorded so we could account for every penny of every contribution. I had gathered some of the waiting people into a committee to begin to decide the criteria for who should receive relief, how much each should receive, and how it should be dispensed. I knew from experience that there would be chaos when we came to actually distributing the relief packages, if this was not done first. And I knew if I had not paid strict attention and organized the stacking, it would have taken twice as long to complete. But I lacked the energy to argue with my ever-energetic brother. I sighed. "I admit it, Alden, I don't know what you are talking about."

"Debs," he said with a self-satisfied air. "Eugene V. Debs of the American Railway Union. He's downstairs and he brings with him the aura of success."

NINE

Debs organized the American Railway Union," Alden told me, "but more importantly he led it to a major victory in April. There was a strike on the Great Northern Railway up in Minnesota. James J. Hill is the owner and he's a tough one. But Debs went up and negotiated. They were out eighteen days and they got the wage increases in the end. Everybody thinks he'll do it again here. And if he does, every man, woman and child connected to any railroad is going to join the ARU. He's here, downstairs in a secret committee meeting."

I'd heard of James Hill but, unlike George Pullman, I had never met him. From what Alden was saying, Debs had been able to deal with one wealthy industrialist, so perhaps could manage another. I only hoped he would have better success than Miss Addams and Mr. Safer. I couldn't believe in it, however.

"There is supposed to be a general meeting. That's what I've been waiting for," Alden told me. "But the crowd is getting so big, they may have to move it out of Turner Hall. There's a grandstand on the other side of Pullman. It's on what they call Athletic Island. I'm just waiting to hear when the meeting will be and where." He looked around at all the boxes. "Of course, I would have helped if you needed it. With the boxes, I mean." He looked up at the crates around us. "You've got to leave this and come, Emily. You don't want to miss seeing it."

Looking at my little brother, I realized that I would always think of him as the child I had followed around when he was just learning to walk. I would never be able to see him clearly as the young man he was now, when I always had that picture of a toddler superimposed on the figure before me. I had a hard time thinking of him as a newspaper reporter.

"Alden, how is Clara? Have you seen her?"

His eyes widened and I thought he flinched. "She'll be returning to Kentucky soon. Then she goes to Woods Hole for the summer. She's finishing her classes."

Clara was a tall, striking woman I'd befriended during my first year at the university. She came from a wealthy family in Louisville and was pursuing graduate studies in chemistry. Blinded by my own prejudices, it had been a shock for me to realize that a mutual affection had grown up between her and Alden. But the deaths of our parents left us very poor. I sensed that he saw that discrepancy in fortune as a great impediment. "She sent a note about the date of her departure, but I was given this assignment and I had no time to see her off."

"Oh, Alden."

"She'll be gone to the East soon enough. Chapman is supposed to go, too, you know. I heard he got a fellowship to work in the laboratory at Woods Hole."

There was a whistle from the stairwell and Alden jumped down from the crate on which he'd perched. "That's it. I posted one of the boys outside the meeting, to warn me when they were done. Come on, Em. They must be leaving for the Athletic Island."

He disappeared through the door and I looked around for more organizing to do, but decided Alden was right this time. I really did need to hear what Mr. Debs had to say. So I put away the ledger and locked up, then followed my brother down to the floor below where half a dozen men were just filing out of the meeting room. We followed them down to the street where a large number of people had gathered, just as Alden had told me. The committee began to lead them all in an impromptu parade across the town of Pullman. Alden had his notebook open and he skipped along in front of one of the leaders asking questions as he went. This must be Mr. Eugene V. Debs, president of the ARU. He looked about forty years of age and was nearly six feet tall. His hair was thinning to the point where he was starting to go bald and he wore spectacles, but his clean-shaven face was open and pleasant. He seemed amused by my brother as he strode along, answering his questions willingly.

"Why, the boys all over the country are clamoring to tie up the Pullman cars. They are in an inflammatory mood and longing for a chance to take part in this affair. The Pullman conductors—who get salaries of twenty-five dollars a month and are obliged to depend on the charity of the public to get enough to live on—would be glad of the chance to go out. Such men are in the mood to get even with the company that compels them to work under this system. The whole country is in an inflammable condition. I never saw it in such a condition before. When a man gets two dollars a day he can live and is therefore a coward—afraid to try to get more—but when he gets cut down to one dollar and forty cents, or worse yet, one dollar, he gets desperate. The difference between that and no money at all is so slight he feels he has nothing to lose and everything to gain by a strike."

As we walked along 112th—a great crowd of people by then, perhaps twenty abreast—I could see across the park to the hotel, where guests stood on the veranda watching us march by. But Mr. Jennings and his cronies wisely chose to stay inside until we passed.

A shorter, vigorous man with a big smile on his face was walking beside Debs. I learned later that he was Mr. Howard, second in command of the union. He told Alden, "The international convention of the ARU will meet in Chicago next week. Then we'll see what happens."

It was very hot in the late afternoon sunshine. When I slowed down and dropped back, wiping a sleeve against my forehead, I found Mr. MacGregor beside me. Repeating his thanks for the efforts to provide relief, he seemed more energetic and optimistic than he had been before.

"We believe the strike will not last long, Miss Cabot. We've learned the company kept twenty clerks on the payroll so they must not anticipate it will last long. But we expect them to try to lure the men away by opening again. I should not be surprised to see placards on the gates next Monday." We could see the front gates in the distance and he gestured towards them as we passed. "They'll announce that all who want to return to work at the old wages can do so. When the company finds no one will come back, then it will be ready to negotiate. The officials are talking nonsense when they say they can get repair work done at railroad shops, for they know that this would cause a strike in the shop where it was attempted and the railroads will not try it." He shook his head knowingly.

The man beside him was Mr. Stark. He said, "They say the notices to the men will tell them that, unless they go to work at once, they will never be given employment in the Pullman shops again. It's got some of the men nervous."

"All we have to do is all hang together," Mr. MacGregor corrected him. "That's all. You'll see. We hope we will not have to depend on your relief for too long, Miss Cabot. There is great hope that this will all be over by next week."

We reached Athletic Island then and filed onto the wooden grandstand. It faced Lake Calumet, so there was a slight breeze. I shaded my eyes and watched as Mr. Debs jumped up onto a wooden table placed in front of the stands. The crowd grew quiet in order to hear him. He had a voice that carried but seemed never to be raised.

"It is unnecessary for me to say that I am with you heart and soul in this fight. As a general thing I am against a strike, but when the only alternative to a strike is the sacrifice of rights, then I prefer a strike. There are times when it becomes necessary for a man to assert his manhood. I am free to confess that I do not like the paternalism of Pullman. He is everlastingly saying, 'What can we do for our poor working-men?' The interrogation is an insult to the men. The question is not what can Mr. Pullman do for us? It is what can we do for ourselves." There was a burst of applause at this as if it was the one thing they had been waiting for someone to say. He went on. "Under this system of paternalism in vogue it is only a question of time until they have your souls mortgaged. It will not be ten, nay five, years before they will take you forever under this system. If you will follow Mr. Howard's advice there is no power on earth to make this strike a failure. Division means defeat and disaster."

There was a huge round of applause and hooting as he waved to the crowd, and eventually he hopped down from the table, to be replaced by a more nervous-looking Mr. MacGregor, who urged the men to stay at home and to abstain from drinking whisky. He told them, "The strike will be ended by this time next week. The officials are already growing sick of it, and would be glad to have you go back to work. The receipts of the Pullman Palace Car Company have fallen off one-half since the strike began, evidence that the public means to show its disapproval of the Pullman Palace Car Company's treatment of its workmen. The dispatch from St. Paul in the *Tribune*, saying that American Railway Union men would refuse to haul Pullman coaches, is the announcement of the beginning of the end." This brought another cheer and ended the session on a high note of enthusiasm.

When I stood to look for Alden and Dr. Chapman, feeling it was time to take a train home, I found Mr. Raoul LeClerc at my elbow. "Mr. LeClerc, will the railroad men really boycott the Pullman cars?"

He looked around. The other people around us in the stands were already filing down the stairs. "There will be no formal action until the convention next week, but they still want to wave it like a threat at the company. You can be sure, Miss Cabot, that there were at least a dozen Pinkerton men here today, ready to report every word back to the company officials. It's how they work."

My eyes strayed to the departing crowd. It would be impossible to know all of them. I saw my brother and Mr. MacGregor waiting for me at the bottom, so I started down followed by Mr. LeClerc.

"What do you think, Emily? Aren't you glad you came now?" Alden asked.

"Mr. Debs is a very good speaker. I hope he's right and that the men will prevail. From the people I've met I've learned that conditions are very bad and have been for some time. I only hope we can provide sufficient supplies to relieve the needs of the most desperate here. And I hope desperation will not drive the men to attack the company. Detective Whitbread has been investigating the report of a bomb plot."

Mr. MacGregor denied this vigorously. "We are going to protect the property of the company with our lives if necessary. We have one hundred men patrolling the vicinity day and night. If a stranger goes near, he is followed until his business is found out. We are not afraid of our own men, Miss Cabot, but we are afraid of toughs from the city, who may take advantage of the strike. We shall make no effort to prevent the company from putting new men to work if it wishes to." He noticed Alden taking down his words in a notebook. "Yes. You should print that, young man. We will destroy no property and make no effort to prevent the company from doing as it pleases. We rely on the sympathy of the public and other workingmen to pressure the company. Now, if you will excuse me, I must see to the patrols. Thank you again, Miss Cabot."

He left, surrounded by a crowd of men asking questions about their assignments or the plan of action for the next day. Mr. Debs and Mr. Howard stood among a group of other men who wanted to shake their hands and speak to them. I turned to Alden. "Where is Dr. Chapman? I think it's time to get the train back to the city."

"He left, went back by an earlier train. Didn't you know? He looked very tired. I think he must have seen twenty patients today." He consulted his notebook. "There were five cases of malaria—it seems the swampy nature of the land leads to it. I'll take you back to town, only first Mr. LeClerc, here, was going to take me to meet some of the people on Fulton Avenue. From what he tells me, they'll be in need of your help over there all right."

TEN

I was disappointed. Despite the awkwardness at the start of the day, I wanted to tell Stephen of all I had seen and to hear the same from him. I was curious about his impressions of Mr. Debs and Mr. MacGregor. I planned to argue that Brian O'Malley could not have been a company spy and I was confident I could convince him now. But he had escaped my arguments. Just as he suddenly disappeared after I refused his proposal—again he had just left me. I had to admit that he never treated me as if I required his assistance in order to do something as simple as taking a train back to town. I was glad of that. And I knew he would have duties to attend to in the laboratory. But I was disappointed nonetheless. I found I wanted to talk to him. Instead, I walked off the island with Alden and Mr. LeClerc and found myself on Fulton Avenue at the far eastern side of Pullman.

Here, there were long rows of brick tenement buildings three stories high with nine families in each house, each family having two or three rooms, with five or six people to a family. Before we entered the first one, Mr. LeClerc stopped.

"You should understand that most of these people have been used to earning a living and enjoying the comforts of life. It is only in the last year that most of them have fallen into the current conditions and you will find them extremely reluctant to give their names. Many would rather suffer the pangs of hunger than the embarrassment of allowing their condition to be known. I have assured them you will not print their names, Mr. Cabot."

Alden agreed eagerly and we began our tour, visiting many of the rooms. It was much worse than I expected. The first man we met was a carpenter who supported a wife and two children aged one and four. They had two small rooms with four pieces of furniture and not a bit of food in the house at all. He told us that many a night in the past year they had gone to bed with no meal whatsoever. Although skilled in his trade, he earned only seventy-five dollars a year on the Pullman wage scales. He paid almost eight dollars a month in rent, and was currently twelve dollars behind, plus he owed thirteen dollars to the doctor. He was very fearful of being evicted.

In another building, we met a family with three small children. The man was gaunt and stood at attention, telling us he was a cabinetmaker who made only enough to bring home two dollars for two weeks work after paying the rent of nine dollars and ten cents for their three rooms. His wife sat wrapped in a blanket on one of the two chairs in the room. It was obvious that she was ill. But the man seemed to want to have his story told. He said that on the last payday he drew seven dollars for his work but decided to take it all home. He said the rent collector had been after him the next day, but he kept the money and now owed eighteen dollars rent.

While he was talking, his wife hugged the blanket around her shoulders, rocking back and forth. She shut her eyes and seemed to listen, but when Alden turned to her and politely asked about how it was for her and the children, she stared into his eyes for a moment and made an effort to speak. Her lip trembled and she dissolved in tears.

"There's nothing, not a thing. They cry all the time for something to eat, but I have nothing. We go to bed and get up and have nothing, nothing all day. He fainted on the job even. He fainted because he had nothing to eat." She shook her head and pulled the blanket tightly about her, despite the warmth of the evening. Her husband patted her awkwardly on the shoulder. "I don't want to live this way any longer. I sometimes think I will take the children and jump into the lake."

The men were embarrassed. I took her hand and knelt to

look into her eyes. "You must not do that, Mrs. Miller. You must promise me not to do that. I am Emily Cabot and I have been sent by Jane Addams at Hull House to set up a relief center. We've brought food, Mrs. Miller. You shall have some tomorrow, I promise you." She pulled away her hand and covered her face, sobbing quietly. I stood up and faced her husband. He looked very gaunt. "You must come to Turner Hall first thing tomorrow morning. We just unpacked the food this afternoon and will be ready in the morning. You must promise me you will come." I sensed that Dr. Chapman and Mr. LeClerc were right about the people. They did not want to admit they needed help. It was not the strike that had caused this want, it only brought it to the brink. These people had been living like this for months. As we left the bleak atmosphere of the Millers's rooms I promised myself that, no matter how busy I was the next morning, if I did not see Mr. Miller I would bring them the food myself.

I thought this would be the most memorable visit of the day, but Mr. LeClerc took us up and down Fulton Avenue where we met many others in similar circumstances. There were many families who had gone with no meal for the whole day. In fact, more often than not, that was the case. There were shop-girls supporting aged mothers, who earned so little they lived in daily fear of being evicted for being overdue with their rent. There was sickness left untreated because there wasn't even enough money to buy a loaf of bread, never mind to pay for the doctor. I lived for a year among the tenements of the West Side of Chicago, where Hull House resides, and I thought I had seen enough of poverty and squalor that I could not be shocked. But the contrast between the prosperous-looking town with its lawns and flowerbeds, and the hunger within the walls of these tenement buildings, was somehow more shocking. That day I had eaten at the Florence Hotel, while so many of these children had gone hungry. My stomach turned as we passed the hotel, on the way to the station, after our tour. "They certainly have need of your services," Alden said uncertainly as we walked along. I could see that he was as shocked as I was.

"Yes, but now I am afraid we will run out of food. I must tell Miss Addams—I don't think she has any idea of the number of people in such distress."

"Now you see what Debs means when he says Pullman would own them," Mr. LeClerc said, as we reached the clean and pleasant little Illinois Central station. From here you could not see Fulton Avenue. The view was designed to show off the impressive mass of the administration building, with the clock tower in the middle, overlooking an artificial lake to the north. It seemed like a picture painted on top of a glass window that, if you reached out and touched it with your hand, would smear, and if you wiped it away, the view would be no better than the rickety tenements of the West Side.

Raoul LeClerc waved his arm at the town behind him. "Pullman owns all of this and he would own the workers, too, if we let him. That's why we have to stop him. We have to break him. Even if we have to blow up every building in his model town."

ELEVEN

I spent a restless night troubled by Mr. LeClerc's parting statement. I also worried that the delay in getting food to the desperate Mrs. Miller would cause her to drown herself and her children in Lake Calumet. Yet, I knew that concentrating my efforts on one family would be an empty gesture. My value was in organizing the relief, assigning people to tasks, and setting up an efficient process to track the needs of the people. It would be tedious, but I knew it was the only way to get the most relief to the most people. I informed Hull House that we had probably underestimated the needs and I had to trust to Jane and the others to raise the amounts of money we would need. I had no faith in Mr. MacGregor's optimistic prophecy that they would be back at work the following week.

That morning, I was comforted by the sight of Dr. Chapman waiting for me to board the train, and the trip to Pullman allowed me to describe to him all that I had seen. He listened quietly and agreed to go to Fulton Avenue again to see the sick who had no money for a doctor. I told him of Mr. LeClerc's words and he grimaced.

"But he was only speaking in haste and anger," I insisted. "You could not help but be angered by what we saw. I'm sure he did not refer to any real plot. It was an expression."

"How can you be so sure, Emily? Do you know these men so well that you can vouch for them? Are you quite sure LeClerc did not tell you this to impress you, so that when an explosion happens you will know it was his act and admire him for it?"

I felt myself redden at this accusation and replied angrily, "Admire him? Of course not. I would never condone such a thing."

But, in reality, I could not help but admire LeClerc for his vigor and action in fighting against the current circumstances. He gave me hope. Compared to us, he seemed full of color. I thought the doctor and I, and even the Hull House supporters, seemed pale and weak in comparison. I did not say it out loud, though.

"Wouldn't you? Are you quite sure you wouldn't be impressed by such an act? I am afraid with the coming of Debs and the American Railway Union we will see this struggle become a contest of wills between the union leader and the industrialist. The pride of each will be on the line."

"But you didn't hear him. Debs said he didn't like strikes and they say he was able to negotiate with James Hill. He and Mr. MacGregor told the men repeatedly to stay away from the works and out of trouble. I heard them."

"Oh, each side will claim to be the innocent party, Emily. But how much is bluster and posing? You will find Debs and Pullman are both powerful men and, in the end, the struggle will be about power. But let me show you something." He opened out the newspaper he carried, folded it back to an inside page, and handed it to me. On the top of the page was an article by Alden, in which he described our visit to Fulton Avenue. He kept his promise and disguised the names, but his careful telling of the circumstances of each family filled two columns.

"This is wonderful. This will help Miss Addams and the others to raise money." I was proud of Alden—it was so much more than I had expected of him. It was the first of a series of articles he was able to publish during the next week before the real troubles began and I do believe they helped—at least in those early days—to promote the cause of the people of Pullman.

We spoke no more of LeClerc.

When we reached the town, worries of bomb plots and potential violence gave way to the work of setting up the relief station. I found that Fiona, and the others in our hastily formed committee, had spent the evening drawing up a list of those in most dire need. Under the watchful eye of her father they came up with a set of criteria for eligibility that made it much easier to begin the distributions. An excerpt from one of Alden's articles describes the system as we set it up that day:

> Relief headquarters open at eight o'clock in the morning, and from that hour until well along in the afternoon a line of men, women, and children file in at the open door, some with baskets, some too poor to afford a basket with only their hands to carry away the supplies received. A counter extends along the west side and across the south end of a room some forty feet in length. If the applicant is making his first visit to the relief headquarters he hands his union card and slip from one of the investigating committee to a man seated behind the counter near the door. A slip is filled out with his name and address and the articles required are handed to the applicant.
>
> He passes farther along the counter to a group of clerks, who take his slip and pass it to a young woman at a desk, who, if the slip calls for meat, writes an order on Secord & Hopkins for the small quantity allowed to a family. The applicant is handed a twenty-five pound sack of flour, a pound of sugar, a pound of tea or coffee, and a bar of soap. As he passes out another clerk at the door takes up his slip and cancels it. Care is used to see that no one gets provisions who is not in urgent need. Two separate records are kept of the applicants, and the slips and the stubs of orders on Secord & Hopkins, so the committee may be able to give an account for every cent received.

The Kensington businesses were extremely generous at that time, supplementing the supplies with fresh loaves of bread and contributions of money.

It was mid-afternoon by the time everything was set up and running to my satisfaction. I saw Mr. Miller from the day before and made sure his application was quickly accepted. But there were others, equally destitute, I did not see. When I consulted

Fiona, she told me that the residents of Fulton Avenue and the Dens who we had not visited the day before were not likely to be aware of our efforts. At her suggestion, we loaded a wagon with supplies and headed east, accompanied by Mr. LeClerc, who had volunteered his assistance. I left the two of them with half the goods at Fulton Avenue and drove on to the Dens by myself.

As I headed south I purposely drove the cart away from dreary Fulton to Stephenson, which took me past the handsome row houses. They were small, but each had its own particular characteristics—a mansard roof here, a different doorway there. And the road took me to the Market Hall with its arches. Unlike Mr. LeClerc, I did not want to blow it all up. On the contrary, I wanted people to be able to live and work in the pretty town. Whatever reasons compelled George Pullman to build the town (and I was sure they were mercenary), I thought that Beman—the young architect he had hired to design the place—had understood only that it was to be a pleasant, wholesome place for people to live in peace. It seemed a great shame that it could not be inhabited in that spirit. I could see that it would take so very little, just a small reduction in the profit of the Pullman Company, for the people to be able to inhabit that dream.

As the horse walked along towards the Dens, I could see the great brickyard shed, stranded alone on the dreary mud flats. When I got closer, I heard shouts coming from the O'Malleys' shack. Gracie Foley's voice carried across the empty landscape and I recognized the clipped tones of Detective Whitbread in the responses. I pulled up beside the policeman's carriage and climbed down.

"'Tis no business of yours where I work, or where I've been, or why I left. Your business is to find who killed my brother. You'll not be coming here to hound *me*. I'll not let you do it. The rest of them in this place may cringe and fawn, and do whatever you tell them, but I'll not. You should go out there and find who killed Brian, I say. Go."

"Madam, I merely asked for an account of your actions on the day in question. Don't you want your brother's killer found? Have you no desire to see justice done? Or is there some more sinister reason why you refuse to answer? Do you deny there was bad blood between you and your brother and that he had forbidden you to come here?"

Looking in the doorway of the shanty, I saw Joe O'Malley sitting at the table, whittling a piece of wood. I thought about how recently the corpse of his brother had been laid out there and wondered how he could bear to use it. But then he had little choice, for there were few pieces of furniture in the shack. In the shadows, Gracie and the detective were both stalking up and down as they argued. I heard another horse and turned to see Mr. Mooney's shiny, black carriage pulling up. Gracie had seen it, too. She must have been expecting him, since she marched out of the cottage tying her hat under her chin with a perky bow and taking Mr. Mooney's hand as he helped her into the carriage. Detective Whitbread followed behind her.

"Madam, I am not finished."

"But I *am* finished. I'm quite finished. I have to return to my work, if you please . . . or even if you don't please."

I noticed that Mooney stayed out of the dispute but I thought he was trying to disguise a smile as he climbed aboard and took up the reins. He must have known arguing with Gracie was a lost cause.

"Madam, I must warn you that I can get a warrant if necessary."

She did not deign to give a reply but only urged Mooney on as he flicked the reins. Detective Whitbread was quite red in the face and I was afraid he would burst with indignation.

"But, Detective, it seems very likely she does need to return to work in the city. You don't really suspect that she killed her brother, do you?"

"It is not a question of suspicion, Miss Cabot, it is a question of getting the facts from everyone involved. The woman is a lunatic. She rants that the officials are in the pay of the Pullman Company and yet she will not answer a few simple questions to assist with the investigation. It is the most perverse behavior I have encountered in such a case."

There was a sharp squeak, and we turned to find Joe O'Malley leaning on the open door and trying the little whistle he was carving.

"She's ashamed is what it is."

"I beg your pardon," Detective Whitbread said with a frown.

Joe O'Malley looked gaunt in too-short trousers, held up by suspenders over an undershirt, and bare feet covered with mud, but he did not seem indignant. "You'll have to forgive her, Detective, sir. She couldn't bear to repeat it, you know." He looked at me over the little carving he was still working at. "Gracie hated the works. The woman she had to report to in the laundry didn't like Gracie and she always gave her the worst of the work and the least of the pay. But it was because of Brendan Foley that she became with child and my father threw her out. He told her he never wanted to see her again. He was hard about things like that. On everything else he was as mild as a May breeze, but about that—about her having a child with no husband—he wouldn't stand for it and he told her she had to leave. She went to Foley in Chicago and he didn't want to marry her, you know, but even he couldn't stand up to her in a thing like that, where she knew she was right. So she marched him down to the local parish—downtown, where they weren't really known—and she got the priest to marry them. I'm sure he was probably afraid of her, too, no doubt. But it turned out that he was a bad choice, was Brendan. He was all right when he could get his stomach filled at his parents and flirt with the girls around here, but his folks were just as put out and they threw him out when he took some money from his da's pocket. He didn't have it so comfortable in the city and it made him cantankerous, so they say. And he would take it out on Gracie. They had a room above a saloon and she wasn't working, waiting to have the child as she was. But he should have known once that was done she'd have taken care of him. She's always been a prodigious hard worker, Gracie has. She makes no friend of them she works for, but no one would say anything but she's a prodigious hard worker.

"But she wasn't working then, and neither was Brendan most of the time, and he took to hitting her. Of course we didn't know that because our own da had forbidden us to talk to her and we were all working our backbreaking jobs. Well, as you can imagine, Gracie fought back and one night he threw her down the stairs. She lost the baby then, but she still had Brendan Foley. He was sorry, they say, after it happened. And Gracie got herself work as a laundress. That's the one kind of domestic work where you can live out, you know, and she could not bear to live in and be under some housekeeper's hand all the time. She could come and go as she chose and, being a hard worker, pretty soon she was in demand and it's on Prairie Avenue no less, for a family named Glessner and some others, that she works. She would never work for Pullman, you understand, although they live there, but she made a good job of it for the others. Then Brendan got himself killed in a barroom brawl—no one was really surprised by that—and she was on her own. She wanted to come back and bring the little ones presents, and show as how she had got on, but my da wouldn't allow it and Brian was as straight as an arrow like our da. She couldn't even come to Da's funeral. Brian wouldn't let her."

He lifted his head from his work to see how we were taking in this story. Detective Whitbread stood with his arms folded, listening, and I was trying to imagine how awful it must have been for poor Gracie to be left so alone.

"She'd never have killed Bri, if that's what you're thinking, and she came down on an afternoon train. She was working in Prairie Avenue all the morning, so she only got here right before Brian was found." He sighed and blew shavings from his work.

"What about your brother, Mr. O'Malley? Do you have any knowledge that he was spying for the company?" Whitbread asked.

"Brian was no spy and any that say he was are lying." Joe dropped his hands to his sides. There was a deep frown on his face, which was lined much more deeply than it should have been as he must have been less than twenty-five. "Brian was just like our da. He was too hard-headed sometimes, he was too much on the straight and narrow. But he would never, never, never betray MacGregor and the rest by spying for the company. It's a lie and no one that knew him will believe it."

I watched Detective Whitbread, who gave no indication of what he thought on the matter. It was true that as far as I had heard, people who knew the dead man did not believe he would have spied. Besides Jennings, the only one who seemed to think it possible was Dr. Chapman and I could not understand why he thought that.

"When was the last time you saw your brother, Mr. O'Malley, and do you know anything that could lead us to the person who hung your brother in the brickyard shed?"

I noticed he did not mention the fact that Brian O'Malley had been dead before he was hung. Joe looked down at the ground.

"I saw him only at breakfast that morning. He went over to the hall in Kensington to hear the speeches. But I was tired of the speeches—they do them morning and night and it's just to give the men somewhere to go, it's not that they say anything. I stayed to look after the little ones and to play my pipe. And I expected Gracie, for I was the one who got a message to her asking for her to bring food for the little ones, and I wanted to get to her before my brother saw her. So I was here."

"You did not see anyone in the vicinity of the shed?"

He looked across the mud flats, squinting. "I did not look that way and if I had, I would not have noticed. I was playing the pipes, you see. Then Gracie came and we were talking when we heard the screams and we went with everyone else to see. Gracie never expected such a thing. She was all geared up to see Brian in the flesh and to have a knock-down, drag-out fight, verbally, if you know what I mean." He turned to the detective. "She won't tell you the story because she is ashamed. She's ashamed for what happened with Brendan Foley and our da throwing her out. But it's them that should be ashamed—him and Brian—for treating her like that. But she found Mooney. Brian would have been mad to know he's not Catholic, but she's happy for once. He's a good man. I don't suppose she loves him, like, not really. But she loved Brendan Foley and see what that got her. I'll be glad to see her marry Mooney and I cannot see that it matters which church or office it's done in. But Brian would have forbidden it. As if he had any right to tell her what to do after all that." He shook his head at the sorry story of his near relations.

"Mr. O'Malley, where are the children?" I asked. Detective Whitbread had done his questioning and I still had my task to complete, but the silence of the Dens seemed ominous.

"Most of the men have gone round the lake to try to catch some fish. The company says they cannot do it from the shore here. We sent the children with them as there's nothing for them here and they whine about their empty stomachs. Gracie will bring more food when she returns, but she must work to be able to do so."

"I've brought stores from the relief station. Can you help me distribute them?"

His face lit up when he saw the contents of the wagon. To my surprise, Detective Whitbread took off his jacket and, in his shirtsleeves with his bowler hat still firmly on his head, he helped us take the sacks around the Dens. I had not expected them all to be in need but, with the help of the men, we did some repacking to stretch what I had brought. We were able to leave something with each of the sixteen shacks. I was alarmed by what I saw. Hollow-eyed, exhausted women, some of them ill, several pregnant, were pitifully grateful for the supplies. With Joe to help me, I filled out the applications for each family, but by the end I was extremely worried. What I had brought, after we divided it again, would only last a few days. How would we ever manage to replenish the stores often enough when the numbers of needy kept increasing?

"Perhaps Mr. MacGregor is right and they will all be back to work next week and no longer need the help," I said, as I climbed into the cart to head back. Detective Whitbread was putting his coat back on and preparing to leave. He had been unnaturally quiet during the food distribution.

Joe O'Malley looked at me with large, sorrowful, brown eyes as he handed me the reins. "If this were a fairy tale, perhaps, Miss Cabot, but I'm afraid this is a dark tale, full of curses and spirits and foul deeds. And it will be a time longer before it comes to whatever end the fates have prepared for us."

He slapped the horse to get him started and I headed back to the town, followed by Detective Whitbread in his rented carriage. We traveled some minutes until we had almost reached the streets of the town again when I pulled up and waited for him to stop beside me.

"Detective Whitbread, you don't really believe Gracie Foley killed her brother, do you? From what Joe said she had only just arrived when he was found."

He tipped up his hat and wiped a handkerchief across his forehead. It was another hot day. "With the information from her brother it should be possible to verify the claim that she was working in town that morning. Why the woman could not have just said so is beyond understanding."

"Detective, you see the terrible straits the people are in here. At least the O'Malleys have Gracie to help them. You won't arrest her, will you? I am very worried about how much longer the relief supplies can last. Someone must do something to end this strike."

"I will arrest whoever is shown to be guilty by the evidence, Miss Cabot. I would remind you that it was you, and Miss Addams, and Mr. Safer who petitioned the mayor to have me assigned to this case. As for Mrs. Foley, I will consult the Glessners. And, as for the strike, I am afraid that is far beyond my authority. It would seem that some of the striking workers are enjoying the holiday." He nodded in the direction of the town and I saw a young couple walking hand-in-hand towards us. She looked up at him with a smile on her face and he walked along with his cap pushed to the back of his head and his jacket swinging from a finger over his back.

"It's Fiona MacGregor and Mr. LeClerc," I told him, surprised myself by their air of happiness. "I left them distributing supplies at the Fulton Avenue tenements."

TWELVE

They saw us and, releasing their hands, hurried towards us. "If you would be so good, Miss Cabot, please do not move your horse forward, as mine would follow." With that cryptic request, Detective Whitbread dropped the reins of his carriage and disappeared over the far side.

Meanwhile, Fiona and Raoul LeClerc greeted me. "Miss Cabot, we were coming to find you," the girl said. The strain on her face had been smoothed away and she was flushed with some anticipation.

"We finished handing out the stores and thought we would meet you." Raoul LeClerc gave me a warm smile. I had the impression he was sharing some secret with me that was over the head of the young girl, as if he appreciated my age and intelligence.

"Mr. LeClerc has made a suggestion, Miss Cabot. I wanted to ask your advice," she told me eagerly. But the tall detective had come up quietly behind them.

I nodded at him. "Miss MacGregor, Mr. LeClerc, you have met Detective Whitbread? He is investigating the death of Brian O'Malley."

Fiona froze and both of them turned to face the policeman.

"Miss MacGregor, if you will, there are one or two questions I would like to pose."

She looked up at me as if for permission. It occurred to me that Whitbread must have spoken to her before in the presence of her father. I was sure he wanted to take the opportunity to question her without him. I tried to look reassuring. Her expression fell and the strain that had been there in the morning returned, but she waited for his questions.

"Miss MacGregor, would you tell me again how you came to find Mr. O'Malley's body in the brickyard shed that day?"

She glanced across the flats toward that lonely building and shivered. "I served lunch for my father and his visitors—Miss Cabot, Miss Addams, and the banker. Then I went out while they ate."

"You did not eat with them?"

"There wasn't enough." I thought of the weak tea and cheese and bread at that table. "I didn't mind, but I wanted to get out, so I went for a walk." Fiona was looking at the ground.

"Pardon me, Miss MacGregor, but are you sure that is all? I have been told there was a certain affection between you and the dead man and that, despite the disapproval of your families, you continued to meet in secret. Didn't you go to the shed to meet Mr. O'Malley? Come now, Miss MacGregor, this is a murder investigation and you must tell the truth."

The girl's face began to twist and she put her hands up to shield it.

"Fiona," I encouraged her, "you must tell Detective Whitbread if you were to meet Brian. You must help him to find whoever did this."

With her face still hidden in her hands, she nodded her head, then looked up. "Yes, we met sometimes. I knew my father would be busy all afternoon. So we were going to meet. But when I got there, he was . . . hanging." She sobbed into her hands and Raoul LeClerc reached out and put his arm around her shoulders. I thought it was the most natural of actions.

"Did you see anyone else?" She shook her head. "Miss MacGregor, was Brian O'Malley spying for the company? Did he say anything to you that would lead you to believe he was working for the company in that way?"

She looked up, wiping her eyes. "No, no. Oh, I don't know. He said that soon he would have enough money so that we could leave here. He wouldn't say where he would get it. I didn't believe him. I didn't believe him."

"Was Brian O'Malley afraid of anyone? Did he mention anyone who might be a threat to him? Did he particularly avoid anyone that you know of?"

"No, no." She sobbed again, this time turning her face into Mr. LeClerc's shoulder. He raised his eyebrows at that, but patted her back awkwardly and looked at me over her head.

Then Whitbread interrogated the ARU man about his own actions that fatal afternoon. At first I thought he would pretend he had been present for the entire lunch but, after a speculative gaze at me, he must have decided I would not support that. He described how he and Mr. Stark had been excused, and how he became restive and decided to go off on his own to investigate the Athletic Island, where they thought they might need to hold the meeting with Mr. Debs if it got too big. It was on his way back to MacGregor's house that he heard Fiona's screams and followed others from the town out to the brickyard shed.

"Were you aware that Mr. O'Malley was acting as a spy for the Pullman Company?" Whitbread asked him.

Raoul grimaced. "I did not know him. The company was rumored to have hired Pinkerton men to infiltrate the locals. We face that all the time. The companies won't raise the wages of the workingmen, but they will pay for detectives to spy on them. Sometimes they manage to corrupt men into spying on their own comrades. Can you blame them, when their families go hungry? But I was not aware of any specific man who was suspected of being a traitor."

"And if you were, Mr. LeClerc—if the ARU became aware of a traitor in their midst—what would you do?"

"We would not hang him, if that is what you mean, Detective. It is not revenge that we seek. Mr. Debs wants to unite the workingmen and women. It is only by uniting that we can fight the likes of George Pullman. You will see us do it. You will see us united and victorious in this struggle and it will not be done by hanging our own comrades. Now, if you are done, I think we need to get Miss Cabot to the station so that she can get her train back to the city." He helped Fiona to climb on to the seat beside me, then walked around the horse and, tossing his jacket into the back, he swung up on my other side and took the reins from my hands. He smiled at me and nodded to the policeman. "Detective." He started off and I remembered too late what Whitbread had told me about his own horse. Looking back, I saw the policeman scrambling to catch his carriage and climb back in as it followed our cart. Raoul LeClerc grinned and slapped the reins on the back of our horse to move him along.

"He has to question everyone for his investigation," I told them.

"It doesn't matter," Raoul said. He looked across me towards Fiona, who was sniffing and wiping her eyes with the back of her hand. "Miss MacGregor, you didn't finish telling Miss Cabot our plans."

The girl looked at him with hero worship in her eyes. "There will be a rally. And Mr. LeClerc wants me to speak."

"The railway men are already in sympathy with the Pullman workers," Raoul said, as he urged the horse into a trot and we passed by the Market Hall and turned towards the Arcade. The movement stirred a breeze in the hot afternoon air. "When they hear how it really is, direct from the lips of Miss MacGregor and the others, then George Pullman will find out what can happen when workingmen unite for justice. You'll see, Miss Cabot. Things are stirring and there will be surprises in store for the likes of Pullman."

THIRTEEN

No, I will not attend a rally of the American Railway Union, Emily. I am here to tend the sick, not to take sides in this conflict." Dr. Chapman was stubbornly adamant in his neutrality, but I argued that such a stance only hurt the cause of the workers. He would not listen.

"But Mr. LeClerc is sure the ARU convention will vote to support the Pullman workers by boycotting the Pullman cars. It is the only way to force the company to be reasonable."

"No matter who is right or wrong, Emily, action by the ARU will only broaden the conflict and more people will suffer. You will see. You must do as you wish, but it makes me heartsick to see the sickness and hunger here. I have no stomach for rallies and speeches."

"But Mr. LeClerc also believes the ARU will make a donation to the relief fund and he asked me to attend so that I might accept it. You know how desperate we are for contributions." It was only too true. Miss Addams and the others were valiant in their efforts to raise funds, but it was increasingly difficult to keep our shelves stocked. By early afternoon these days they were empty, even when we reduced the amounts given and regulated eligibility. I was discouraged to have to turn people away every day now. And I was angry.

"Nevertheless, Emily, I cannot see my way to go. Your brother will no doubt welcome the opportunity to escort you."

"Oh, don't worry about me, Doctor." I was really very angry with Stephen Chapman. "Mr. LeClerc has begged me to come with the Pullman contingent. He has recruited several speakers, including Jennie Curtis and Fiona MacGregor. I'll go with them."

"I've noticed that Miss MacGregor has little time for nursing now that Mr. LeClerc is around."

The comment was unusually spiteful for the doctor. But he looked quite worn out and I was sorry to have to argue with him. It was true that Fiona MacGregor had at first arrived every morning to help the doctor with the clinic. It irked me a bit to know that he missed her. I could not bring myself to believe that he was jealous. Fiona was so young and so uneducated. I knew that Dr. Chapman had once been in love with a wealthy young woman who married someone else. The thought that he might be interested in Fiona MacGregor, after proposing to me, was unthinkable.

"Mr. LeClerc is representing Mr. Debs and the ARU in trying to help the people of Pullman. He is attempting to keep their spirits up by organizing activities," I protested. As we all came to feel more pressed by the worsening conditions, Raoul LeClerc's warmth, vigor, and élan had eased our hearts. I couldn't help but admire him for insisting on enthusiasm. It was as if we were all traveling through a dark tunnel but he was sure he could see the light of day at the end. He believed the ARU was the beginning of a new and better day for the workingman and he made others believe it, too. It was too bad that the doctor could not imagine it.

So I found myself at Ulrich's Hall, on Clark Street in Chicago, that night, surrounded by the Pullman contingent. We had traveled up together and were greeted kindly by the large number of men standing in groups around the hall. The officials on the raised platform at the front had not yet called the meeting to order when I saw a rustling in the nearby crowd and heard a familiar voice.

"Excuse me, it's them there we want to get to." It was Gracie Foley, elbowing her way through. "Come, Joe, come along. We'll stand alongside the rest of them right here and there'll be no more talk of spies in the O'Malley family." A few of the Pullman crowd turned their backs as she reached us, but Gracie was not to be put off. "Miss Cabot, it is, isn't it? And here's my brother,

Joe, that you know. And Mooney, where's Mooney?" She was dressed in green taffeta with velvet trim and a tall hat with new ribbons and a wisp of a feather. Swinging around, she gestured behind her. "Ah, here he comes. He knows many of them, you see, being a saloon keeper and a man about town." She glowed with pride as she watched the short man shake hands and move to join us. "And what did you find out?" she asked him, brushing a speck of dust from his lapel when he reached us.

"Debs and Howard are against it," Mr. Mooney told us confidentially. "But the men are for it. They want to teach Pullman a lesson."

"Lot of good it'll do them," Gracie said in a low voice. "But here is our union man who has come to help us now," she said more loudly as Raoul LeClerc moved to my side. "You see, we've come at your bidding, Mr. LeClerc." She looked around at the backs turned towards us. "We'll have no one saying the O'Malleys don't come out and support their comrades. Here's Joe come to the rally like the rest."

"We need every bit of support we can get, Mrs. Foley." I was glad Raoul did not reject her as some of the others seemed to be doing. I felt him squeeze my elbow. "We're grateful to have Miss Cabot representing Hull House, as well, and all our other supporters." Pushed by the growing crowd, I felt him move close behind me until his breath was almost in my ear. I felt a jolt at the familiarity of the physical contact but I told myself not to be prudish. It was a momentous night and we were all fired by a special kinship.

Fiona MacGregor waved frantically from across the room. She looked nearly panicked.

"I see I must go and help our speakers. Miss MacGregor and Miss Curtis have agreed to help us plead our cause. Miss Curtis is the union leader for the women workers in the Pullman shops. I only hope they can touch the hearts of the convention as they have touched mine. But, Miss Cabot, you will go up and accept the contribution for the relief station, won't you? Come over and wait with us. Excuse me, they are almost ready to begin." With a final touch of my arm, he hurried away.

Gracie watched him go with narrowed eyes. "Hmm. Yes. And I'm sure Mr. Raoul LeClerc will touch the young women involved just as deeply. With his honeyed words, of course." Mr. Mooney snickered and turned away to watch the movement on the stage where they were about to begin, but Gracie put a hand on my arm. "LeClerc is just after skirts," she said in a low voice. "But there's another one here tonight I have some real doubts about." She nodded and I followed her gaze to where a man with a wool cap pulled low over his eyes was slouched against a wall. Someone pounded a gavel to call the meeting to order while she whispered in my ear, "I'll not say a thing if you don't, Miss Cabot, but I've an idea your friend over there might not be welcomed by this crowd if they found him out now."

Startled, I looked again and realized what Gracie's sharp eyes had already found out. Attention had turned to the stage where they were introducing Jennie Curtis as one of the first speakers. She began her simple but wrenching tale of how the death of her father had left her with his debts to the Pullman Company for past rent, and the support for her elderly mother, just when her wages were reduced. Meanwhile, I worked my way through the crowd. Coming up behind the slouching form, I reached up and gave him a sharp poke in the shoulder. When I had his attention, I led the man out a door and into the corridor.

"What are you doing here? Spying on them?" I asked in a whispered hiss when we were finally out of earshot of the crowd. I could hear reactions to Jennie's story in the background.

"Miss Cabot." Detective Whitbread stood upright here. "I would not call it spying. I am pursuing information pertinent to my case."

I knew the detective frequently adopted disguises while undertaking investigations—I had been surprised by him before.

But this time it seemed an awful betrayal for him to pretend to be something he was not in order to trap someone from Pullman. "This meeting has nothing to do with the murder of Brian O'Malley," I insisted.

"You cannot know that. If O'Malley was murdered because he was a spy for the company, his murderer is probably here."

"That's just an excuse. Why shouldn't I tell them who you are? How do I know you are not here so you can report back to the company and the local authorities what the union is doing?"

He pulled himself up even straighter. "Miss Cabot, I am sure if the Pullman Company wants to know about these activities they are quite capable of hiring Pinkerton agents to pose as workingmen. They do not get their information from me. However, if even you can misinterpret my presence as some kind of threat, then you are probably correct in your insinuation that the members of the ARU would not take kindly to my being here. Since that is the case, and since you threaten to expose me, I will take my leave. I would give you a word of caution, however. The company claims that there are plans afoot to plant a bomb in the Pullman works. You must consider how you will feel if such an explosion takes place and causes a loss of life. You will have to ask yourself whether any of your own actions—or lack of action—could have prevented such an event. You may sympathize with the plight of the striking workers, Miss Cabot, but I advise you to be very careful to gauge exactly how far you are willing to go in supporting their cause."

With that, he turned on his heel and disappeared before I could think of a reply. It was with an uneasy mind that I returned to the meeting. Detective Whitbread had been my mentor and guide since I first came to the city. He had even put his job on the line to find the truth in difficult situations. Yet, in this matter I had to disagree with him. I could not be neutral. I was sure the workers were right and Pullman was wrong. It grieved me to have to part ways with the detective, yet I felt a glow of independence.

The time had come for me to think, and speak, and do what I thought was right, without seeking the approval of Detective Whitbread or Dr. Chapman. My time had come.

Jennie Curtis was just finishing her speech.

Mr. President and Brothers of the American Railway Union: We struck at Pullman because we were without hope. We joined the American Railway Union because it gave us a glimmer of hope. Twenty thousand souls, men, women, and little ones, have their eyes turned toward this convention today; straining eagerly through dark despondency for a glimmer of the heaven-sent message which you alone can give us on this earth. Pullman, both the man and the town, is an ulcer on the body politic. He owns the houses, the schoolhouse, and the churches of God in the town he gave his once humble name. And, thus, the merry war—the dance of skeletons bathed in human tears—goes on; and it will go on, brothers, forever unless you, the American Railway Union, stop it; end it; crush it out.

The room broke into wild applause. It was deafening and many stamped their feet to make it even louder. I found my way back to Gracie Foley and Mr. Mooney and the others from Pullman.

"Who'd have thought it from a little mouse like that?" Gracie shouted in my ear. It was a surprise. Miss Curtis appeared to be a small, timid young woman, but she had been carried away by her passion. I saw Mr. LeClerc leading Fiona MacGregor to the podium to take her place. She looked overwhelmed by the noise, the lights, and the smoke from the cigars. She appeared to swallow convulsively and then to stare at Mr. LeClerc in panic. He realized she would not be able to perform.

Holding her hand as she clung to his arm he addressed the room. "And now Miss Fiona MacGregor of Pullman will help us present our contribution to the relief station run by our friends at Hull House. If Miss Cabot will join us on stage, we will present the check."

I had been told the ARU would make a contribution, but I had no notion that I would need to accept it in front of this gigantic crowd. But I could see Raoul LeClerc searching for my face. He must have hoped he could alleviate the awkward situation caused by a dumbstruck young woman by appealing to another. I straightened up, took a deep breath, and headed for the stairs at the side of the stage.

Meanwhile, Mr. LeClerc reached down to a table of union officials on the floor in front of the stage, and was handed an envelope. He was busy checking inside for the amount while I reached the podium as gracefully as I could. The crowd welcomed me with warm applause. LeClerc quickly announced the donation of four thousand dollars, then stepped away, with Fiona still clinging to him, attempting to hide her face.

I felt I would have liked to hide my face, too, as I looked out at the huge crowd that waited for me to speak. A feeling of expectation hung in the air and the sheer force of humanity gathered before me frightened me for a moment. Whatever could a bookish, intellectual, social reformer have to say to this contingent of hardworking men who kept the iron horses of the country's railroads running from day to day? There was a sea of upturned faces, most of them hard-favored men, and a few women, extending out to the doors at the sides and back and up to a balcony and boxes above. I almost wavered, but I knew I must represent not myself but the women of Hull House and the university. If Jennie Curtis, a seamstress from the Pullman works, could ignite and inspire these men, I must at least be able to face them. I cleared my throat.

"Mr. LeClerc, Mr. Debs, gentlemen and ladies of the American Railway Union, on behalf of Hull House I want to thank you for your very generous contribution to support the relief station in Kensington." I was greeted by polite applause. I fumbled with the envelope Mr. LeClerc had put into my hands and removed the check to wave it at them. "We will use this to provide the very basic staples of flour, sugar, and coffee for the suffering people of Pullman. I confess, I have never before seen such want, such pain from hunger, as I have seen in Pullman. On behalf of those people who line up every day at our doors, I thank you. And I pray, with your help, that this cruel situation may be brought to a happy end."

It was all I could think to say, but it was heartfelt and the crowd responded warmly. Mr. LeClerc took my elbow and guided both me and Fiona to the stairs. Applause was still loud when we reached the bottom and I felt myself pulled back to him so that he could whisper in my ear, "I thank you. The little MacGregor, she lost her nerve, but a woman like you would never let us down. I thank you." It was said so close and softly in my ear I felt a tingle run down my spine and blushed.

Meanwhile, Mr. MacGregor was to have the final say before the vote. I noticed a lot of activity at the table below the stage. Mr. Mooney had said that Debs and Howard were against a strike, but emotion was running high in the room and there seemed to be an argument going on about how to word a resolution. The final appeal did nothing to restrain the feelings in the room.

Mr. MacGregor was once again enumerating the difficulties of the Pullman workers, the lowering of their wages, and the high rents. He went down a list of figures proving this yet again and then made a final, rousing statement.

"Now this, brother delegates, is what the Pullman system will bring us all to if this situation is not faced fairly and squarely in the American way, for Americans by the American Railway Union. It is victory or death." There was a huge response of applause and stamping of feet. "And so to you we confide our cause. Do not desert us as you hope not to be deserted. Be brothers in deed as well as in name, even as we are brothers in need. Every man of you, every honest heart among you, every willing hand stands ready. You know you can; will you?"

This was answered by a huge uproar of yells, applause, and

foot stamping. Tears ran down the little man's face. There was a flurry of activity at the table until Raoul was handed a sheet of paper. He rushed to the podium, shook the hand of Mr. MacGregor, and then started to speak several times before the room quieted enough to hear him. "Moved... hereby moved..." he took a breath and shouted out, while reading directly from the sheet of paper, "Moved that, unless the Pullman Company should consent to an arbitration of existing difficulties by twelve o'clock Tuesday, June 26th, the members of the ARU will place a boycott on their cars."

The roar in response was deafening and in the resulting turmoil of shouting, stamping, and the tossing of hats, the necessary second was made and the voting was done. The vote was in. The ARU would refuse to hook up the Pullman palace cars to the trains.

FOURTEEN

This will bring an end to the strike," I insisted. "Pullman will have to agree to talks or else none of his coaches will be carried by any train manned by ARU members and that is most of them. Certainly it is all the lines in and out of Chicago."

We were in the makeshift clinic above the S & H Grocery where I'd found Alden and Dr. Chapman in conversation. Despite the check from the union, it was necessary to close the relief center early again for lack of stores but I was still elated by the result of the previous evening's vote. I wanted to prove to Stephen Chapman that I was right about the ARU and how the support of that larger union was going to bring the stalemate to an end.

"I hope you are right." He looked weary and I remembered it was only a few months since he had suffered the shotgun blast that shattered his right arm. I wondered whether he was fully recovered. The long days at the clinic were taking a toll on him. I felt guilty for arguing with him, but I also felt a spurt of joy in my heart. I was convinced that Raoul LeClerc and Eugene Debs and the ARU had come to the rescue of Pullman and soon all would be right again. I didn't mean to gloat but, for once, I was right and he was wrong, despite my comparative lack of experience in the world.

"Emily, come to the city with me if you're done here. There's something you've got to see," my brother told me.

"What?" I could see that, whatever it was, he had already told Stephen. "Will you come, too, Dr. Chapman?"

"I am not finished here. I'll close up when I'm done. You should go with Alden, Emily."

"To do what?"

"You'll see." Alden took my arm and led me to the coatroom. He insisted on keeping his secret. That was tiresome of him but I was in a good mood. Good enough to humor him. It was such a relief to know we were not alone in trying to sustain the striking workers. Now that they had the power of the full ARU behind them I was convinced they would succeed in reaching a just settlement.

We took the train into the city and Alden led me through the crowds. When we reached his destination I recognized the red brick of the building known as the Rookery. Inside, he led me to a light-filled central atrium. It was one of the very tall, impressive buildings that Chicago was becoming famous for.

"It's on the eighth floor. Come on, we'll take the elevator."

Upstairs, the operator let us off and the door clanged shut behind us as Alden hurried down the corridor. When we stepped inside a large open room, it appeared that Alden was already well known there. A couple of dozen desks piled with papers, and several having telephones on them, were placed in rows around the room. Bells were ringing and men were talking, while one man in shirtsleeves chalked things on a board at the other end. But Alden headed for a row of glassed-in offices on the side. I followed him, getting a few curious glances from the mostly male office workers. There were only a few women here and there, mostly sitting at typing machines.

"Hello, Cabot. This your sister, then?" Alden was greeted by a rotund, balding man who was hurriedly donning his coat as we approached. He waved us into his office.

"Yes, my sister, Emily Cabot. Emily, this is Mr. Spike Morgan, general manager of the Michigan Central Railroad."

"How do you do, Mr. Morgan." I was a little confused. "Excuse me, but my brother has not informed me of much. What is this place?" We sat down inside the glassed-in office where we still had a view of the room full of people.

"This, Miss Cabot, is the General Managers' Association. It is a voluntary, unincorporated association made up of twenty-four railroads centering, or terminating, in Chicago. As I have been telling your brother, here, we men of the roads have found it necessary to cooperate just as much as the men who have organized the ARU. The ARU's members are drawn from many railroads and many different trades across the railroad business. Our organization is a cooperative on the management side, you see?"

As we were looking out towards the room, I half rose from my seat when there was a sudden movement at the doorway. It was Mr. Jennings. "So, the Pullman Company is part of your organization?" I asked.

Mr. Morgan was staring at the Pullman assistant manager with a glum look. "Not officially. It's not a railroad and furthermore, Miss Cabot, some of us—perhaps most of us—do not approve of the way Pullman is treating his workers. No wonder they strike. No, as I have been informing your brother—so he can have the complete story to tell his readers—we don't particularly care for Pullman. If that were the only consideration, the General Managers' Association would not be involved. I can't see any of us lifting a finger for Pullman." He shrugged and turned away from the glass window. "But the ARU is a different story. Eugene Debs and his outfit are out to try to take control of one of the most vital industries in this country and we're not going to stand by and let them do it. No, siree. Not in my lifetime.

"Look here. If Debs has his way, his group will be able to paralyze us. We can't let that happen and we won't let it happen. You see those men over there? They're on the line to Baltimore where we've got two hundred out of work railroad men ready to step into jobs if the ARU strikes. Debs says the ARU members will refuse to hook up Pullman cars, does he? Well, we've got men that will. Any one of his men who refuses will be fired and replaced. They think they can take us down because the roads won't run. But we're ready for them. One call and a trainload of them are on the way." He was using two fingers to point to the board where figures were chalked. "And there'll be violence. We know it and we're prepared for it. We can't let them close down transportation and we won't. You see that contraption over there? That's a hot line directly to the White House. It's a special telegraph line direct to President Grover Cleveland and Attorney General Richard Olney. We've got your brother here and other reporters from all over the country and we're going to make sure they know the truth about what is going on, once this thing starts. And when the ARU shows its true colors, and starts destroying property and threatening lives, we are going to be sure the government does something about it."

I was stunned. This was a far greater reaction than I ever would have imagined. "But the ARU only wants Pullman to agree to arbitration," I protested. Suddenly, this room filled with so many powerful men was making me feel very small.

"That's what they say, Miss Cabot, but that's not the real story. They really plan to wreak havoc. They are dangerous men and they are planning violence even as we speak. That's what brought Jennings here." He pointed at the tall man from Pullman, who was talking to several others. "He's reporting on a plan to blow up the clock tower down there. That's the sort of people we are dealing with in the ARU, Miss Cabot. Don't be misled by them."

I stood up. "That may be true of some people in the ARU, Mr. Morgan, but it is not true of the men and women of Pullman. I know them and I know they have no plans to damage property or endanger lives by doing any such thing. I thank you for your time. It was a mistake for my brother to bring me here."

"I'm sorry if I upset you, miss, but it's good for you and the others at Hull House to know who you are supporting." He held open the door. "I'm afraid we are in for difficult times, but it's Debs and the ARU who are bringing it on. We're only trying to defend ourselves and our stockholders' investments."

I stood up and looked out at the rows of desks. "Mr. Morgan, none of these men look undernourished. None of them have to go home to hungry children. And you say they don't even want to support George Pullman. Even you can see he is a stubborn, arrogant man. Yet, here you all are prepared to oppose the poor workers of Pullman with all the wealth and power at your fingertips. No, I do not understand your position. I do not understand it at all."

"I'm very sorry to hear it, miss. Good day. You're welcome back any time, Mr. Cabot. We want to keep the press informed."

I marched out through the desks. It was appalling. As I made my way out to the corridor, suddenly I was afraid. I could no longer count on a timely end to the problem. With this type of response in readiness, the struggle was going to continue. We would need so much more at the relief station and our supplies were coming to an end.

"Miss Cabot, I'm glad to see you. I told Dr. Chapman we will be happy to provide you with a room at the Florence Hotel." It was Mr. Jennings, who joined us to wait for the elevator. Appalled as I was by the thought of the power of the General Managers' Association, I looked at him with a total lack of comprehension. He seemed to realize it. "If the ARU carries out their threat and the trains stop running. Dr. Chapman came by and asked if we could accommodate you in that case. He thought you might need to stay down in Pullman if you could not get back to the city. I told him we would be happy to oblige you."

I tried to cover the repulsion I felt at this suggestion. Dr. Chapman had already assumed the worst would happen and officiously arranged things for me. After what I had just seen, I was afraid he was right. But that only made me more angry. "It will not be necessary for me to stay at the Florence Hotel, Mr. Jennings, if Mr. Pullman will only have the common decency to meet with his own workmen. The only request is for a meeting to discuss the matter."

"Oh, no, I'm afraid that won't happen, Miss Cabot. Mr. Pullman has already left."

"Left? What do you mean?"

"He and his family have gone to their summer home, in New Jersey."

FIFTEEN

H ow can they let him do this? How can he be allowed to pack up and leave town?" It was the next day and I was stalking back and forth across the clinic floor, in front of a quiet Dr. Chapman, who was eating a sandwich, and Alden, who straddled a chair.

"Who do you think could stop him?" My brother shrugged. "No one even knew they had left till the company spokesman announced it. Did you know he has a track that leads right up to the back door of his mansion on Prairie Avenue? They were all out the back door without anyone knowing." To my exasperation, Alden seemed to admire the plan.

"And what will happen to the people of Pullman?" I was angry. "I had to close early again because we ran out of supplies."

It was that which had driven me down to the doctor's clinic. I could not bear to turn away any more people that day.

"Now that Pullman's fled and there's no chance for talks, they are sure to stop hooking up the Pullman cars tomorrow. That's the deadline," Alden reminded us, as if we could forget.

Dr. Chapman crumpled up the brown paper from his sandwich. "There will be trouble with the trains. Have you brought your things down to the Florence, Emily?"

It was infuriating. "Yes, yes. We sent them over from the station this morning. But how can I stay there with all those company people happily eating full meals while everyone around us goes to bed hungry?"

Dr. Chapman sighed and rubbed his forehead. "You are here to distribute relief supplies, Emily, not to take sides. What use is it to the Pullman workers if you are stranded between here and the city or, worse yet, if you come to some harm? There will be trouble over this." His dark brown eyes appraised me. I knew he doubted whether I knew what I was getting into.

"What about you? Have you taken a room at the Florence? Or will you return to the university and forget all this by working in your laboratory?"

"Emily," Alden scolded me. "How could you?"

"It's all right, Alden," the doctor interrupted. "In some ways perhaps I believe I would do more good in the laboratory at the university. The situation here will only get worse. However, I have some patients who require my continued attention and when I answered Miss Addams request for my help here I put no time limit or reservations on my acceptance." He closed his eyes and took a deep breath. "Besides, the conditions are not so very different from my upbringing in Baltimore. I have a bed," he pointed to his examination table and I saw a pile of blankets in a corner. "That's more than I've had sometimes, I can tell you." He was raised by an itinerant preacher of a father who brought the boy into the slums with him when not abandoning him to his mother's wealthy family.

"Oh, Stephen, if you will stay you must come to the hotel as well. Why should I have a hot meal and a soft bed while you are here?"

He raised an eyebrow and shook his head. Alden answered for him. "Because you're a young lady, Em, and you can't be roughing it over the corner store. Besides, look at it this way, perhaps you can find out what the company is up to and tell MacGregor. Who knows what you'll find out. Keep your ears open."

"Alden, you are despicable. I am not taking advantage of Mr. Jennings offer in order to spy. You *would* think of that."

"Oh, Emily. Make up your mind, will you? You don't have to be such a prig. Come on. I'll walk you as far as the station. If you don't hurry a bit you'll get no hot meal tonight. They'll close the dining room."

I allowed myself to be shooed out by the doctor, who looked quite tired, and I continued to argue with Alden all the way to the station. He ran for his train then, and I headed for the Florence Hotel.

It irked me to realize I would have to enter by the ladies' entrance on the north porch. The evening was warm and dark with a slight breeze you could hear rustling the young trees that lined the road. The smell of roast beef and beets still hung in the air, although the sounds from the dining room were of clearing up, not the gentle rattle of cutlery created by diners. I was too restless to go in, and the night was warm, so I walked past the north porch and around the side where I saw a curious sight. Light spilled out from a doorway and the clatter of dishes made it clear the kitchen was beyond. A woman wiping her hands on an apron was talking to a man who held a carton in his arms. I caught my breath at the distinct voice that I could recognize even at that low tone. It was Raoul LeClerc.

The woman heard my approach. She twisted the apron in her hands and frowned with suspicion. He turned then, and saw me. I stopped, not wanting to intrude as he spoke again to the woman. He stepped quickly to a small cart and added the box to some others. I saw that Fiona MacGregor was with him. She looked up at him, glowing with adoration, as he smiled, whispered in her ear, and gave her a pat on the shoulder.

As she turned to pull the cart away, using a long handle, he took two quick steps to stand in front of me. "Miss Cabot, you have caught us." He took my elbow and told me confidentially, as Fiona disappeared into the shadows, "The kitchen staff, they have leftovers . . . things that would only spoil . . . not good enough for the company men tomorrow." The woman still stood in the doorway glaring at me, but he smiled and shook his head at her and she finally turned back into the kitchen. "At first we came to pick through the garbage. But the staff, they know what they cannot keep and would only throw away. So they give it, you see? Only it would be trouble for them if Jennings and the others knew. But you would not tell them, would you?"

"No, no, of course not."

"Of course not. You, who have come to feed the hungry with the help of Hull House. We are all so grateful for that."

"I only wish we had more supplies so you did not have to dig in the garbage of the company managers. I am so sorry there is never enough."

"No, no, it is not for you to be sorry. Not at all." He looked around and gestured to the road. "Come, a little walk? I do not wish to be seen—you understand? And there is the lake. One of Pullman's many little artificial beauties. This way."

I let him guide me across the road to the path around the little lake in front of the empty factory. The moon had just risen and was reflected on the serene face of the water. I had to admire Mr. LeClerc. While we were all becoming discouraged by the situation, he remained optimistic. When I admitted to having taken a room at the Florence, he was enthusiastic. "But, of course you must, Miss Cabot. Emily, may I call you Emily? You see, you must eat every meal there and not feel guilty, really. You will know that all the leftovers and scraps will go to good use. The more they have staying there, the more they can prepare, and the more they can pass out the door to us at the end of the night." He put an arm around my shoulders and squeezed. I couldn't help but be warmed and invigorated by him, yet I was worried.

"Mr. LeClerc . . . Raoul . . . I don't understand how you can be so cheerful. Haven't you heard that Mr. Pullman has left town? Now there can be no arbitration without him. He has left and tomorrow is the deadline. Even the threats of the ARU not to hook up his parlor cars had no effect on him."

"Exactly." His face was close to mine in the darkness, almost touching. "Tomorrow. Tomorrow, Emily, will begin a new day.

A new world. Because tomorrow they will learn the power of workingmen when they unite. Not just Pullman, but all of them. The railroad men."

"Raoul, there is something you should know. There is a group of railroad men, in the Rookery. They are prepared for a strike."

He laughed. "The General Managers' Association? Do you think we don't know? But we know, Emily, and we are prepared, too." We had stopped and he stood facing me now, hands on both my shoulders. His excitement ran through me like an electrical current. He stroked my cheek lightly. "You must not worry. You will see."

And then he kissed me, lightly at first, and then with strength and passion. I knew I ought to pull away but, for once, I wouldn't let myself. I returned his passion with my own. I felt his hands moving down and with my own I felt the muscles of his shoulders. I stroked his hair. I knew it was wrong but somehow it did not matter. How could it be wrong to share such warmth? To depend on and explore each other? I felt a small dread of what I was getting into, but I squelched it and pressed myself into his arms. His mouth was on my neck.

Suddenly he dropped his hands. "I must take you back to the hotel, Miss Cabot." He began to walk and I had to pull myself from a trance and trot to keep up with him. I was afraid for a moment that I had done something wrong, but he grabbed my hand and swung it.

"Tomorrow," he told me. "Tomorrow at noon. You must come to Twelfth Street Station. Bring your brother. It will be worth his while, I promise you." He stopped. We were back opposite the hotel entrance. "You will come, won't you?"

"I . . . yes . . . certainly. I will come." I could get someone else to cover for me at the relief station.

"Until then, Emily." He faded into the darkness, but I could hear him whistling as I climbed the steps to the ladies' entrance. I found my heart was beating rapidly.

SIXTEEN

It didn't happen quite as soon as Raoul expected. I arranged for someone else to cover for me at the relief station and contacted Alden. But when we arrived at Twelfth Street Station at noon we saw no unusual activity. Alden found out that the Illinois Central Railroad had made up trains of cars ahead of time, including Pullman cars. Then they had chained, padlocked, and sealed the couplings. We did not see Mr. LeClerc and I felt badly for him that the action had not started as he had hoped. It was another disappointment and it did not bode well.

"Don't worry, Em," my brother told me. "It'll happen all right. Just not so fast. You'll see. This is going to be really big."

I decided to go to Hull House while in town and report on the problems down in Pullman. Miss Addams had received bad news about her sister, who was very ill. She welcomed my visit, as I could help her to put things in order before she left for what she feared might be a final visit. Her absence would make it even more difficult to resupply the relief station, but a death in the family waits for no other circumstance—something that I had learned with my mother's death in Boston a few months previously. My heart went out to Miss Addams—there is such a dread when going to see a loved one with the knowledge that it may be for the last time. One feels so inadequate.

I had already planned to return to Pullman later that day, but received a message from my brother saying that he would come and escort me after dinner. When he arrived, he was full of information about the suspense.

"Nothing yet," he told me on the cab ride to Twelfth Street Station. "Your friend Jennings, and some of the others from

Pullman, will be down there for the send-off of the Diamond Special for St. Louis. It leaves at nine. They're already calling the ARU action 'ineffective'. We can get you on the nine-thirty local down to Pullman. We're here. Come on."

He jumped out and I followed him into the new, modern terminal, which had been built for the World's Columbian Exposition the year before. The tall structure housed many tracks and was always bustling with travelers. I had been there many times during my two years in the city, but never before was I conscious of the men who actually ran and serviced the streamlined mechanical monsters we had come to take for granted. Where would the country be without the continual throb of these engines that pulsed in the air of the huge shed? The roads, as they were called, had become the arteries that carried the life-blood of the nation. Chicago itself had grown thick and prosperous as the crossroads where food and goods and people from the East and West passed through.

The crowded tenements of immigrants from Europe who surrounded Hull House on the West Side had all been delivered here by the railroads—coming from Eastern ports already overburdened with new arrivals. And Pullman had designed his palace cars to allow the privileged among us to ride along in style, cushioned from the noise and smells and sounds, in an atmosphere of luxury comparable to a Prairie Avenue parlor. And it was the carrying of just that small part of the whole that was going to stop. Looking around at the lines of sturdy metal boxes all preparing to depart, I could only think that the Pullman cars must be a very small part of this picture. If only George Pullman would have a little pity on the people of his town, there would be no need for even this comparatively minor disruption of the vast movement of goods and people across our continent.

Alden beckoned me towards a man in a worn tweed jacket who was slouching against a column. "Emily, this is Piper from the *Times*. He thinks there's going to be some action. Piper, this is my sister. She's at Hull House and she's been running the relief station down in Pullman."

The man nodded, not bothering to remove his hands from his pockets. "Over there, that's the Pullman Company contingent. Track Eight." I looked across and saw Jennings towering above some of the other men I was familiar with from the Florence Hotel. "That's the Diamond Special."

"Are they palace cars?" Alden had his pencil and notepad out.

"Yeah, but made up ahead of time. They're gloating, but they may be in for a surprise. The ARU is here too, over there." He nodded in the other direction. This time I recognized Raoul LeClerc. I took a step back so the pillar blocked my view. Somehow I did not want him to see me if this would be another demonstration of failure for the ARU. I thought it would gall him to see me there, and I had no wish for that. I also felt a little uncertain of how I would feel, meeting him for the first time after our encounter the night before. I feared my brother's ever-inquisitive eyes.

"But the men at the union rally last week were so firm," I objected. "How can they not go through with it?"

"Oh, they'll go through with this. You wait and see. The union hasn't declared a strike on the railways, see. They want to make sure that is clear. They are only refusing to handle Pullman cars. All they want the railroads to do is to leave those in the yards, that's all. It's a small number of cars. By delaying the action, they are trying to make that clear."

"So, will they just move the trains without the Pullman cars?" I asked. "The rest of the trains will continue. Surely the railroads can agree to that."

"You would think so, and most of the railroad men don't care for Pullman."

"That's what they told us at the General Managers'," Alden said.

"But they've laid it down. The General Managers put out a statement yesterday that the proposed refusal to hook up the

Pullmans is an action in support of something they have nothing to do with—the Pullman Company isn't even a railroad. So, they say any employee who refuses to hitch up a Pullman car will be discharged, even if he'll do every other duty. Most likely the first ones will be the switchmen. If one of them refuses to switch a palace car onto a train, then he'll be fired, right there. They tell someone else to do it, and he's fired for refusing. They fire a switchman, and the other unions come into play and the others—engineers, etcetera—all walk off. Like dominoes falling. But the managers say they'll just hire others in their places. It's a poker game. Got to see who's holding and who's bluffing. Look, there goes the Diamond."

I looked as the steam from the engine filled the shed and the wheels started turning. The crowd around Jennings clapped and whooped. I peeked out to see where LeClerc was standing with some workingmen. He showed no emotion.

"Was that one made up ahead of time?" Alden asked.

"Not sure." Piper stood up from the column he had been leaning against. "Here it comes, watch this now."

As the Diamond Special slowly moved out of the station, the track beyond it was revealed. I heard a yell and saw one of the men in LeClerc's group trudge away and take a ladder down to the tracks. He stood beside a box on the ground and folded his arms.

"Switchman," said Piper.

A man with a clipboard shouted down to him from above. The switchman looked at him, raised his eyebrows, and shook his head.

"That's it, he's firing him for refusing."

Sure enough, the man quietly climbed the ladder and walked back towards LeClerc. The men around him were silent. They did not seem angry or surprised. They expected this. Jennings and his crowd had started to leave but they stopped and watched now, frowning. The man with the clipboard shouted again. I couldn't hear the exact words, but the whole station had gotten unusually quiet. There was still the clatter of wheels, and the occasional shriek of a whistle, and the pounding of the engines, but people seemed frozen like statues.

Another man shook his head, was fired by the man with the clipboard, and walked away. A shout from the departing man started an exodus of others. We saw the engineers from another train walking away. The man with the clipboard was shaking his head angrily and shouting out their names. He was writing down names as he recognized the men. As a group they walked to another track further down. There they joined a parade of men quietly walking away from their jobs.

"Oh, boy, the Pullman crowd is unhappy."

I looked across and sure enough, Jennings was getting redder in the face every minute. The men in his group shook their heads and talked loudly, although I couldn't hear what they said. Jennings found Raoul LeClerc in the crowd of workingmen and glared at him. LeClerc merely nodded, then spoke a few words to the men around him and they dispersed.

"The ARU doesn't want trouble," Piper commented. "Here comes their man."

Raoul came over to us.

"So it has begun?" Piper asked. "How many do you expect to walk off?"

"It depends on the workers," LeClerc told him. "All types of workers have been urged to participate, whether they are ARU or not." We all watched as the walkout quickly spread to other tracks. There was a quiet and orderly parade of men just walking away. "It seems that many of the workers want to participate. We'll see."

"Look at that, would you?" Piper whistled. "I wouldn't have believed it. That's a few hundred already. I need to go get some numbers, and some reactions."

"Me, too. Emily can you catch your train down to Pullman without me? I need to go." Alden was clearly eager to pursue the story.

"I'll take her to Track Two," Raoul offered. "There are no Pullman cars on that local, Miss Cabot. And I happen to know that it will continue to run, despite the action."

Things were beginning to stir as passengers realized they might be delayed or even be unable to make their trips. Raoul took my elbow and led me to the train.

"I'm glad things happened so smoothly for you," I told him. "I know the people of the town of Pullman are very grateful for the support of the ARU and the railway men. It will make such a difference to them. I hope above all that this will bring Mr. Pullman to his senses and that he will make a just settlement with his workers."

He gave a small smile. "We can only wish it will be as simple as you propose. However, we will have to see." There was a blur of activity behind him as we said goodbye. There was tension in the air and uncertainty about the future. I was glad the strike had come off and the workingmen were standing together. But I was uneasy as we pulled out of the station and I saw several engines stopped with wisps of smoke lingering around them. I had heard that once an engine was cold, it would take a long time to get it going again. Certainly some of the engines would go cold that night. How long would it last? And how long would it take to get this mighty surge going again, once it had come to a halt?

And now that it had started, I couldn't help wondering when I would see Raoul LeClerc again. The memory of our walk by the lake lingered in my mind.

SEVENTEEN

And you brought the letter to Mr. MacGregor first of all, is that correct, Miss Cabot?" Detective Whitbread was obviously not happy with me about that fact, but I could only admit it.

"Well, yes. You see it was slipped under the door when I arrived here this morning." We were in the relief station with the door firmly closed—Detective Whitbread, Mr. MacGregor, and myself. I was especially hoping not to rouse the curiosity of Dr. Chapman, downstairs in his clinic. He would be unhappy with this turn of events and sure to scold me. "It seemed the best thing to do under the circumstances, and Mr. MacGregor was the one who insisted, he absolutely insisted that we bring you into it immediately."

Mr. MacGregor was sitting in a hard-backed chair looking small and uncomfortable. The lanky detective was tipped back in his chair, balanced on the two hind legs in a manner I found alarming. He was reading the scrap of paper that had been folded and forced under the door. The words were carefully, almost painfully, spelled out in rounded letters, printed in pencil.

"I know it is important to report such a threat to the authorities . . . to you . . . "

"Miss Cabot." Detective Whitbread landed all four legs of the chair on the worn, wooden floor with a bang. "This letter threatens a bomb. A bomb, Miss Cabot. How could you even consider withholding it?"

"I never meant to do that. I mean, of course I knew we would spread the alarm. It's just that, well, you know how difficult the struggle has been down here. This letter makes it seem like the striking workers will set off a bomb. But it's really a trick; it's not legitimate."

"But a bomb, Miss Cabot. Exactly what did you hope that Mr. MacGregor could do about this?"

"Call you, just as he has done. But won't it be better, much better, if he and the other strikers help you to foil this plot?"

"Ah, I see, you expected Mr. MacGregor to find the assassins, expose them, and save the day?" I blushed then because I had had something like that in mind. "And what of the bomb, Miss Cabot? How did you expect Mr. MacGregor to deal with that, may I ask? At least the man has the common sense not to try to handle this without police help. I'm sorry I cannot say as much for you. What did you think would happen? Two groups of men fighting, a bomb blast, and people killed? Of course the very strikers you wish to help would be blamed. Have you no sense at all?"

"Of course, I . . . Listen, Detective, I know that the very idea of a bomb is just terrifying, especially here in Chicago. I know that ever since Haymarket it has been the thing most feared of all. And I know they never really found out what happened there. Look at what they did—they arrested, and even convicted, men who were later proven not to have been in the city at the time. The governor pardoned some of the men because it was so obviously unjust. To this day people still believe what they want to believe and the truth about what happened is still not known."

"Exactly the danger in allowing this type of incendiary device to go off, Miss Cabot. Exactly why this must be prevented—*not* allowed to happen and *then* proven to be the result of some conspiracy that justifies the actions of one side or the other. This is extremely dangerous and it is essential to use this intelligence to stop it." He waved the scrap of paper that threatened a bombing at seven o'clock that evening. It indicated that the intruders would enter by the east door of the factory.

Mr. MacGregor coughed and moved in his chair. "Miss Cabot

did come to me, and I know this is a great danger to us all. It is something we have feared all along. It is why we have scheduled the men to patrol. We know our men would not do anything to harm the works, but if the company could make it seem like we would, then people might believe it. So we have been afraid of something of this sort all along."

"Yes, and that Jennings was at the General Managers' in the Rookery claiming someone would try to bomb the clock tower. How do we know he didn't set it all up?"

"There is no proof of anything of the kind, Miss Cabot. Have you considered that this note, itself, might be a trap? It could be an attempt to lure you to the place so that you would be harmed. Or it might be to dupe you into believing the company is behind the action, when it is actually the ARU They have some very suspicious characters in their ranks."

"Oh, how can you say that? They are just standing with their fellow workers to help the people of Pullman get a just wage. And why is it that—just when the ARU is taking action, an action that is much more liable to have effect than anything the poor workers down here can do—suddenly there is a bomb plot to blow up the clock tower? Never."

"Detective," MacGregor broke in. "I have an idea that the one who wrote the note may be one of our men. I'm thinking he was coerced by money, maybe, to be a part of this but he had second thoughts. I'm thinking he sent the note to Miss Cabot here because if the company men are in on it, then there's some in the police down here are owing to them. And if we reported it to them, you see, then it would get right back to the company—if the company men were behind it. I'm very much afeared some of our men may be involved," he sighed. "It's lacking money for food that would do it. But, if one of them has exposed this plot, I'm thinking they may feel Miss Cabot here and the ladies of Hull House would stand firm and not be swayed by the company, unlike many others down here, if you see what I mean."

Detective Whitbread frowned. "It is a concern. MacGregor is right. If it turns out it is the company, then if we used the men from the station down here, well, they've all got an interest in helping Pullman, I've seen that."

"I could get some of my men I know would never have been corrupted."

"No. You cannot be sure of that. Any of them could be involved."

"There's the ARU man—LeClerc—he could get some men from in town."

"Never. How do you know the ARU is not behind this, Mr. MacGregor? And what do you think the Pullman Company would say if we were to expose a plot and we were to have ARU people in the room? Impossible. No, I'll go to town and return with some men from the Harrison Street station. They have no contacts down here and are beholden to no one. It will be a small number, but it should suffice. Meanwhile, you will tell no one. I will recruit Miss Cabot's brother. The two of them will be external, impartial witnesses who we can be confident will not alert anyone in the company ahead of time. They, too, will accompany us. At five o'clock we'll meet near the Florence Hotel."

"But Detective Whitbread, surely you won't have the young woman come along on such a dangerous assignment. What if we don't stop the bomb in time? There could be injuries."

"I am willing to come," I insisted.

"It will be an object lesson, Mr. MacGregor. If Miss Cabot is going to take a matter like this into her own hands, I think she must learn exactly how dangerous it will be. I will attempt to ensure no one is harmed, of course. But if she will mix herself into such matters, she must take her chances like the rest of us."

○ℬ

So it was that I found myself sneaking into the east door of the Pullman factory after Whitbread and several plainclothes detectives shortly after five o'clock in the evening. I had not returned to the Florence for a meal, unsure of my ability to keep my excitement at the prospect of the evening's activities to myself. I made do with some bread and cheese from the relief station.

It was warm, with a wind whipping up. As we approached the factory, from a wooded section between it and the lake, I looked sideways and thought I saw a figure. One minute I could have sworn it was Raoul LeClerc, and the next I realized it was my memory of walking with him that other evening that was tricking me into feeling his presence. The next moment I felt a tap on my shoulder from Alden and took my turn hurrying into the factory.

MacGregor had shamefacedly admitted he had access to a key to the east door. That probably explained why the conspirators also planned to come that way. Whitbread had brought half a dozen men—silent, hard-faced men—who took his orders without question. I had a feeling they were used to dealing with much rougher characters than any of the Pullman strikers.

With very little conversation, and a single lantern, Whitbread stationed his men around the building and locked, or boarded, doors until there was only one means of approaching the base of the clock tower in the center. The ground floor was made up of a warren of fairly large-sized workrooms with wooden floors and bare brick walls. They were careful to padlock any doors to the sheds where they worked on the cars, and to the stairs up to the offices on the second and third floors. Whitbread located a large closet, opposite a broad table at the base of the clock tower, and opened the wide door, gesturing for us to go in. Mr. MacGregor found a stool for me to sit on, while he, Alden, and Whitbread would have to make do with the floor. Before he joined us in the closet, the detective lit a small gas lamp mounted on the wall above the table in the hall. We had seen such lamps set around the building. Perhaps there was a watchman who came through.

"And now," Whitbread said in a low voice. "I must ask for silence and meditation. We have come ahead of time so as not to risk detection. They will undoubtedly send someone in to make sure all is clear. No talking. And when they come it is especially important to maintain silence. Nothing will happen until I blow this." He held up a silver whistle on a line around his neck. He had left the door ajar, providing just enough light to see by. "It is especially important that our impartial witnesses, Mr. and Miss Cabot, hear the voices and it is essential that we capture the bomb-making materials. Otherwise, they will run away and strike again when we are unaware and unwarned."

So we sat. After a while it was painful to remain perched on the stool in the dark, without the possibility of conversation. I could hear my brother twitching—he had never been much good at staying still. The detective and Mr. MacGregor seemed to have much more self-control than either of us. I thought the wait would never end.

Finally, I heard a soft shushing sound from Detective Whitbread. Sure enough, in the flickering gaslight, a shadow passed across the opposite wall. But then it was gone. Alden moved to stand and I heard Whitbread push him back down. Footsteps shuffled in the hallway and a voice softly counted, "That's two, three . . . where are you . . . four and five . . . and six. That's it."

MacGregor moved then and I saw the shadow of Whitbread's long arm move swiftly and silently to cover his mouth. I, too, had recognized the voice. It was MacGregor's second in command, Leonard Stark. I put a hand to my own mouth to keep from exclaiming. This was the worst possible thing. Stark? How could he be involved? He was one of the main organizers of the strike. I realized how this would end—it was not good, not good at all. It would turn out that some of the strikers had decided on violence, on destruction of the property of the company that was treating them so cruelly. But who had warned us with the note?

Could it be that the company had found out and planned to have us discover this? I was deeply disappointed. Why had I been the one to bring about this discovery? It would go very badly for the striking men and women of Pullman, the people I so wanted to help. It would be a huge embarrassment to the ARU and all its representatives would suffer.

"When I light this, you want to scram," Stark said, and I heard the swish of a match. At the same moment, MacGregor stumbled and knocked against the wall. I heard Whitbread and my brother both swear. There was a sizzling sound outside, then the earsplitting screech of the detective's whistle, and all was pandemonium.

There was shouting and grunting and banging. I held back in the closet but could see Whitbread jump up and scrape along the floor with his shoe to put out the lit fuse. He pulled out another lamp, and lit it so that we could see more clearly what was happening. Meanwhile, his men had reappeared from their hiding places and dragged Stark's followers to the center of the room. Mr. MacGregor was doing a painful little jig as he recognized them.

"Martin Allen, how could you? How could you, man? And George Devine, I might have known you'd be a fool. Where's Stark? Where is that lying, thieving, double-crossing son of a bitch? I'll kill him." Suddenly, a body came flying from the hallway to land on top of them. It was Leonard Stark, who quickly rolled to one side and jumped to his feet with his arms out and a knife in one hand. MacGregor faced him, squatting as if to attack.

"Here, here now, it's over," Whitbread told them, nodding to his men. They grabbed Stark and MacGregor, while the others lay on the floor, as if afraid to move. Another of Whitbread's men looked in from the doorway. "Did we get the third one?"

"Yes, yes. That's all of them? Three is it?"

Stark was struggling, trying to shake off the men who held him. Whitbread stepped over and twisted Stark's hand until he let go of the knife. "Jennings. I want to see Jennings. The Pullman Company. I work for them."

"Not any more you don't, you liar," MacGregor was still restrained by the policemen.

Stark struggled again. "Let me go. I'm an agent of the Pullman Company. Let me go. I demand to see the general manager."

"You LIAR!" MacGregor screamed. The two men on the floor flinched.

"Stop it. All of you," commanded Detective Whitbread. "MacGregor, get a hold of yourself or I'll have them put you in handcuffs. Do that for the others," he nodded, and his men put handcuffs on the three men. Stark was red in the face.

"I'm telling you I'm an agent of the company. I work for the Pinkerton Detective Agency and I am assigned to the Pullman Company. I demand to speak to Jennings."

Whitbread crossed his arms and regarded the red-faced Stark with raised eyebrows. MacGregor howled and had to be restrained from attacking. The detective turned to one of his men and quietly told him to go to the Florence Hotel and return with the Pullman manager. When he turned back, he said, "Mr. Cabot, I hope you are getting all of this down, then."

To my amazement Alden began interviewing everyone and taking down names. Only Stark turned away in disgust when addressed. He got the names of the policemen and the Pullman men. MacGregor, practically in tears, provided background on the latter, while berating them as idiots for getting involved in a bombing plot. They admitted it had been for money promised by Stark.

Finally, Jennings came trooping in, followed by a dozen company men all sporting their little enamel flag pins. They looked outraged. "You see, Detective, it's just as I told you. Look at that. They were trying to blow up the clock tower. I told you, it's your duty to protect us from this kind of violence. It's up to the city to protect private property."

"And I would point out that we have succeeded, so far, Mr. Jennings. However, this man—who is the main culprit in the crime—claims to be in your employ. Is that true?"

Jennings had the grace to blush but he didn't let embarrassment stop him. On the contrary he began to bluster. "This man is from Pinkerton. He is assigned to us. If you and the mayor and the rest of your department were doing your jobs the Pullman Company would not have to go to the expense of hiring protection such as Pinkerton. And I can tell you it is costing us a lot of money. Yes, he works for us. Let him go."

"Let him go, Mr. Jennings? But this man has just been caught in the act of planting six sticks of dynamite at the base of your clock tower to blow it up. Why would we let him go?"

"Because he was working for us. He was working for the company. Tell him," Jennings turned to Stark, who had a devilish grin on his face.

"Yes, sir. As per directions I engaged to determine the likelihood of an attack on the company property. It was suspected that some of the ARU men had engaged in such sabotage in the past and it was necessary to do a thorough investigation to forestall such an attack."

"ARU men, you're mad," MacGregor broke in. "These are no ARU men. These are Pullman men who have no money and families that are starving. They're no ARU men."

"Exactly. They are your men and they are open to such plots," Jennings shouted. "We have to protect ourselves. We have a right to protect company property from such plots. Tell them, Stark."

"Yes, sir. So this one, Martin Allen, and George Devine along with Joseph O'Malley, participated eagerly and with full understanding in the plan to blow up the Pullman Company clock tower."

"Joe O'Malley. There's no Joe O'Malley here, you lying, thieving traitor." MacGregor would have lunged at Stark again, but Whitbread put a long arm out.

"I would assume Mr. O'Malley is the one who alerted us to the plot," the detective suggested.

"He didn't show up, but the others did," Stark sneered.

"Yes, well, we will be taking all of you down to the station for booking."

"Oh, no, you don't," Stark said. "The company won't press charges against me. I'm their agent. Ask Jennings."

"That's right. Of course." Whitbread looked at him sourly and MacGregor howled again. Jennings was insistent. "Let him go, Detective. I am telling you the Pullman Company will not press charges against this man. He is in our employ and I want to emphasize, once again, that if your department was doing its job protecting us it would not be necessary for the company to incur this extra expense."

Whitbread signaled one of his men to release Stark, who smiled smugly. "I suppose the company *is* willing to press charges against these other two men?"

"What? Of course, that's the point. Oh, really, take them away. They would have blown up the building for God's sake."

"Wait," I yelled, unable to believe what I was hearing. "You cannot do this. These men were being paid by your agent, by you, to do this bombing and you want them arrested for it? You planned this bombing."

Jennings was red-faced when he turned to me. "Miss Cabot, I cannot imagine what in the world you are doing in such a place, at such a time. Nor do I see what this could possibly have to do with you or Hull House. Furthermore," he blustered, unable to think of what to say to me, "you are on restricted company property. Leave immediately, or you will be arrested for trespassing."

I glared at him. Whitbread's men were hiding grins as they moved around, getting the prisoners ready for removal. The detective himself was standing in the middle of the room shaking his head with a raised eyebrow. "Alden," I shouted, "are you getting all of this down? Be sure to mention how Mr. Jennings was going to have me—the Hull House representative to the relief station down here—arrested for trespassing after witnessing his agent provocateur trying to plant a bomb in his clock tower. By all means include that." And, realizing we had lost, and that there was nothing to be gained if Whitbread had to release Stark, I stalked out of the room and over to the Florence Hotel, up to my room to go to bed with no supper. When I saw my brother later in the week I learned that only two of the six sticks of dynamite had been recovered. Detective Whitbread was furious when he realized that, in the confusion, someone had walked away with the other four.

EIGHTEEN

S o they took those two men away and let Stark go. I couldn't believe it. Jennings refused to press charges against Stark but he insisted they arrest the other two men, and they had only done it for the money. If the Pullman Company hadn't given their Pinkerton agent the money to bribe those men they never would have tried to blow up the clock tower. It was all Stark's idea."

"They went along with it, though. They were the ones who brought in the dynamite, from what you said." Dr. Chapman was being obtuse again. I'd been forced to wait until he was free of patients to get his attention. It was the following day and once again I'd quickly run out of supplies at the relief station upstairs and I was at loose ends. I was still absolutely incensed at how the evening had ended.

"But that's not the end of it. At least Alden was there and he rushed out to make sure he got the last train so he could make the newspaper deadline—he took down the whole story. When people see how the company has acted, when they know the truth about it, Pullman will be so disgraced. How could he not give in after such nefarious, felonious, reprehensible behavior is exposed? You'll see, he'll have to give in now."

There was a roar from the meeting room where MacGregor and the other strikers were assembled.

"It must be another line that has joined the strike. Besides the Illinois Central, the Chicago and Northwestern; the Chicago, Burlington, and Quincy; and the Atchison, Topeka and Santa Fe have all had men strike. They are estimating there must be almost eighteen thousand." I had been keeping track.

"I know. I think even Debs is surprised. It's already gone beyond what they planned for."

"It's wonderful. It's all in support of the workers here. Pullman will have to come down from his high horse."

"I hope you're right, Emily. But I've heard from a number of my patients that some of these railroad men are striking because they have grievances of their own."

"Well, what's wrong with that? If they have grievances?"

"It could complicate the solution. The strike is spreading like a rash and there's some doubt as to how much control the ARU actually has of it."

"After the way Pullman's behaved, I'm glad it's happening. Someone has to do something to prove to him that he can't just do anything he wants without even talking to anyone else. Here's Johnny—I sent him for a copy of the *Sentinel*. I'll bet Alden's article is on the front page." I grabbed the paper from the boy and couldn't help letting out an exclamation of disgust. On the front page—instead of Alden's article telling the truth about what had happened the night before, how the Pullman Company had used an agent provocateur to hire men with starving families to try to plant a bomb in the factory—there was a huge cartoon of Eugene Debs wearing a crown, titled *Dictator Debs*. I searched through the paper and finally found a small article on the fifth page. It merely reported that a bomb had been planted in the factory but that police—aided by a Pinkerton agent in the employ of the Pullman Company—had prevented any damage and arrested two strikers, charging them with the deed. "How could they? How could Alden let them?"

Dr. Chapman read the article over my shoulder. "I'm sorry. I'm sure your brother wrote it up as you described."

"But how could they not use it?" I protested.

"They're afraid of Debs and the ARU It was one thing when

the strikers were only the Pullman workers down here—then there was sympathy for their plight."

"Sympathy, but no one would do anything. No one could make Pullman talk or arbitrate. He just kept saying there was nothing to arbitrate. It's only by enlisting the other workers that they can do anything to make an impression on him." I was really finding all this most frustrating.

"But it's not Pullman who is hurting. You said yourself that his contracts have a clause so that he loses nothing if there is a strike. It's the railroads who are hurt by the ARU strike and it's not the Pullman issues that they care about. It's the ARU flexing its muscles. It's the ARU proving their work actions can have an effect and then turning around and using that power to raise wages or address the other issues of their members. That's what the railroad men want to fight and they have the newspapers behind them."

"This is so unfair!" I flung the paper across the room, but it just fluttered apart and drifted to the floor.

"I'm afraid it is."

At that point there were footsteps on the stairs and then Gracie Foley appeared in the doorway, breathing a little heavily from her climb. "Miss Cabot, Dr. Chapman. I'm wondering now, have you seen my little brother or sister by any chance, or my brother, Joseph, who's gone missing?"

I shook my head and Dr. Chapman assured her that we had not seen the children. I'd told the doctor about Stark's claim that Joe O'Malley was one of the conspirators, and Detective Whitbread's belief that Joe had been the one to send me the note warning of the bomb plot.

"Did you hear what happened last night, Mrs. Foley?" I asked.

"That they found out that Stark was really a Pinkerton and they arrested those damn fools Allen and Devine? Of course I heard it, it's all over. There's no truth in that blackguard's claim that my brother Joseph was involved, no truth at all, and he'll never prove it. I've an idea the news of that is what caused him to go missing. But I'm afraid for the young ones. It's all upside down outside, you know. They sure have made an impression with this ARU strike, I'll say that for them. It's thrown most everyone for a loop, it has. It's like a holiday or something. People can't get to where they need to, so they're just walking around. And the rumors. You wouldn't believe it. I met a union man downstairs. He was coming in from Rock Island and they told him the train couldn't run because of riot crowds on the line. So he switched to another line. He got a few miles further on and they stopped the train, telling the passengers they couldn't go any further for there were unruly crowds of strikers on the tracks making it unsafe. Well, this man, he'd had it by then. So he took his bag and walked the whole five miles but didn't see a soul. They're trying to start something is what it is."

"I would believe it after what I saw last night," I agreed. Dr. Chapman looked amused.

"So I said to Mooney, I said, we need to go find the young'uns because if there is any trouble they'll be only too likely to find their way to the middle of it and I'm sure they're hungry at any rate. So I brought down some baskets of food for them, but the young'uns aren't at the Dens and they're not here. And they say there really is a crowd gathered about a mile south. So what do you say, Miss Cabot, Dr. Chapman? Will you join us in Mooney's surrey? We'll go down and round them up and tell them there's food for them, but not if they don't come away with us right now. That'll get 'em. And then we'll find a spot and have a picnic. It's a fine, warm day for it and time they thought of something besides this strike. Will you join us?"

"Thank you, Mrs. Foley, but I have patients coming in a little while," the doctor told her.

"God bless you, doctor. They all love you for it. What about you, Miss Cabot? Mooney is downstairs awaitin'."

"Go ahead, Emily," the doctor told me. "You said you are out of supplies upstairs anyhow. I'll look out for anyone who comes asking for you."

So I got my hat and gloves and joined Gracie Foley in Mooney's open carriage. He sat up front driving us, and I sat in the back with Gracie, for all the world like a couple of Prairie Avenue matrons out for a drive. Three wicker baskets were stowed by our feet and I knew the O'Malley children would have the relief of a real meal that day.

It was not long before a large, restive crowd appeared on our left. When I saw what they were doing I became alarmed. A train car—disconnected from others on the track—was surrounded by rows of people five or six deep on both sides, mostly men but with some women interspersed. They were chanting, and I realized that they were rocking the car back and forth, and from side to side. They threw up some lines, attached them to the corners, and then groups pulled down on the ropes as the car was rocked to their side. They were chanting, "One and two, one and two, one and two," louder and louder until the car tipped towards our side of the track, hung for a moment, and fell with a great boom, as people scurried out of the way. A cheer went up, along with a cloud of dust, as it landed on its side. I saw then that another car had already been overturned.

As they were cheering a whistle shrieked from an engine approaching very slowly from the south. Men with rifles and shotguns were perched all over the engine and the car behind it. All had their badges prominently displayed. It was only then that I noticed a few regular police officers at the edge of the crowd. They had been watching, helpless to disperse the large, angry mob. But the men on the train started yelling at the protestors, ordering them to disperse. They were greeted with jeers.

I was becoming quite uncomfortable. What had seemed like a lark—while the crowd was happy with their actions—was fast beginning to feel very dangerous. Gracie stiffened beside me and bent forward to speak quietly to Mr. Mooney. He climbed down and began to saunter through the crowd.

"I told him to take a gander. See if he spots the young'uns . . .
Look, there they are, he found them." Sure enough, he'd located
Patrick and Lilly and sent them hurrying towards us. We helped
them up into the front seat and gave them each a slice of bread
to eat.

Gracie shielded her eyes, pointing at the engine. "God in
heaven, I don't believe it. The gall of that man. Look who's
over there."

Leonard Stark straddled the fender, wearing a badge and
pointing a rifle at the crowd.

"There he is, big as day, your Pinkerton man. Look at him."

It seemed he'd been recognized by some of the crowd, who
were probably shouting insults at him, although we were still too
far away to hear. Something nettled him as he jumped down from
the engine, cursing at the crowd. They backed away from the rifle
as he approached. We could see Mooney on the side, hands in
his pockets watching the drama.

Stark angrily fired into the air. Some of the crowd jumped
away, but their verbal insults must have increased. Glaring at
them, he did the most incredible thing. I was looking right at him,
and it seemed as if the world stopped for a moment. He turned
towards Mr. Mooney—who was standing, watching from a few
yards away—aimed his rifle, and shot him in the head.

I couldn't believe it. Mooney was not threatening him, or
even yelling at him. He was just watching from the sidelines. It
was impossible. The whole scene hung there for a few moments,
none of us able to comprehend it.

Then Gracie growled in a low voice that rose in pitch and
volume until she was screaming. "No, no, no! Nooooo. Mooooney."
She jumped down from the carriage and ran towards where he'd
fallen.

Meanwhile, the crowd broke into a roar, rushing as one body
towards Stark. He was quickly surrounded by the men who were
with him. (I later found out that they had all been appointed deputy

marshals.) They closed in around him and retreated back towards the engine, guns raised to ward off the crowd. They yelled that they were taking him to the police station, where the wounded man should be brought, too. Soon Gracie was swept back to the carriage with a group of men carrying Mooney. She climbed into the carriage and the men handed Mooney up to us. We held him on our laps while one of the men took up the reins, urging the horses towards the police station, which was only a block away.

The crowd ran along beside the carriage until we reached our destination. Gracie followed the men, who carried Mooney inside, while I stayed in the carriage with the children. I climbed into the front seat and wrapped my arms around them, for comfort and to keep them safe. The angry mob milled restlessly around the front of the station. Only a few minutes later, a cart came out of a nearby alley, driven by a tall, thin man I recognized as Detective Whitbread. "Out of the way. This man is injured, we must take him to the hospital, out of the way!" The back of the cart was covered by a tarpaulin and the crowd—when they heard it held the injured man—made way for the nervous horse being egged on by Whitbread. I couldn't see who was in the cart as it sped away, but I suspected that Gracie wasn't one of them. After making the children promise to stay in the carriage, I made my way into the station house to look for her. I found her just inside the entryway keening over Mooney, who was lying on a wooden bench. She was frantic with worry.

A beefy police officer was turning away a group of angry strikers with the words, "He's gone now, I tell you. He was in that cart that just left." There was a roar of anger as this news was passed back to the others. They wanted Stark and they were furious at being tricked, but I don't think any of them were as furious as I was when I realized what Whitbread had done.

As the policeman cajoled the crowd into settling down and leaving, I screamed at a couple of men, grabbing them and forcing them to carry Mooney back to the carriage. Gracie was wild.

"We have to take him to Dr. Chapman," I told her. "It's not far. They're not helping him, Gracie, we have to do it."

They lifted him up into the carriage, laying him with his bleeding head in her lap. She had tied a handkerchief with lace edging on the wound, but it was deeply soaked with blood already. He was still breathing at least. Furious with all of them, I climbed up to take the reins. I had only driven a carriage of this size a few times, but I trusted no one else. I yelled at little Patrick to show me the way. He reached over to help me with the reins and even pulled out a whip to get the horse moving through the crowd. One man wanted to stop us to make sure they weren't being fooled again, as they had been by the first cart, but hands reached out and pulled him out of my way. It was as well for him because I had no intention of pulling up the horse for any more foolishness. I would have run him down.

With the help of young Patrick we made it to the clinic over the grocery store. The men standing outside did not need any urging to carry Mooney up the stairs for us.

It was only when I saw the grim look on the doctor's face, as he directed them to lay Mooney on the table, that I realized it was all for naught. He was already dead.

NINETEEN

L ace curtains drifted in a very slight early morning breeze. I woke to the sound of birds and the smell of frying bacon. My room at the Florence Hotel was over the kitchen. As I was an unchaperoned woman, I was required to enter and leave the hotel through the ladies' entrance. My room did not have a private bath, so I had to travel down the hall to the water closet. I always waited for complete quiet in the corridor before making the trek. And arrangements for a bath were tedious, so I hadn't indulged very often.

My limbs felt heavy, as if it would take a great effort to move that morning, and my head was already starting to ache. I kept seeing that moment when Stark shot Mr. Mooney, perhaps hoping that eventually it would fade or somehow the action would change. It made staying in bed a torture, so I pulled myself up. I had offered to stay with Gracie the night before, as she kept vigil over Mr. Mooney's body in the clinic, but I was soon elbowed out by women from the town. They may have shunned her when her father threw her out, but in her time of trouble they surrounded her like a picket fence. Dr. Chapman told me plainly to go home. But I had no home to go to, only my room at the Florence. I would not call that home. I longed for Hull House where I could have had companions to talk to. Here I was neither fish nor fowl. I was not, after all, part of the town of Pullman, nor did I have anything in common with the men from company management who were staying at the hotel. The place was permeated with the stench from the pipes and cigars they smoked late into the night in the front rooms where women were not allowed. The tramp of feet and sound of male voices was somehow a threatening background music, although they all treated me with the utmost politeness.

It was a warm day for my dark clothes of mourning but certainly they fit my mood. They reminded me of my mother's passing, which had left me and my brother so alone in the world. It seemed death was inescapable that year.

A freshly laundered blouse had been hung from a peg on the wall. At Hull House we sometimes dispensed with a corset. That morning it would have been a relief in the warm weather to escape its rigidity. But as the only woman in the hotel, and as the representative of Hull House and the Civic Federation at the relief station, I knew it would be inappropriate. With a sigh, I used the washstand to perform my morning ablutions, then dressed to meet this very unfortunate day.

Descending the steep staircase by the front desk, I realized that the men bustling around the lobby had either not heard of the tragic events of the day before or were unmoved by them. I turned into the dining room. My head pounded and my stomach was unsettled, but I seemed only capable of following my daily routine. The waiter led me to the small table by a window that they kept for me and quickly returned with a plate of fried eggs, tomato, hash browns, and thick slices of bacon. He plopped it down before me and filled my cup from a teapot, which he left on the table. My stomach turned, but I attempted to eat a little, dividing up the portions with my fork.

At the next table, a group of men debated the situation. "There's rioting all over the city. They've turned over boxcars and set them afire. The authorities have got to do something to stop it or the city will burn."

"People are afraid to go out their doors. There are packs of them roaming like animals." This man sounded pleased. "This will show them what Debs is really up to. They'll see what we're up against now."

"I heard there was a crowd with bats that attacked the sheriff and his men on one of the Rock Island lines. They barely escaped with their lives."

"And the women are worse than the men. They're yelling all sorts of nasty things trying to provoke them, the hags. They'd pull down everything and murder us all in our sleep if they got the chance."

"You heard about how they tried to blow up the clock tower, didn't you? What do Hopkins and Altgeld have to say about that? They are worse than useless. If the roads didn't hire their own men to protect their property the politicians would let it all be destroyed."

"I hear the general managers are documenting everything. They're on the line to Washington, warning them that the whole thing will blow up and there'll be a massacre if they don't do something."

"What can they do? The city police stand by and let these mobs run rampant. They're standing right there while the mob pulls over cars, tears up the tracks, and blocks the engines. They are worse than useless. Sometimes I think they're in league with the strikers. At this rate Debs will be running the country, calling the shots for everybody. It's a revolution. If they don't put a stop to it, it's going to be a bloody revolution."

"What right do they have to stop the whole transportation system? Debs just wants to be able to dictate terms to everyone. If they let that happen, it'll be the end of our system of government. They need to do something. They need to do whatever it takes to break this strike and get the trains moving again."

My head throbbed with the noise, and I wanted to yell, "What do you want them to do, shoot innocent people? Like Mr. Mooney?" Did they think that would somehow improve things? Mooney wasn't even a striker, nor was he part of the railroads. He was just trying to find the children to keep them safe. I couldn't eat the food and pushed the plate away. But I dreaded going to Kensington. There were no stores left at the relief station and I didn't know when any would come. Much as I disliked it, I had to find Mr. Jennings to ask for the use of his telephone.

"Certainly, Miss Cabot, come to the office." He led me to the room where we had talked when I was with Detective Whitbread.

"Mr. Jennings, did you hear about the shooting yesterday? It was Mr. Stark, that Pinkerton man who was working for you. He shot Mr. Mooney. He just shot him without provocation, right in front of everyone."

"Oh, come now, Miss Cabot, I hardly think it was without provocation. From what I heard, there was a huge crowd blocking the line. Stark was surrounded and outnumbered and he shot in self-defense."

"I was there, Mr. Jennings. Mr. Mooney was not threatening anyone. He was just standing there. Mr. Stark shot him for no reason. The Mr. Stark who you let go after he tried to plant a bomb in your factory. The very same man."

"You should not have gone to that area yesterday, Miss Cabot. Perhaps this will show you how very dangerous it is. In any case, Mr. Stark is no longer in our employ. He has been deputized by the sheriff. With all of these troubles, they've had to add men to help get the lines opened up. He was working for the sheriff, not the Pullman Company."

"What have we come to, Mr. Jennings, when we have criminals in charge of our law enforcement?"

"You must ask your detective friend, Miss Cabot. But if Debs and his union had not provoked the situation, none of this would have happened. Here is the telephone, you can connect to the exchange." With that advice, he stomped out of the office.

I managed to get through to the pharmacy near Hull House and they got Miss Giles to come to the line.

"I'm so sorry, Emily, but Miss Addams is in Milwaukee. She's trying to reach her sister, who is very ill, but with the train stoppages she has been unable to get there. We are all very worried about her."

"Oh, I see. I am so sorry to hear that. But, Miss Giles, we have run out of supplies down here and the people are in a very bad state. They have had nothing from us for three days now and there is no other source of supply."

"Yes, well, with all of the disturbances people are afraid to go out into the streets, although I must say we have not seen any actual trouble here on the West Side. Nonetheless, some of our most dependable volunteers have had to stay at home due to concerns about travel. I am afraid there is no one to solicit donations. In any case, many people are not in favor of the strike now, due to the unrest that's been the result. I am not at all sure how successful any solicitation would be right now."

"But, you don't understand. The people are really on the verge of starvation. There is no food down here." I thought of the full breakfast plate I had pushed away. How cruel that the managers in the hotel had full plates while the children went to bed with empty bellies. It was an impossible situation. It made no sense at all. "I'd hoped something might be managed. I hoped a wagon might be on the way. I don't know what to tell people."

"I'm very sorry, Emily. I'll call a meeting of anyone who is here today, but I cannot promise anything. You might think of returning yourself, to try to organize something. I will do my best, but we'll have to see."

I had to be content with that, but I still dreaded returning to the relief station where I knew there would be people waiting in hopes that we would get in some more supplies. I had nothing to tell them.

It was a beautiful day. The trees were lushly green and the flowerbeds around the little artificial lake were brimming with colors. It was a day for a picnic. I stifled a sob as I thought of the picnic baskets Gracie brought from town just the day before. On such a gentle, warm summer day the people of Pullman were suffering from hunger gnawing at their stomachs and grief clawing at their minds. It was quite cruel to see the contrast.

When I reached the offices above the S & H Grocery, there was quiet. I expected angry wailing at the uncalled for death of Mooney. But then I realized that he was not a striker. He wasn't even a Pullman resident. This was not his fight, and his death had made no impression on the people locked in this battle. Except for Gracie. I went up to the relief station and gave the bad news to the half a dozen workers waiting for me. I looked over our wonderfully systematic arrangement for carefully distributing supplies, now useless with empty shelves. There was nothing to distribute. I found a few small caches of flour and coffee and distributed all that I had to the volunteers, then I sent them home. I went to lock the door, but what was there to steal? I shook my head as I locked it up anyhow.

As I descended, I heard voices coming from the clinic. Recognizing the doctor first, I realized the other voice was Detective Whitbread. Suddenly resolute, I flew down the remaining steps and through the clinic door.

"Detective Whitbread, how could you do that? How could you allow that man to escape? He shot Mr. Mooney!" I cringed as I looked at the sheet-covered body on the stretcher in the middle of the room. I was glad Gracie was not there to hear my outburst, but I could not restrain myself. I had thought so highly of Whitbread that I could not believe he had helped Stark escape the crowd the day before.

"Miss Cabot. What would you have me do, allow the mob to tear him limb from limb? Because that is what would have happened. The death of Mr. Mooney was a tragedy, but there was no need to compound it by another killing. In any case, you should not have been there. If you and Mrs. Foley had only avoided such a dangerous scene, this would not have happened."

"We were only there to find the children and bring them away. Gracie had a picnic . . . " I suppressed a sob.

"It's true, Whitbread. Mrs. Foley asked Miss Cabot to accompany her to find the O'Malley children."

"In any case, Mr. Mooney did nothing to deserve to die. Stark just aimed his gun at him and shot him in the head. Have you arrested him, at least? You haven't let him go, have you?"

I saw Whitbread exchange a look with the doctor. "It is not as simple as you think, Emily," Dr. Chapman told me. "He was an authorized deputy sheriff when it happened."

"Authorized? Authorized for what? Authorized to shoot an innocent man who was just standing there?"

"According to him and the other deputies, there was a large crowd," Whitbread told me. "He was outnumbered and surrounded. The crowd surged towards him and he fired in self-defense. The fact that he hit Mooney was a tragic accident."

"They lie. I was there. Didn't you talk to anyone besides the deputies? I saw the whole thing. He just aimed at Mooney and shot him. It was murder, out-and-out murder. Surely you won't let him get away with that?"

"Miss Cabot, the man is currently employed and vouched for by the sheriff. Unfortunately, the sheriff has recruited a force of somewhat questionable, unsavory characters. But in the face of the roaming mobs and general unrest, there is no way to control the actions of such an authority. The incident with Stark yesterday was by no means the only occurrence of questionable legality, I assure you. In ordinary circumstances a full investigation would be pending, but at the moment the police are stretched to their limit just responding to the many calls that are coming in."

"You let him go! You saved him from the crowd and then you let him go on the word of the other men who were with him. He murdered Mooney, and you are letting him get away with it."

"Emily," Dr. Chapman interrupted me, "Whitbread is only doing what he can. He has no authority to override the sheriff. And when the situation is this unstable, innocent people get hurt. What did you think would happen in a strike? Did you think it would all be rallies and speeches? This is what happens. This is your strike that you so whole-heartedly support. No matter who wins this struggle, there are many who will only be hurt by it. Whitbread is doing his job. He has come to allow me to release Mooney's body to Mrs. Foley so she can bury him." He waved some papers in his hand. "He has a cart to move the body. What are *you* doing? Where are the supplies for the relief station? Every day I see more and more people weakened by lack of food. They are getting sicker and sicker. Instead of telling the police what they should be doing, why don't you attend to your duties? And where is Miss MacGregor? Isn't she helping you with relief? She is a very young, inexperienced girl. Couldn't you use your influence to help her?"

I fell back from his accusations as from blows. The issue of Fiona MacGregor was completely unexpected. What did he want me to do?

"There are no supplies to be had. I talked to Miss Giles this morning, but Miss Addams is on her way to see her dying sister and there is no one to find the money needed. As for Miss MacGregor, she is on my committee, but with nothing to distribute I have had to send them away. In any case, as you yourself remarked, since the arrival of Mr. LeClerc she has chosen to spend her time assisting him rather than handing out supplies with me or helping you in the clinic. If I see her, I will be sure to let her know you were asking."

TWENTY

I turned on my heel, quickly leaving the clinic. I left the doctor and the detective to each other. I was sick of them, sick of the strike, sick of the violence, and furious at my helplessness. As I hurried down the stairs I was frustrated yet again. A crowd of men was flooding out of the meeting room on the floor below, blocking the stairway. As I waited for the crowd to thin, I saw Fiona MacGregor lingering in the meeting room. I was about to continue on my way when I saw that Raoul LeClerc was there as well, tidying up after the meeting. He saw me and his face lit up with a smile as he came towards me.

"Miss Cabot, you are here. Have more supplies come?"

My face started to burn with embarrassment. No, there was no food. If there was food I would be upstairs handing it out. I restrained myself from snapping at him. "No, unfortunately. I have had to turn people away again." I noticed Fiona move up until she was between me and LeClerc. "I'm glad to have found you, though, Fiona. Dr. Chapman was just asking for you. He sorely misses your help in the clinic."

She frowned. LeClerc put a hand on her arm as she turned to face him, staring up into his large brown eyes. "Go," he said, and nodded towards the stairs. "Go to help the doctor. It's all right. Go."

Reluctantly, she allowed him to turn her towards the door, where he gave her a little push. Passing me, she hesitated. "Go." He waved a hand at her. "Shoo, go." When she clambered up the stairs he smiled at me, putting a hand on my arm. Then he looked to see if there was anyone else around. Before I realized what he was doing, he had pulled me into the room, out of sight of the doorway, and pushed me against the wall. I felt his breath on my face, then his lips on mine. I felt the pressure of his kiss for a long moment before I pushed him away with both hands.

"What are you doing?"

His hand caressed my cheek. "Don't be alarmed. I couldn't resist. You were so beautiful, standing there, in the doorway."

I slid away from him until I was in the hallway once more, then I turned to him. "You mustn't do that. Have you heard what happened? Have you heard that the Pinkerton man, Stark, shot and killed Mr. Mooney? And they let him go. They didn't even arrest him." My face was burning with embarrassment. I should not have let him kiss me, I should have protested more, but for all of that my anger at the death of Mooney was more compelling. I thought at least Raoul LeClerc would understand. I hoped he would, because no one else did.

His large brown eyes seemed to have tears in them as he shook his head. "I know, it is tragic. Very tragic." He reached out to touch my arm as if to calm me. "Listen, Emily, don't you see what it means? They are desperate. They will do anything. It means they are at the end of their rope. They will shoot a mere passerby, they will try to starve the people, they will ride the engines aiming their shotguns at the crowd. But it won't work. They cannot run the trains without the workingmen, the union men. Can't you see how close we are to winning? Mooney's death is tragic, but he is a martyr. And there are others. But we are so close. If only the people can hang on and stay together a little while longer. We will win. The ARU will win, and it will be a new day for all working men and women in this country."

"You really believe that, don't you?"

"Of course I believe it. That is what we are doing here." He took me by the shoulders. "I promise you, Emily Cabot, when this is over, and Eugene Debs and the ARU are in charge, men like Stark will not be tolerated. But we must win this struggle and to do that we must find a way to feed the people. You know they are desperate. Can't you help? Can't your friends at Hull

House help us to hold out just a little longer?"

I closed my eyes and clenched my teeth in exasperation. When I opened them, I was looking directly into his warm brown eyes. He reached up to caress my cheek. I brushed his hand away, confused by the feelings he had stirred in me, and distracted by the more pressing situation. "All right. I'll go myself. There is no one at Hull House who can help. Miss Addams is not there. Others are staying away out of fear that they might meet mobs in the streets. I'll have to go up there myself and hound them all until they give me supplies, just to make me go away. I can do that. I *will* do that."

He smiled and stole another kiss before he put an arm around my shoulders, hurrying me along the hall and down the stairs. "Come, I trust you to find someone to help you get a cart for the supplies you'll bring back. You can do this. We will be waiting for you to return." When we reached the street Ian MacGregor was standing there holding a clipboard. Raoul pointed to him, giving me a slight push in that direction, and then headed back inside.

I marched over to Mr. MacGregor and demanded his help. As it turned out, it was easy for him to recruit two men to take me to the city in a wagon, in the hopes of returning with supplies. But when I reached Hull House I learned that Jane Addams was still stuck in Milwaukee, completely taken up with the imminent death of her beloved sister. Florence Kelley was managing the settlement house's affairs in her absence. She told me that the people in the city viewed the strike very differently. People were afraid to go out now, fearful of meeting marauding bands of strikers.

I thought of the sturdy men at the ARU meeting I had attended and could not believe they would suddenly turn into a rowdy, destructive crowd. The crowd I had seen at the crossing where Mooney was killed had not been striking railroad men or strikers from Pullman. I was sure they were not. More likely, they were people already out of work or unable to get to work due to the strike. From the Hull House residents themselves I learned that people were beginning to believe the newspaper claims that

Eugene Debs was out to force industry and government to do as he dictated. There was a tangible fear of rioting and the general managers were calling for the federal government to intervene.

"But it is a labor action, it is a dispute between the workers and the railroads. Why don't they make Pullman return from his country house and just talk to his working men and women? Why is that too much to ask? How can the government get involved?"

Mrs. Kelley grimaced at my naïveté. "The local government does not want to intervene. The mayor is on the side of the strikers, as you very well know, but the police are wary. Governor Altgeld refuses to intervene although there have been calls for the National Guard to be brought in. It's the general managers. They are trying to say the United States mails are being interfered with."

"But I heard that the strikers are *not* interfering with mail trains."

"Who is to say? There are powerful men who own the railroads and they are determined to break the strike. Debs has been more successful than he may have wanted. The strike has spread, especially out west. The railroad men will do anything they can think of to force the government to act. They want to force a crisis. The governor is afraid of what the attorney general might do."

"You mean in Washington?"

"Oh, yes. The general managers are in constant contact with the president and Olney, the attorney general. They are taking the battle to the courts, to get injunctions against Debs and the ARU."

"They cannot interfere. Surely they cannot interfere."

"We shall see."

Frustration drove me to action. We scoured Hull House for supplies to take back to the starving town. The previous winter, the settlement house itself had been a relief station during the terrible smallpox epidemic. We turned out the closets and pantries for stores left from that time. We solicited from visitors, but it was little enough in the end. With Miss Addams gone there was no one to go to the parlors of Prairie Avenue asking for money, so I did it myself. I begged and bullied and made a pest of myself. I approached Mrs. Louise Bowen, who had saved us on Christmas Eve, when the turkeys we were to distribute were destroyed. I timed my arrival to coincide with her likely preparations for dinner guests and demanded an audience. She heard me out with a grim expression. She wrote me a check but advised me that her acquaintances were no longer sympathetic to the strikers, or even to the Pullman families. The tide had turned. People wanted an end to the violence being reported in the papers and a return to normalcy. This was not the way to recruit sympathy. There was nothing more that she could do. And she pointed out the injustice of Miss Addams's inability to reach her dying sister, due to the effects of the strike on the railroad lines. I realized I had received as much aid as I was likely to get.

I arranged for my purchases and returned to Hull House, eager to pack up the wagon and make my way back to Pullman. But when I entered the front door I heard angry voices coming from the library. Miss Giles was attempting to ignore the noise while she led the kindergarten in ring-around-the-rosy. She looked worried as she came to greet me.

"It's Mr. Pullman," she told me, with a furtive look at the closed door. "Miss Addams had only just arrived back when he came in. He sounds very angry."

TWENTY-ONE

I sent Miss Giles and her toddlers out to the kitchen for cookies. The loud shouting coming from the library was muffled but alarming. I took a deep breath and clenched my teeth, then opened the door and stepped in.

Miss Addams was seated behind her small desk opposite the door. George Pullman stood in the middle of the room facing her. He wore neither hat nor gloves and his cravat hung slightly off center. I had only met him that once, at his home, but he seemed like a shrunken version of himself. Perhaps it was the pasty color of his skin, replete with brown age spots, or his slightly disheveled hair, which was much whiter than I remembered. He held a silver- topped cane that he swung around wildly as he spoke. He was no longer the immovable rock that he had appeared to be on our first meeting.

"You will cease and desist from your interference, madam. You will stop it now. What right have you to complain of my actions? What business is it of yours?" He was shouting, but the tirade, which had apparently been going on for some time, flowed over Miss Addams. She saw me, however, and appeared glad for the interruption.

"Emily, Mr. Pullman is seeking his children, his younger children. It seems they have had a disagreement and left home. You will remember Miss Cabot, Mr. Pullman. She has been running the relief station down in Kensington, providing food and medicine for the people. Perhaps your sons and younger daughter have gone there." I shook my head and she hurried on. He stood with his voice barely restrained, ready to start raving again. "I regret it very much if I have done anything to displease you,

Mr. Pullman. It is the duty of each of us to try to understand and alleviate the suffering of our fellow man. We try . . . "

"Suffering, suffering. Who are you to judge suffering? What do you know about it? I built this company from the ground up. I employed these people. I took them away from the dirt and temptation of the city to a town conceived and built by me. I saved them from the squalid surroundings where you choose to live. Where do you and these union agitators come from that you think you can tell me how to run my business? The town of Pullman is named for me. It is my town, my company. You have no say in the running of it. None at all and neither do Debs or his radical extremist followers.

"Don't you see what you have done?" He gestured with the cane towards me, raising his voice even louder. "If those people are without food it is your doing and the doing of those vicious radicals who have infiltrated the works and bribed the men with false hopes." He whacked his walking stick on the wooden floor as if he would beat his message into it. "Ingrates. Never have there been such ingrates. I cannot work in my own offices for they are closed. I cannot use my own desk. I cannot entertain at the hotel named for my own daughter for fear of actions by these violent strikers."

"Oh, really, Mr. Pullman," I interrupted. "I have been staying at the Florence myself. I assure you no harm has come to me. The actions of the strikers have been greatly exaggerated."

But he spread his arms widely and screamed, "Will you let me speak? Will you hear me out? Can I not even speak once without contradiction?" His aspect was wild and he quivered with rage. Miss Addams clucked, waving her hands gently as if to tell me to be quiet. I obeyed, fearing for the man as his face reddened and his eyes protruded.

"I, who have built this company with my own hands over thirty years, cannot even go to my club without being spurned. To the society of this city, which I have helped to flourish, I am no longer welcome. I am a pariah. Where is gratitude now? Who remembers my contributions now? No one. It is all because of the despicable lies about me from men and women who would never have had the homes they live in if I had not built them. Do they thank the provider of these good things? No, they demand MORE! They refuse to work unless they may dictate the terms. To me—ignoring the fact that without me they would still live in these miserable slums." Here he made a wide gesture to encompass our neighborhood. "These slums where you and your like come to stir up envy and discord. Well, they can go back. You may have them back, all of them. But you may NOT have MY CHILDREN." Another crack of the stick on the floor.

My face was burning. It was only with a great effort, clenching my teeth painfully, that I kept myself from yelling back at these accusations. But Miss Addams gave me a stern look and rose from her seat behind the delicately carved desk in the corner. "Mr. Pullman, I assure you again that I have no knowledge of the whereabouts of any of your children. But, please, I can see that at this time you too are suffering from this awful situation, just as your people in the town of Pullman are. Please, will you allow me—or Mayor Hopkins, or someone else, anyone of your choosing—to begin a conversation, to call all the parties to sit down together to arbitrate this disagreement? I know in my heart that, if we can only begin to talk, all other obstacles will fall away before us."

She stood and walked towards him with her arms outstretched, but even Miss Addams could feel the waves of rage emanating from him, as he stood there glaring. She stopped before she reached him.

I thought he would burst. His face was so red the word apoplexy popped into my mind. He struggled wordlessly for a moment, gripping the cane so fiercely in one hand that his knuckles were white. His other fist was clenched and he raised both fists before his face, shaking them like a baby. "There is

NOTHING . . . TO . . . ARBITRATE." It was a bellow that made me fear he would explode, and collapse from the effort, but he abruptly banged his stick on the wooden floor a final time and dashed from the room.

Miss Addams and I rushed to the window to see him fling himself into his carriage, which then hurried away. She returned to her seat wearily. I could not even think of any response to the display we had just witnessed. She buried her face in her hands and I noticed the black-banded stationery on which she had been writing.

"Miss Addams, you were trying to reach your sister in Wisconsin . . . "

She raised her head. "Poor Louisa passed away before I could reach her."

"I am so very sorry." I remembered how I had been called to my mother's bedside in the spring. How would I have felt if a train strike had kept me from her deathbed? I would have been furious. It had given me some peace to be there at the end. "I am so sorry these circumstances kept you from her. I know how very hard that must be for you. I wish I could do something for you and your family."

There were tears in her eyes. "Thank you, Emily. We are grateful for the prayers of all of our friends. But I understand that you have come for more supplies for the people of Pullman. You must return with them. Tell me about it." She generously put aside her own grief to hear my report, and then said, "You must start back as soon as possible. This is a great tragedy."

"It could have been so good," I couldn't help complaining. "He is right about the slums. The town is so much better. But they are truly starving."

She sighed. "Mr. Pullman thought out in his own mind a beautiful town. He had the power with which to build this town, but he did not appeal to, nor obtain, the consent of the men who were living in it. There is an arrogance inherent in philanthropy that can completely spoil the offering. And when that happens, the loss seems worse than the original lack it was meant to help. It is truly tragic."

TWENTY-TWO

J ake and Pauley, the two men who brought me up from Pullman, were happy enough to stay the several days it took me to organize supplies. At least at Hull House they were fed, which was better than down in Pullman. When we finally loaded up the wagon I was disappointed at the paucity of the amount I had been able to purchase. It appeared to be so little, when I knew that the need that would meet us at the other end would be so great. But it would have to do. At any rate, it would be an improvement over the completely empty shelves I had left behind. I thought even the Hull House residents were happy to see me leave, so demanding had I become with my begging.

It was a hot and dusty ride back down to Pullman. We did not see any of the mobs so feared by the people who read the newspapers. When we arrived it was easy to recruit some of the weary men in the meeting room to help carry the supplies up to my relief station. They were only too quickly unloaded and I gave a small amount of food to my helpers to take home, saying the rest would be distributed the next day when I had managed to round up my committee, who would once again oversee the fair distribution of the goods.

I locked the doors and descended to the clinic on the second floor to let Dr. Chapman know that I had returned. His door was shut but in the corridor, on the hard bench, there was a single waiting patient. I felt a thrill of recognition.

"Raoul."

He looked around as if in a fog. I was so glad to see him. I was so tired of being angry, of having to hammer at people to make them understand the crisis. I was so happy to be able to tell him that I had returned with supplies. Not enough, perhaps, but at least it was something. I longed to feel his arm around my shoulders in a confidential manner, as when we had last met. I was so excited to reconnect that I sat down close beside him and put a hand on his arm. I had worried I would feel embarrassed, seeing him after the kisses he had surprised me with the last time, but now my scruples seemed ridiculous to me. He had a warmth and an enthusiasm that I felt a great need for. He still had hope for success and I needed to feel that. It seemed that he was one of the few who felt the same passion for this situation as I did.

But he looked at me, as if I were a stranger, then looked down at my hand on his arm and moved away from me, pointedly sliding several inches to the side with a distinct frown on his face. I was mortified. It was such a forward thing I had done, sitting practically on top of him, touching him. I was so wrong about how I assumed he felt about me and it was all obvious to me in that second. I jumped to my feet in a useless attempt to hide my shame.

"Mr. LeClerc. I have just returned from the city. I have managed to bring back some supplies. Not much. Not enough, but some. Is there news of the strike? Is there any hope of it ending?"

He looked sullen. It was so unlike him. In the weeks since I had first met him, his hair had gotten longer and so had his moustache. He had let a small goatee grow on his chin. He looked more foreign than ever, I thought. More like the idea of a wild-eyed anarchist. But his eyes were not wild. They were dull under the lowering brow of his frown.

"I cannot say at this time. It doesn't matter what we do, they lie. They provoke trouble to blame the unions and Debs. They want to crush us but it will come at a cost to them. They want to gag us, but we will be heard. They are turning the full force of the government and the money people against us, but they will learn. They will find out that the workingman will fight back."

At that moment the door to the office opened and

Dr. Chapman ushered out a very ill-looking Fiona MacGregor. I realized Raoul was in the corridor because he was waiting for her. The doctor seemed angry. Fiona was very pale as she shuffled forward, leaning on his arm. Raoul leaped up and took over solicitously, with one arm around her as he gave her support.

"She needs bed rest. Complete bed rest," the doctor said. "There is nothing else I can do for her. Take her home. I have nothing else to say to you." Then he turned and went back into his office, closing the door with a bang. I jumped.

"Miss MacGregor, you're ill. I'm so sorry to hear it. I . . . I've brought back some supplies from Hull House. I was going to come and see you, to get our committee together." She looked at me vaguely and slumped against LeClerc. "But don't worry. I will gather the others. You go home and rest, like the doctor said." LeClerc was taking her to the stairs, ignoring me. Soon I was left alone in the corridor. It was the end of the day, dusk coming on, so all of the doctor's patients were finally gone. I stepped over and knocked on his door.

"Come in."

I opened the door and left it open, as it usually was. He had his back to me, tidying up instruments on a table in the corner of the room.

"Dr. Chapman. I came to let you know that I've returned from the city . . . with some supplies." I thought he would approve of my actions. "I saw Mr. LeClerc in the hallway. Poor Miss MacGregor. She's ill, it seems?"

He banged a metal instrument into a container, his neck red. It made me wonder whether he was angry that Fiona had gone away with Raoul LeClerc. It seemed to me that he had some affection for her. Was he disappointed by her so obvious admiration for Mr. LeClerc? The doctor and Fiona MacGregor? But she was so young, and so uneducated. Yet clearly he was moved by some strong emotion. It shocked me.

"Miss MacGregor is ill and presumably she will recover if she rests. It is not something to be discussed. This miserable town and this miserable strike. They do nothing but drive people to awful choices. Men like Pullman and Debs are only too willing to sacrifice the ordinary people in their quest for power."

"I believe that Mr. Debs and the ARU are trying to build a better future for all of the workers. How can they fight back against someone like Pullman without such an organization?" I thought he was more angry for the effect on little Fiona than for anything else. He really was angry on her account. But it was Raoul who was comforting her and taking care of her now. I felt the need to swallow my own disappointment about the feelings I'd thought Mr. LeClerc had for me. There was a greater good to be considered. The doctor was wrong about the ARU at least. "I'm sure Mr. LeClerc continues to want to help the people of Pullman."

"LeClerc! He'll help them to hell if he can."

He was jealous of Raoul. I would never have thought it of the doctor. So much was happening before my eyes without my understanding any of it. Of course, the doctor had proposed marriage to me before all of this began. I turned him down believing he made the offer only from pity. And I was mortified to find I was correct. Perhaps in Fiona MacGregor, he had found a woman who truly raised his affections, only to lose her to the union man. I felt a knot in my throat.

"Dr. Chapman." Alden appeared in the doorway. "Oh, Emily, I didn't see you. I haven't seen you since the clock tower incident. I tried to write that up the way it happened, by the way, but they changed it . . . they edited it."

"'Dictator Debs', Alden? Instead of exposing how the Pullman Company used that Pinkerton man to trick those men, it becomes a condemnation of the strikers, as if they planted the bomb. It was all Jennings and Stark."

"I know, Emily, but the newspapers are all against them. They were with the strikers while it was just Pullman, but once the

ARU got involved, they turned against them."

"Do you know what Stark did, Alden?"

"Shot Mooney? Yes, I heard."

"And he still got away with it. Whitbread hid him in a wagon and drove him out of the police station so the crowd couldn't get him."

"He had no choice, Emily. That's his job."

"To save a murderer?"

"To protect him from a mad crowd. They would have torn him apart. You know Whitey couldn't let that happen. Stark has to be dealt with by the law—although that's not going to happen 'til this is all over. Right now he has the protection of having been deputized by Sheriff Arnold. But if he killed Brian O'Malley, you know Whitbread will get him in the end."

"If he killed him. What else could have happened? Jennings and Stark planned the bomb plot. Brian O'Malley was going to tell on them, so they killed him and hung him up with the spy sign so they could blame the strikers."

"Whitbread will have to prove it—but that will have to wait."

"Wait for what?"

"For the end of this."

"The strike? You see an end in sight? Well, good, because I don't. I don't see how any of this will end. What have you heard?"

"Same thing that you're hearing. Listen."

"What do you mean?"

"Listen, don't you hear that?" He ran to the window and threw up the sash. There was a pounding noise and some shouting, but regular—not confused—shouting, then more pounding, tramping. I stepped over to stand beside him at the window.

There were rows of men in dark blue coats, with rifles on their shoulders, marching down the street. Stamp . . . stamp.

"It's the army," Alden explained. "The president sent the army."

TWENTY-THREE

resident Cleveland ordered them in. It's supposed to be to protect the mails," Alden told us. "Attorney General Olney got an injunction against Debs and the ARU. They haven't arrested them, but they can't talk to any of the unions or send messages. All communication is banned. If you see any ARU people, they're not supposed to be here."

I remembered how distant Raoul LeClerc had seemed. He was not supposed to be here in Pullman. His presence would be taken as an effort by the ARU to communicate with the Pullman strikers. I tried to excuse his coldness to me with that thought. But, if that was the case, why had he come? For Fiona?

I could not believe what I was seeing with my own eyes. The files of men were stamping past below us. "But how can they do this? How can they bring the army into Chicago? By what authority?"

"They haven't called it martial law yet, but it's close. At first they had the police—Detective Whitbread, in fact—directing the local militia. But they were being sent out whenever there were problems at the railroad crossings. The Pullman Company people and the railroad managers complained. They want their property protected. They complained so much that General Miles came down, having ordered in the regular troops from Fort Sheridan. Now the police and sheriff all have to report to the local military man. City Hall is furious. We heard Governor Altgeld has protested, too. But what can they do? It was Olney in Washington. He had a federal judge issue an injunction based on interference with the U.S. mails and then they ordered the troops in. It was the general managers. They demanded it."

"Excuse me, is Dr. Chapman here?"

We turned from the window and saw a very young-looking man in a dark blue serge uniform with a shiny black leather belt.

"I'm Stephen Chapman."

"Sir, my commanding officer, Colonel Turner, requests that you come to headquarters. That's at the Florence Hotel, sir."

"For what purpose?"

"I don't know, sir, but he wants to meet with you, as the representative of the clinic, and with the organizers of the relief station—a Miss Cabot from Hull House, I believe?"

"That would be me," I said, equally surprised.

"Oh, very good, ma'am. I am to escort you both to headquarters, please."

"Headquarters is at the Florence?" Alden took out his notebook and pencil.

"Yes. We took over some rooms a few hours ago. And you are . . . sir?"

"Well, I'm . . . "

"This is my brother, Mr. Alden Cabot," I interrupted. Dr. Chapman raised an eyebrow but did not contradict my attempt to give the impression that Alden was also running the relief station. I thought it better not to mention that he was a member of the press. I suddenly felt that such a witness might be useful. I wanted him to come with us.

"Well, if you would all come along with me then."

I looked at Stephen and Alden and shrugged. It seemed a way to find out what was really happening. We followed the soldier out the door.

The four of us walked over to the hotel, seven or eight blocks away. The troops were still marching in the middle of the street. The public had come out to watch, as if it were a parade. But there was none of the holiday spirit of a parade. There was wonder and unease. More than one man I passed on that walk removed a hat to scratch his head as if trying to decide what to think of it all.

More than anything the march of the men in the middle of the street seemed menacing.

When we reached the Florence, we saw that the lawn in front, and surrounding grounds, had been turned into a campground. Tents were laid out in rows and fires were being set under iron kettles and skillets. Amidst all the activity there was no question of using the ladies' entrance. We followed our escort up the stairs of the main entrance through which I had gone on my earlier visit with Detective Whitbread.

"Miss Cabot, Miss Cabot."

Before we entered I heard Mr. MacGregor's voice calling. I turned and saw that he and several other men were being held back by a group of soldiers at the base of the steps.

"It's all right," I told our escort, "I know Mr. MacGregor." I stepped back down the steps. The soldiers still blocked the Pullman strikers from getting any closer.

"Miss Cabot, they won't let us in to see the man in charge. They won't let us do our patrols. They've stopped us from doing anything. You have to tell them. You saw what the company did, how they tried to make it look like we were causing damage. We must protect the works or they could sabotage it again."

"Can't you allow him to come in with us?" I asked our escort.

"No, ma'am. Colonel's orders. No strikers in headquarters."

I turned back and talked across the impassive forms of the soldiers blocking the strikers. "Don't worry, Mr. MacGregor. I will tell them what I know."

At that I had to return to my companions and enter the hotel lobby. It looked just as it had on my previous visits, but the smoking and billiard room to the right had been turned into the military headquarters. I could see that one of the billiard tables had been pushed under the windows and maps were spread across its surface. Others had been moved against walls and at least two typing machines had been set up at smaller tables, with chairs I recognized from the dining room. They were manned by uniformed soldiers. Other men in uniform milled around and I could see that a telephone and telegraph had been set up on another table.

We weren't the only people waiting in the lobby when our escort left us to find out if the colonel was ready to see us. At the far end of the hallway Mr. Jennings was arguing with an officer with epaulets on his shoulders and a sword at his side.

"But I must see the colonel," he was telling the officer. "You don't seem to understand. We are officers of the Pullman Company. We own this hotel and this town. You cannot just take over rooms like this."

"I'm sorry, sir, but the colonel is not free at the moment. He asks that you wait in the north parlor. He will send someone for you when he is available."

"But that's the ladies' parlor," Jennings protested in frustration. Then he saw us standing there and his face reddened. He became even more agitated. "This is ridiculous. I demand to see your commanding officer. We are the ones who have demanded protection for the property of the company. By what right do you move in and take over here?"

The officer signaled several soldiers who calmly surrounded Mr. Jennings and the two men at his elbows. "I'm sorry, sir, but we have had to commandeer these rooms as part of our deployment. The town of Pullman falls under our control, sir. I must ask you to retreat to the parlor, sir, or I will have to tell these soldiers to take you into custody. We would prefer not to have to do that, sir, but I cannot allow you into the colonel's presence until he calls for you."

"Mr. Pullman will hear of this. And you can depend on it that he will contact the attorney general personally to protest this treatment."

"Yes, sir. That is as it may be. Now, if you will wait in the parlor . . . " Alden snickered as the soldiers quietly followed a defeated Jennings down the hall to the ladies' parlor.

There were several other groups of civilians standing around the lobby waiting to be called. Dr. Chapman suddenly turned to me and took me by the shoulders. "Emily, listen. This is a serious situation." He looked around and spoke in a lower tone. "I don't know why the colonel summoned us, but we are here as representatives of Hull House, the clinic, and the relief station. This is no time to be speaking up for the cause of the strikers or anything else. We are here to try to tend to the well-being of the people down here and not to take sides in this conflict. I know it has been difficult to get supplies but, however meager the stores we can offer, it will be disastrous if the army were to close us down. Do you understand? For the good of the people we are trying to help, we must try to keep the relief station and the clinic open."

I glared at him until he remembered himself and released his grip, patting my shoulder as if to apologize.

"Uh, oh," said Alden. "That was the wrong thing to do, Doctor. I know that look." I turned my glare on him. "It's stony. It's the sphinx gaze, the one that turns you to stone."

Too late, the doctor realized his mistake and there was a look of alarm on his face as our escort came up behind him. "Colonel Turner will see you now, if you will follow me, please."

He led us through the men in uniform scurrying around the first billiard room and into a room at the far end of the building. I had never been there before. The man in charge had chosen to position himself behind the barriers of lesser men as a good demonstration of military tactics. Jennings and the other Pullman men might lay siege, but they would be hard put to reach the man in the inner sanctum. He was a broad-shouldered man, in a double-breasted dark blue uniform with gleaming brass buttons. He had short, clipped hair but a full beard and moustache. He looked about forty-five years old, bronzed and bitten by the sun. The troops had probably been out West fighting red Indians before being called to the wilds of Chicago.

"This is Miss Cabot, Mr. Cabot, and Dr. Chapman, Colonel. Ma'am, gentlemen, this is Colonel Turner." Our escort looked relieved to have completed his duty and stepped aside. For a moment I was distracted as I recognized the large table behind which the colonel stood as one from the dining room. I could not imagine how it had fit through the doors, as it was so large. An armchair, also looted from the dining room, was pulled out behind it. It gave me a hint of the power the commands of such a man held. Let there be a desk commanded, and no mere doorway could stand between the order and its completion.

He spoke. "Miss Cabot, gentlemen, I am here to establish order and protect the property of the United States."

"Excuse me, Colonel Turner," I purposely interrupted, "there are men outside who wish to speak with you. Mr. MacGregor, who is well known to us as a leader of the peaceable strikers in this town, is trying to get an audience with you. He has important information."

The colonel glanced at our escort as if to blame him for delivering such a noisy package and grimaced. "Madame, it is not the policy of the United States Army to negotiate with people who are out to disturb the peace."

"But Mr. MacGregor and his men have been trying to prevent violence and the destruction of property ever since the strike began. After the incident here last week in which the Pullman Company itself hired men to plant a bomb—in order to implicate the strikers in a treacherous manner—they have every right to be concerned and to want to talk to you. Are you aware that the man Leonard Stark was used as an agent provocateur by the company? And are you aware that Mr. Stark is guilty of the out-and-out murder of an innocent man, and was implicated in the hanging murder of another man before the strike even began? Yet this man, Stark, is allowed to go free. But you will not speak to Mr. MacGregor? I protest, Colonel Turner. I fail to understand how you intend to protect anyone if this man Stark is allowed to roam around shooting people."

The colonel's frown had deepened during my speech. "Miss Cabot, if you please. I have heard something of this person." He turned to our escort. "Corporal Giles, go and get that policeman. Tell him I need him immediately." He held up a hand to me as the man quickly left. "Please wait, Miss Cabot." A moment later, the young corporal marched in smartly, followed by Detective Whitbread.

"Detective Whitbread, sir."

"Yes, yes. Detective, this young lady complains of a certain Leonard Stark who she says has been guilty of murdering various people. Is this the man you told me about?"

Whitbread avoided my gaze. "Yes, Colonel. Mr. Stark is a Pinkerton agent. He was employed by the Pullman Company to ferret out a conspiracy to blow up the clock tower."

"Ferret out! He created the conspiracy," I objected.

"Miss Cabot, be quiet," the colonel demanded. Before I could point out to him that I was not a soldier and thus not required to take his orders, Whitbread continued.

"Miss Cabot is probably correct in her description. She and her brother were present when we foiled the plot. However, as she knows, the company as represented by Mr. Jennings refused to press charges against Mr. Stark, but insisted on doing so against the other two men."

"Who only did it for the money Stark and Jennings paid them," I pointed out.

"Quite possibly true. Nonetheless, they did take part in the attempt and have been arrested. They await trial in the county jail."

"While Stark is allowed to roam around shooting people."

Detective Whitbread looked grim. "Miss Cabot refers to a shooting that took place on the Rock Island line several days ago."

"Ah, yes. I believe I heard of that."

"I was not present. However it would seem that a large crowd had gathered. Mr. Stark, along with a number of other men of questionable character, had been deputized by Sheriff Arnold. I have warned you that the sheriff has been unwise in his recruitment of men who are untrained and irresponsible. Some are no more than ruffians."

"Yes, yes, you have made the point before. Go on."

"Confronted by an unruly crowd on the tracks, the deputies attempted to move an engine through. When the crowd would not move, Mr. Stark descended from the train, had words with the crowd, and eventually discharged his weapon. There are a number of witnesses who say that the man killed by the bullet was not an agitator, he was only an onlooker."

"He was. I saw it with my own eyes. Mr. Mooney was only standing on the sidelines when Stark just shot him. I saw it. Not only has he not been arrested, but you helped him get away. You pretended it was the poor wounded man and drove him away from the police station. How could you?" I turned on my old friend and mentor, Whitbread.

"Miss Cabot refers to a subterfuge we undertook to remove the man Stark from the local police station when the crowd followed us there. It was necessary when they threatened to take him by force."

"And afterwards?" the Colonel asked.

"Sheriff Arnold insisted the man's action was taken according to his directive. He refused to allow us to charge him. The accusation is still outstanding. The intention is to press charges, but the sheriff has refused to give him up. He insists his deputies were in danger from the crowd and the action was in self-defense."

"What about Brian O'Malley?" I asked. "How is knocking a man on the head and hanging his body from the rafters self-defense?"

Detective Whitbread considered this. "There is no proof at this time that Leonard Stark was responsible for the death of Brian O'Malley." He looked at the colonel. "That death happened before the ARU strike. It is still an open investigation that has been set aside while we deal with the other disturbances."

"Of course he did it," I insisted. "Brian must have found out about the bomb plot and like his brother—who did eventually betray the scheme—he was going to give them up. Stark and Jennings found out about it and killed him to stop him from telling."

"Miss Cabot, there is no evidence to justify your accusation. None at all."

"But they were the ones who planned the bomb plot, you know it. And Stark was already pretending to be a striker when really he was working for the company all along."

"Nonetheless . . . "

"Enough," Colonel Turner broke in. "Miss Cabot, these matters are for the local authorities to sort out. They are not what I am here for. The army has been brought in to stop the violence, to protect the property of the United States, and to reinstate the regular delivery of the United States mails. Until that is done, these other matters will have to wait. Tomorrow morning my men will begin the job of clearing the tracks and making sure the mail trains get through. We will not tolerate any disruptions. Until peace is restored and transportation is back on schedule, the police and sheriff's departments down here will be reporting to me. Their primary duty will be to arrest anyone who prevents restoration of the train service. Until we have completed that task, no other matters will get their attention. So you see, the sooner that task is completed, the sooner we will be able to withdraw and leave the administration of law and order to the local authorities."

He had a booming voice. I suppose if you are used to dealing with ranks and ranks of men you must need that. He had an authoritative manner, as well, and it was obvious that he was used to being listened to and obeyed. But this time Dr. Chapman spoke up.

"If you wish to restore order, then you must do something

about the people of Pullman," Dr. Chapman told him. "The people here are sick and starving. They have been in this condition for so long now they are desperate and there is no way to pacify desperate men if they have nothing to lose."

"Exactly, Doctor. That is why I have asked you to come down here. I understand you have been treating the people of Pullman for the last month. Tell me. What is the condition of their health?"

"Very poor. It is not just the strike. It stems from conditions before that, the very circumstances that led to the strike. For the past half-year most of them have not had sufficient money to eat well. As a result they have become weaker and weaker. Due to the dampness brought about by proximity to the lake, malaria has been spreading. There are also a significant number suffering from tuberculosis. The general weakness due to lack of food has led to some other fevers and even broken bones."

"Malaria. You say the lake contributes to this. What of your medicines? You have quinine? Other medicines?"

"Our stores are very low. Originally we brought down supplies from the city. I have had to ask for resupply several times and lately have had to beg some surplus from the university."

"Corporal, ask Captain Robinson to step in." The young soldier was back almost immediately, delivering a white-haired man with an open collar and no hat.

"Dr. Chapman, this is Captain Robinson, our company surgeon. Captain, the doctor reports there is sickness down here and a lack of medicines. There's malaria for one thing. We want to guard against this spreading to the troops. I'll issue a general order telling them to keep away from the locals. Meanwhile, you take Dr. Chapman here and get him fixed up with supplies of quinine and whatever else he needs. We need to keep our men healthy, so we need to help him keep the local sicknesses from spreading."

Captain Robinson led Stephen away to the other room while the colonel called for a Corporal Fellows. A thin young man with wire-rimmed spectacles appeared immediately.

"Miss Cabot," Colonel Turner continued, "I understand there is a problem with food supplies in the town. Exactly what is the situation?" Before I could answer, he stepped over to Alden and took the notebook he had been scribbling in from his hands. "And what is this?"

Alden looked at me with alarm. "My brother is a newspaper reporter."

"I see. What newspaper, may I ask?"

Alden grinned. "*The Sentinel* . . . ah . . . sir."

"And you are down here to get a story?" Without waiting for an answer he bellowed, "Giles!" Our escort appeared in seconds. "Corporal Giles, it seems Mr. Alden Cabot is not down here for the relief station his sister operates. On the contrary, it seems he is a reporter looking for a story." The corporal looked dismayed. The colonel handed Alden back his notebook. "Never mind. Take him around the camp. Show him the preparations. Be sure to impress on him the number of men and the readiness of every company. It will be a good thing to get out the word on how large the force is. The hooligans will think twice when they know what they're up against. Go along, show him all of it."

"Yes, sir."

"Thanks, Colonel Turner," my brother said with a wave as he left.

"Now, Miss Cabot. You were telling me about the state of food supplies."

"Very bad, Colonel. We have been out of supplies for several days and what we had has been very limited for the past two weeks. In fact, I have only returned today with a wagonload of supplies that we plan to distribute tomorrow. But it is much less than I had hoped. We have a list of seven hundred families now, in very desperate circumstances. They have no money and, while the businesses down here had been very good about extending credit, there is no credit left now. In fact, the most common source of food in the last weeks has been leftover scraps from the tables here at the hotel where there is never a shortage." Suddenly I realized that I had given away that secret. "Oh, please. Do not prevent them from sharing that. I should not have told you about it. Please, Colonel."

"Nonsense, Miss Cabot. I don't know what you are going on about. Let me tell you, while we are camped here no one in Pullman will starve. This is Corporal Fellows, our quartermaster. Now our supplies are intended to feed our men and keep them up to snuff. But we certainly can't have them eating their meals while starving civilians look on. We really would have a riot then. No, no. There's nothing fancy about our meals, Miss Cabot. You will find our staples are beans and rice. I believe there is some powdered milk we could share with the children, eh, Fellows? I'll let the corporal take you away, then. He can talk numbers with you." He actually patted me on the back to encourage me to follow the young soldier. "Don't worry, Miss Cabot. No one is going to starve. I promise you that. Not while the army is camped here."

He quickly turned back to bark out more orders and meet with more people, while I followed Corporal Fellows to a corner table where he sat me down and questioned me on the amounts and types of supplies needed and I described what I had originally brought from the city and what I had brought in the most recent load. I told him of the oversight committee, the list we had compiled, and the process we used to distribute food fairly.

"Very good, miss. That is exactly what the colonel wanted as a method of distribution. Now, I've taken into account what you told me and what you were able to do at the beginning, and here's what I think we can do." We discussed a very long and generous list he had compiled of flour, sugar, rice, coffee, and beans. It was incredible to me. It was as if a huge, heavy block that had been on my shoulders was suddenly gone, removed. "No one will starve in Pullman." The colonel had said that as if it were the easiest thing in the world to accomplish. It was only after sitting with the young corporal, with his fast hand figuring the amounts and the sun gleaming off his spectacles, that I realized what it meant. The colonel was not bragging. It was true. No one would starve in Pullman for as long as the army was camped in their yards. It was a huge relief.

"You're sure you don't think it would be a good idea to post a guard?" the corporal was asking.

"Oh, no. Really. We've never had any trouble. I don't think it's necessary."

"Well, we will see. We will be by with these stores tomorrow afternoon. We'll let you distribute what you brought back from the city in the morning and then we'll restock your shelves. As the colonel said, it's not fancy, but what's good enough to keep an army moving should be plenty to help the local population."

"They will be so very grateful, Corporal. You have no idea."

"Very good, miss. We'll look forward to seeing you tomorrow. I'll bring men to move things."

I left him to his tasks, stunned by how easily all my worries had been relieved. I felt light-headed. I couldn't bear the thought of staying at the hotel. Obviously the military men had no idea I was a resident. Nor could I bear to run into Mr. Jennings and the others from the company. Luckily, I saw that Stephen was just finishing with the company surgeon and I left with him. He, too, seemed stunned to find out how much help he would get from the army. We walked through the rows of tents without speaking.

"It's not right, though," he said when we finally reached a corner that was beyond the camp boundaries. He stopped and looked back. "They are being generous with the medicines they can spare. I suppose with the food, too?"

"Oh, yes. Beyond what I could ever have hoped for. The colonel said no one would starve and now no one will. I don't know why I'm not happier about it. I feel like someone has a strong hand on my shoulder and they will never let go. It means I won't fall down as I walk, but I can't get loose from it either."

"Yes. It feels wrong. Ours is not a country where the army

can occupy a city and have it feel right. They usurp the local authorities. They may mean well, but it is so dangerous. They can impose so much. They are too strong." He shook his head. "This may solve the quinine problem and put beans on the table, but I fear that it will bring far more serious problems, Emily. I fear that very much."

TWENTY-FOUR

olonel Turner's hope that the troop deployment would bring the strike to a speedy close was not fulfilled. On the contrary, the presence of the army exacerbated the situation. In the following days the soldiers were assigned, along with police and deputy sheriffs, to clear the tracks and allow the trains to get through. But the people—not just the strikers, by any means—did not cooperate. There were plenty of unemployed men, and just plain troublemakers, who saw the opportunity for chaos, so there were always people available to block the way. They overturned cars on side lines to block the tracks being used or set fire to older cars in various places. When we saw a column of smoke it was sure to be a boxcar set afire by a crowd. They learned to move away when the train bearing soldiers came along, but then they filled in behind it, or went on ahead to block the passage, while the soldiers protected men clearing the tracks behind. Trains began to move, but it was a slow process. I could imagine the frustration of the military men unable to command the crowds of civilians.

The newspapers were completely behind the president and attorney general. They continued to refer to the union leader as "Dictator Debs", claiming he was orchestrating the violence of the roaming gangs. They accused the local police of being sympathetic towards the strikers. They reported that the police stood by as the crowds overturned cars and blocked tracks. The headlines sneered at Mayor Hopkins's effort to bring the two sides to the table to talk. The editorials approved of the general managers resolve not to sit down with the ARU, even though Debs was willing to acquiesce to the mayor's request for a meeting.

They reported the ARU leader's speech accusing the railroads of hiring thugs to cause trouble and blame the strikers, but they questioned the accuracy of the statements.

And the strike was by no means limited to Pullman, or even the greater Chicago environs. The newspapers promptly reported its spread, especially out West. In California, federal troops moved in to try to deal with strikers. As close as Indiana and Blue Island, south of the city, there was a mixed response. Local restaurants and businesses refused to serve military or sheriff's men, so strongly did they support the local strikers. There were reports of men arrested for refusing to report to their state militia duties because they were in favor of the strikers, and of train engineers cajoled or threatened into leaving their cabs when confronted by crowds. After one confrontation Sheriff Arnold claimed the cause was lost because of the defection of cowardly deputies.

Meanwhile, the ARU had purportedly begun to use men on bicycles to pass on information. It was said that they were on the point of recruiting some of the powerful city trade unions of carpenters and gas men to join the boycott. It was hoped this would force the railroad men to the bargaining table where they would have to promise to restore all the strikers to their jobs. The general managers vowed not to give in and claimed they were bringing in men hired in the East—in New York and Baltimore—to take the jobs of anyone who had walked off.

At least my job was easier now, as Corporal Fellows had lived up to his promise. Boxes of stores were brought to the relief station, easily moved up the stairs, and unpacked for me by vigorous young soldiers. He did insist on placing a guard, despite my objections, but I could hardly hold it against the red-cheeked young men who were set the boring task of standing outside the storeroom.

Dr. Chapman continued to worry. He began to see injuries from the confrontations between the crowds and the authorities. The deputies were quick to bludgeon and the soldiers used their bayonets. There had not been any more gunshot wounds, but I heard in the dining room of the Florence that General Miles had issued an order countermanding earlier standing orders. It was now up to the commanding officer, and purely a tactical decision, whether or not to fire into an unruly crowd. When I told the doctor, he groaned and proclaimed that catastrophe was imminent.

On a particularly warm afternoon, I decided to close the relief station early, after turning away the last few people. There would be more supplies the next day, but it was still difficult to see the disappointment in those faces. I gritted my teeth and told myself I would keep back just a little bit for the end of the day the next time.

I knew that I should lock the door behind me as I left, but the key was sticky in the humidity and I found myself nearly cursing as I struggled with it. Really, what was I learning down here? What was I becoming? I hadn't even known the words I nearly uttered before all this started. The young soldier on guard beside the door tried hard not to grin, as if he guessed what had almost passed my lips. It irked me. Just as I managed to extract the key, I heard my name called from the floor below.

"Emily, are you up there? Come down. I want you to meet someone," my brother's voice bellowed. "Emily!"

"All right, all right. I'm coming. Honestly." As I hurried down the stuffy staircase, the young soldier relaxed and slumped against the wall.

Alden was in the doorway of the clinic, beckoning. Beyond him a young woman in a long, dusty, checked travel coat stood talking to Dr. Chapman.

Alden grabbed my arm. "Emily, do you know who that is?"

I pulled away. "Let go. It's stifling in here and no, I don't know who she is."

"It's Nellie Bly." When I looked blank, he shook his head. "Oh, Emily, you are so thick. Nellie Bly . . . *Around the World in Seventy-two Days* . . . don't you know?"

"She's the newspaper reporter?" I looked across to the pretty-faced brunette of medium height with a trim waist who was talking to the doctor with a great deal of animation.

"Yes. She's the one who went round the world, and she met Jules Verne, too. Come on." He grabbed my arm and dragged me over. "Nellie, this is my sister, Emily. She's here running the relief station for Hull House."

The young woman shot out her hand and I shook it. "Pleased to meet you. I've come to find out the truth about the strike."

"Really. And if you find that truth, will you write about it? And will your paper publish it? Because most of the papers are publishing lies about it."

"Emily," Alden protested.

"The proprietor of *The World* hires people to find out and publish the truth about everything, regardless of all other consider-ations, and if the truth is not given it is the fault of the writer, not the paper," she told me.

"Yes. There you are," Alden said, gazing at her with immense admiration. It made me worry for my friend Clara, who had been the object of his affections for some time. "Nellie's here to find the truth. Do you know she once pretended to be mad to get herself admitted to an insane asylum, just to report on the conditions?"

I had heard that. "I don't think that kind of stunt will help you here."

"No, but our readers want to know the truth about this strike, and I'm here to find it. I had quite a time just getting here, let me tell you. I took one rail line and five different streetcars. They wouldn't come far into the neighborhood because they are afraid of the rioting crowds."

"I found her walking a couple of blocks away," Alden told us.

"So, where is this town of Pullman? And why are these workers striking when they have a model town to live in? Why, they're better off than most of the working people in the country. Are they really under the influence of anarchists and union agitators?

Where are these rioters and bloodthirsty strikers and what is their excuse for the havoc they're causing? That's what I've come to find out."

I was disgusted. "Bloodthirsty strikers? For heaven's sake, what we have here are sick and starving people. What do you think we are doing here with the clinic and relief station? Do you know I've just had to turn people away hungry? I had to tell them to come back tomorrow. And this has been going on for months. Tell her, Dr. Chapman."

He was looking at us with speculation. "Perhaps it would be better to show her. What Miss Cabot says is true, Miss Bly. The people I am seeing are sick from many months of poor nutrition. But why don't you see for yourself? It's only a few more blocks to Pullman."

"Yes, that's it. Lead me to it. I want to see for myself, and for my readers. A lot of them would like to live in a model town like Pullman, so they certainly don't understand why these people are striking."

"I wondered that, too, when I first came here," I told her. "But you have no idea how much they are suffering. They aren't bloodthirsty, they're hungry. And they are poor, more poor and in debt than your readers can imagine. They cannot feed their children."

Nellie Bly stared at me, then gave a little shake of her head. "Well, then, what are we waiting for? I need to get the story, the real story, and get back to town to file it."

Dr. Chapman stayed at the clinic while Alden and I took Miss Bly the few blocks to Pullman. The newspapers had turned against the strike and I did not have much hope that even Nellie Bly would be able to portray the true state of things in Pullman. I could see that my brother was hopeful, though, so I went along. With the food gone for the day, there was nothing else for me to do.

"Well, we certainly have the army. But where are these strikers?" she asked. We were walking briskly through the army camp around the Florence Hotel. There were troops of men marching and stacking weapons. We had to scurry out of the way of some, and wait for another group to pass. Officers were self-importantly slapping each other on the back as they came down the hotel steps replete from a plentiful lunch. We could smell the cooking and hear the dishes rattling as we passed. "Where are these bloodthirsty strikers?" Nellie asked again, as we skirted a group of men and got whistles from them.

Alden was ahead of us and he turned back to hurry us on. "It's up here, Fulton Avenue. That's what you want."

A few blocks further on we were beyond the army encampment and the streets were quiet and empty. "You'd think it was the Sabbath," Nellie said. Then she spotted a woman hanging clothes out on a line in her backyard. Nellie walked right up to her. "Can you tell me, please, where I can find the poorest strikers?"

The woman wiped her hands on her clean apron. "Across the street is the letters. They mostly don't speak English. They're not in the unions, most of them, but they are suffering the worst."

"What do you mean by the letters?"

"That row there, they're known by letters rather than numbers," she said, pointing to the Fulton Avenue tenements we had visited in the past. Nellie asked the woman her feelings about the strike.

"It's not our fault it's only a few of them wanted to strike. My husband is not in the union. I have to be careful what I say. Only sometimes I just have to speak out and say what I think. They talk too much, is what it is."

"So, are the unions to blame?"

"Not entirely. There hasn't been work. There was no work and they finally got some orders, only a few though. But Mr. Pullman couldn't put them to work if he had no orders."

"Was that the main cause of dissatisfaction?"

"Not entirely. They put them out of work, but they kept the rents high. And people can't pay them. Then, they had other complaints and a committee went to talk to the managers, but the company laid off three of them from the committee. So they strike. But what good does that do? I told them it doesn't hurt Mr. Pullman's vacation. He doesn't go hungry. I know all about strikes and workmen and I know there are wrongs on both sides. But striking and destroying property and killing rich men isn't going to help the working men."

She directed us across to the tenements and there Nellie heard the same kind of stories we had heard before. They showed her leases with rents they couldn't afford and told of nights of going to bed hungry. By the time we reached the end of the block, I could see that her opinion had changed. She came to see, as I had, that Pullman himself was most to blame.

We were in a doorway when I felt a tug and looked down to see Lilly O'Malley, Gracie's little sister. I bent down to hear her whisper, "My brother, Joe, he must see you. He said it's about the bomb." With a shock I realized she meant he knew something about the dynamite that had disappeared from the clock tower. Joe was still wanted by the police for the attempted bombing, even though they had let Leonard Stark go. Four sticks of dynamite had disappeared that day. The last thing I needed was for Nellie Bly to ask about Joe O'Malley. I stood up and announced I needed to go. "I must check on one of the families who could not come to the food distribution," I lied.

Nellie shook my hand again. "Thank you, Miss Cabot, and I promise you *The World* will print the truth. Anarchists and firebrands, pooh! Why these are poor hardworking folk being ground beneath the heel of that heartless coward Pullman!"

I turned away, hopeful that at least one newspaper would carry a story that supported the people of Pullman. As I reached the street, I saw Joe O'Malley beckoning from a nearby alley and hurried over to meet him.

"Miss Cabot, it's LeClerc and Fiona. They're building a bomb, I fear."

TWENTY-FIVE

W hatever do you mean? Mr. O'Malley, I don't believe it is safe for you to be here. The police will arrest you if they see you." I looked over my shoulder.

"Aye, miss. That Jennings is determined to blacken the name of O'Malley, but it was him and that Stark who were behind it."

"It was you who sent me that note, then? About the bomb in the clock tower?"

"Aye. 'Twould not have been dealt with fairly by the company. I hoped you might get them to stop it and show the truth of it. But that Stark and Jennings got away with it for all that."

"I'm sorry that is so. I've protested, but no one will do anything. I am very sorry, but I don't believe anyone can do more about that until the strike is over."

"If ever it is."

"It must be."

"It's not for that I've come now. There is something else that must be stopped. After they took the men away some of the dynamite was gone, was it not?"

I remembered back to what Detective Whitbread found at the end of that evening. "My brother told me there were four sticks missing. I assumed Mr. Jennings and Mr. Stark had spirited them away."

"'Twas not, 'twas LeClerc."

"What? How? He was not even there."

"But he was, miss. And so was I. I hid myself there most of the day, don't you see. I hoped you would find someone to stop them, as you did. But I could not let them go through with it if you did not, so I hid to watch, hoping I'd not have to show myself. And who should I see arrive before you all? It was LeClerc. I thought at first you had gone to him instead of the police and MacGregor. I was surprised, but as long as they were stopped, I cared not. But then I saw you and the police detective and MacGregor. Well LeClerc, now, he did them a favor. When Stark ran, he nearly got away. 'Twas the ARU man who grabbed him and threw him back to you. I could see it all from above, as I had been watching in the dark all along. But while you were all arguing with Jennings, I saw another thing. I saw LeClerc sneak in and take the dynamite. Well, I followed him then, but he only left. He wasn't going to use it. You'd stopped the trouble, as best you could, but Jennings had still got away with it. To expose the ARU man then would only make it go bad for the strikers. There seemed no reason to do it. They wanted me, too, so I saw no way to expose it without causing myself and the innocent men like MacGregor nothing but trouble. So I kept mum, and I kept low. Even after poor Mooney was killed. It would only make for more sympathy for the company and the sheriff's men, give them more of an excuse if they knew LeClerc was the one stole the dynamite."

"But you are telling me, now. Why? Why are you telling *me*?"

"I'm afraid now he'll use it."

"Surely not. Mr. Debs and the ARU have been against violence all along. They have forbidden it. Just like Mr. MacGregor. They don't want to blow anything up. They want a peaceful resolution. It was the company that wanted to make it look like the strikers were behind the violence. Why would Mr. LeClerc use the dynamite now? I don't believe it."

Joe pushed aside some of the branches to look towards the camp of soldiers around the Florence Hotel. "Things have changed, you see. Times are desperate. Maybe Debs forswears violence but the men as work for him, like LeClerc, maybe they see the end in sight and it's not a good one. Maybe they're losing faith in Debs and the leaders." He let the leaves fall gently back into place. "If he uses the explosives, they will blame the strikers.

What do you think the army will do then?"

"No, he wouldn't. But why do you think he will use the dynamite? He hasn't so far, has he?"

"He's in the brick shed, miss. He's there using the tools to fill a pipe with nails and screws from the machine yard and I'm feared he will use the sticks of dynamite to explode it all."

"How do you know about this? Have you been following him? Working with him, like you did with Stark?"

"No, miss. Not like that. It's not LeClerc I've been following." He hung his head. "It's Miss MacGregor. I've been trying to reason with her. To make her see what he plans to do, but she'll not listen."

"Fiona? But she was ill when I saw her last week. She was with Raoul then." So was Joe O'Malley in love with Fiona, too? Fiona, who had engaged the affections of the doctor, Raoul, and Joe's dead brother. She had certainly been busy. No wonder she had no time for the clinic. "Surely Miss MacGregor is not involved in something so dangerous."

"She's at the shed in the brickyard with him now." He looked across at the army camp again. "I cannot go to her father. Besides the fact I'm in hiding, he would not believe it of his daughter. But we cannot let them make the bomb and we cannot let the soldiers find out what they are doing. We must stop them, but not let anyone find out."

"But why do you come to me, Mr. O'Malley? What do you expect me to do? How can I stop them?" I was bitterly disappointed in Raoul LeClerc. It was possible that Joe O'Malley spoke only out of jealousy, but somehow I believed him. I wanted to turn away and go back to my relief station. And there was nothing to stop me.

"I thought you could get the police detective to help us."

"You mean Detective Whitbread? After he went along with them the last time? And after he saved Stark when he shot Mr. Mooney? I have not spoken to him since then. Why would you think he would help in this? You may as well tell Colonel Turner and have done with it."

"No, miss. I don't think so. I think the detective will see that if the company and the army find out about this, it would be a disaster. I think he can stop them. But you must decide, miss. I cannot go to them. I can try to stop LeClerc, but Fiona will take his side. And if I am not successful, then they will use the bomb. I must go back."

"Mr. O'Malley, you must go and tell Detective Whitbread yourself. I cannot do it."

"No, miss. I'll go back to the shed. You must send the detective if you can see your way to do it."

"No, Mr. O'Malley, don't go." But he had already left.

I stepped out from the alley and looked towards the camp at the Florence. Who to tell? Who to warn? Should I go to Mr. MacGregor again? But what if the soldiers saw a confrontation at the brickyard shed? Surely they would assume all of the strikers were involved in the bomb plot. I could picture them surrounding and shooting MacGregor and his men. And this just when Nellie Bly was set to describe how peaceful and pitiable the situation was for the people of Pullman. And what of Raoul LeClerc? His connection to the ARU would be obvious. They would assume Debs had ordered the attack and all hope of a compromise to settle the strike would be lost. This was all the newspapers would need to crow over "Dictator Debs." Nellie Bly would never get her story published. Could I allow the desperation of two people like Raoul LeClerc and Fiona MacGregor to destroy the hopes of the men and women who had joined this boycott in an effort to bring some justice to the starving workers of Pullman? I did not know why I had to decide what to do—what did I know of such things? But to merely return to the relief station and act surprised when a bomb exploded, ruining everything, was something I could not bring myself to do. I regretted that Joe O'Malley had picked me to tell of the dilemma, but I could not escape the consequences of knowing about it. I kicked a clod of dried mud and headed across the street.

TWENTY-SIX

Q uickly, Miss Cabot, we want to avoid being seen."
I was following Detective Whitbread across the mud
flats to the brick shed. We had come through town and
past the MacGregor house, so we were taking the same route
I had followed that first day in Pullman when we found Brian
O'Malley hanging in the shed. It sent a shiver down my spine to
remember that. Whitbread, with his long legs, was striding too
quickly for me to keep up. I had to run.

It had not been particularly easy to lure the detective away
from the billiard room of the Florence to tell him about another
bomb plot. I had to swallow my blind anger at him for saving
Stark after the man had shot down Mr. Mooney, but I did. When
I confronted him, I realized for the first time exactly how strained
he looked. Ceding authority to anyone would not come easily
to him, and having to relinquish all responsibility and allow a
military organization to take control was not something he would
approve of, especially knowing that the military had been called
in by the influence of the Pullman Company and the railroads.
I knew from past experience that Whitbread did not give in to
pressure and I came to the sudden realization that the only reason
he did not quit his job altogether was that the balance between
civil order and chaos stood so shakily in the current situation,
that his sense of duty would not allow him to desert no matter
how much he objected to the orders of the day. That he was not
above making his own interpretation of orders was something I
was well aware of. That he would use that discretion in this case
was proven by his immediate reaction to my news. He agreed with
Joe O'Malley. The construction of the bomb, using the stolen

dynamite, must be stopped without informing the authorities.

We reached the wall of the shed, and Whitbread crouched close to the door, gesturing for me to duck behind him. He moved until he could see through a slit between the wall and the open door. By standing up halfway behind him, a hand on his shoulder, I could also see. At the workbench along the wall, Raoul LeClerc had his back to us as he worked on something—presumably the bomb. I could see glass jars of nails and screws and a pile of plumbing pipes. Fiona MacGregor was perched on the workbench screwing something together. She looked less weak than when I had last seen her. There was no sign of Joe O'Malley.

Suddenly, Whitbread took my arm and dragged me off to the end of the building. "Miss Cabot. I will attempt to apprehend them. You must stay hidden. In the case that I am unsuccessful, you must go and alert Colonel Turner. Stop." He put up his hand and I shut my mouth, opened in protest. "I know we do not wish to involve the army, however, that is the missing dynamite, at the end of the workbench. We cannot allow them to use it. If I am overcome or incapacitated, you must stay hidden, let them get away, and then go and get the soldiers. Do you understand?"

"Yes."

"It is essential that they do not know you are here. Essential. Whatever happens, you must stay hidden."

"Yes, yes, all right."

We crept back. I stood to take another look and saw Fiona MacGregor reach over to stroke LeClerc's hair. He pulled back. Meanwhile, Detective Whitbread stood up and took out his pistol. He quietly walked forward.

"Stop what you are doing," he announced. I remained crouched down, watching from my hiding place. "Put your hands up and turn around slowly. I have a gun and I will use it if necessary."

LeClerc froze where he was, his hands still on the workbench. Fiona jumped down and stood in front of him, between his back and the detective. "No, no. Leave us alone."

"Miss MacGregor, move out of the way. To the side, please. Mr. LeClerc, put your hands up and turn around. Slowly."

But Fiona wouldn't move and suddenly Raoul swung around and threw something. Whitbread ducked, but I heard a crunch as he was struck. He did not fire, as LeClerc knew he would not. He wouldn't risk hitting Fiona. Raoul grabbed her and kept her in front of him as he moved back through the high piles of drying bricks. There was a gunshot and I saw that Whitbread had fired in the air. Another missile came flying and the detective overturned a bench and retreated behind it.

"Mr. LeClerc, come out."

"Why? So you can arrest me and let a killer like Stark go free?"

"What were you planning to do? Complete the bombing of the factory that Jennings and Stark had planned? Why? You know they wanted to make it look like the strikers were to blame. Why do what they wanted to do and make it real? Surely you can see this would just defeat the purposes of the ARU and play into their hands?"

"What do you want us to do, lay down and die for them? And they can do anything? They can starve the people, organize a fake bomb plot, then use it to shoot innocent people and call in the army to do their dirty work for them. All this they can do and you want to put Debs in jail? You want to put me in jail? While men like Leonard Stark are given stars to wear so they can kill with impunity? That is your justice? That is your law? What do you expect us to do?"

"Mr. LeClerc, the wrongdoings of others do not justify your own. You stole that dynamite with the intention of using it. You may believe you are justified in causing damage to the property of the Pullman Company or the railroads, but your actions are unreasonable and unjustified. People could be hurt by such an explosion."

"People are being hurt by the actions of this company and those railroads. People are starving and dying. They are being clubbed and beaten and shot. Why don't you go and arrest them? Go arrest Stark."

It seemed to me, from the variation in his voice, that he was moving but I could not tell where he was in that large, open barn of a shed. I thought I heard another noise closer to me, but the angle of what I could see was extremely limited.

Whitbread continued to try to reason with him. "I can understand your frustration, Mr. LeClerc. I can only agree with you that Mr. Stark should be in custody. However, he is currently protected by the sheriff. It is something that can be pursued after the current tensions come to an end. After this is over, I promise you Mr. Stark's actions will not be forgotten. If it is possible to charge him with the death of Brian O'Malley as well, that will be done."

Suddenly, I saw a figure stand up in front of the crack in the door. "Stop, watch out," I yelled, but it was too late. Fiona had lobbed a brick at Detective Whitbread and hit him on the head. I heard a crunch and he slumped over. I ran out from behind the door. LeClerc leapt to the fallen man and grabbed his pistol. He had it pointed at me.

"Emily."

I ignored him as I knelt next to Whitbread. He was breathing but unconscious. I called his name, loosening his tie and collar. "What have you done?" I snapped at Fiona.

She stood with another brick in her hand, as if ready to strike again. LeClerc reached out a hand and took the brick from her. "We are sorry, but it was necessary. Come, Fiona. We will get our things and leave before he comes to." He pulled her towards the workbench.

"You can't do this," I yelled at them. "What are you doing? You cannot bomb the factory and hope to create any sympathy for the strikers. You'll ruin everything. Stop!" I was still crouched down, trying to stop the bleeding from Whitbread's head wound. I pulled out a handkerchief and wished the doctor was with me.

LeClerc stopped and turned to face me, still holding Fiona by the hand. "Sympathy? What good is sympathy? Does sympathy feed the starving down here? Does sympathy stop the soldiers? It's too late for sympathy. The only thing that will make an impression is fear. Fear of the power of the workers. Unless we can impress them with that, all the sympathy in the world will do no good." He turned angrily back towards the workbench and ran into Joe O'Malley. "Get out of my way."

Joe blocked him from reaching the pipe bomb. I could see it now. There were wires and two of the sticks of dynamite. "No. No bomb." He held up a hammer in his hand, threatening. LeClerc took a step back.

"No. Go away," Fiona screamed. She ran forward, but Joe grabbed her with his left arm still holding the hammer up towards Raoul. "Let me go, let me go." She twisted herself away as Joe kept his eyes locked with those of LeClerc. Fiona made to attack Joe again, but this time Raoul caught her arm.

"No, stop. We're leaving."

"Fiona, don't go with him," Joe pleaded.

"Let us have it," the girl begged. "Come with us. You can come with us. We need . . . " She started forward, but Raoul pulled her back before she could finish her sentence.

"No," Joe said. "I can't let you take it. I can't let you do that."

As Detective Whitbread began to move with a groan, the others looked around.

"Leave now, before he wakes up," Joe told LeClerc. The ARU man looked beyond him to the bench, as if calculating whether he could overcome O'Malley, but the husky young Irishman stood tall and stubborn. "I won't let you," he told LeClerc.

Whitbread groaned again and began to try to sit up. LeClerc shrugged and stooped to pick up a bag.

"Leave the pistol," Joe demanded. The ARU man set it gently on the ground and with one look over his shoulder at me, he started towards the door. I felt my heart in my throat as I took the imprint of his back and planted it in my memory. I was sure I would never see him again and a whole world of opportunity and possibility seemed to close down with his exit. I still felt something for him, I could not deny it.

Fiona MacGregor stood looking back and forth between Joe and Raoul.

"Fiona, don't go," Joe pleaded. But she glared at him and ran after LeClerc, who was already out on the mud flats. Joe slumped against the workbench, putting down the hammer as he looked at us.

"They're getting away," Whitbread grumbled. "Help me up." I steadied him as he got up.

"You're still bleeding." I tried to stop him, but he pulled away and loped over to where his pistol lay on the ground, bending to pick it up. "I must go after them."

"But the bomb materials . . . " I objected.

"You and Mr. O'Malley stay here and guard them until I can send someone. I told you to stay hidden. When will you learn . . . "

Before he could finish, the O'Malley children, Lilly and Patrick, ran through the open door. "Joe, Joe . . . it's Gracie. She's gone to the railroad," Patrick told him.

"Here . . . stop . . . what do you mean?" Joe stooped down to ask them.

"She's gone. She took Brian's gun. She's gone after them. We don't know what she wants to do. She wouldn't tell us. There's a big crowd out north of the factory. We told her we saw him, we saw the man who killed Mr. Mooney. We told her."

The straggly-haired little girl, Lilly, was near tears. "She went to get him, Joe. I'm afraid. Will he shoot her? Will he shoot her like he shot Mr. Mooney?" She burst into tears then and fell into her brother's arms. He comforted her.

"Detective . . . " I began, but he interrupted me.

"It's Mrs. Foley? She's gone after Stark with a gun?" he questioned and Joe nodded, holding on to his little sister.

Whitbread took a last look at the backs of LeClerc and Fiona MacGregor, retreating across the mud flats. Then he moved to the workbench. He found a burlap sack and started putting the sticks of dynamite into it. "Damn him. Damn him, damn him, damn him."

"What is it?" I had never heard the policeman curse before.

"There's one missing. He's taken it. There's nothing to be done . . . here." He tied the sack with some string and handed it to me. "Hold on to this." He steadied himself on the bench, still dizzy from the blow to his head. Then he took up his pistol and checked it for rounds.

"Detective Whitbread, you're still bleeding. Come with me to the doctor."

"No, we must stop Mrs. Foley before she does something she'll regret." He looked down at the children. "Where did she go? North, you said?"

Patrick ran to the door and pointed to where a cloud of dark smoke was rising north of Pullman. "Up there."

Detective Whitbread began striding away. I heard Joe sending the children home as I ran after the policeman. "But what do you want me to do with this?" I held up the burlap bag.

"Keep it safe. The rest of the bomb making is just nuts and bolts and pipes. Without the dynamite they cannot do the harm they planned. They have only one stick, now. We'll alert the army as soon as possible. Make sure they don't get hold of that lot."

He strode on more quickly than I could keep up with and pretty soon Joe O'Malley came up behind me. He took my arm and we followed Whitbread towards the crowd along the railroad tracks. There were houses here lining the tracks and people were perched on the roofs, as well as standing in crowds down on the ground. Two railway cars had been overturned and there was an engine, attempting to move north, that was blocked by them. Men were making an effort to right the cars and get them out of the way, while soldiers and deputies surrounded them, trying to keep the crowd at bay. Every now and then a bottle or brick flew through the air, hitting the ground near the soldiers.

As we got closer we saw the crowd swaying and swirling around something. I saw Whitbread begin to run, so I hurried as much as I could. Then I saw him. Just stepping down from a cowcatcher on the engine was Leonard Stark, holding a pistol. The crowd in front of him was parting. When Joe saw this, he dropped my arm and began running. Through the bodies I suddenly saw a space clear. There was Gracie Foley, hands extended, pointing a pistol at Stark. Some soldiers with bayonets on their rifles saw, too, and moved in to try to protect Stark, but the crowd was pushing forward. I saw the top of Whitbread's head and his arms flailing as he forced his way through the crowd. Suddenly, I saw a large boulder in front of me, so I jumped onto it in order to get a better view. There was a gunshot, smoke, yells, and screams from the crowd. I jumped up trying to see and as the smoke drifted away I saw Whitbread, down in Gracie's arms. He had taken the shot.

TWENTY-SEVEN

I t was only later that I heard what had happened from some
of the other Pullman people who were in the crowd. The
military had become organized in their attempts to clear the
tracks. But the strikers, and others who banded with them, felt
betrayed that their own country had turned against them and
taken the side of the owners. Without any direction from the
ARU, or anyone else, they organized themselves.

They did it all without any formal plan. With the cunning of
a crowd they realized that there was no way for the soldiers to
spread out far enough to prevent the sabotage of tracks ahead
while they were protecting workers who were removing cars
or repairing rails closer to hand. They also discovered that by
putting women in the front of the crowd they slowed the engines
that were approaching with soldiers and deputies hanging on the
front and sides. By the time a train was able to move, the men
ahead had finished their work overturning the next boxcar or
damaging the switches. It made the movement of the trains an
inevitable stop and go process.

Colonel Turner had a full train moving north on the tracks
that day. Soldiers were positioned all over the outside of the
train. In addition, Sheriff Arnold had stationed some of the three
thousand deputies he had sworn in. When there were more and
more stops, the officers became more and more impatient. They
had their orders to get the train through to the city by evening.
The Pullman people told me that the military men perched on
the cowcatchers and car tops were fearsome to see. They leveled
rifles while they held bullets in their mouths like some kind of
awful metal fangs. It seemed that everyone knew the prohibition

against firing at civilians had been lifted, so the soldiers were allowed to shoot.

It was at one of the previous stops that someone in the crowd had recognized Stark. The O'Malley children heard and ran home to tell Gracie and Joe. Gracie had been sitting in their shack, not eating, and drinking only water, staring into the darkness ever since Mooney's body had been laid to rest. The children were frightened by her reaction. She started muttering about Stark and Mooney and Stark and her father. She pushed the children aside when they tried to stop her from picking up a pistol that had been owned by their father. They ran after her, but finally gave up. Patrick had seen Detective Whitbread and me at the shed. The children knew the policeman and liked him, despite his past arguments with Gracie Foley. It seemed he had returned more than once, bringing supplies to them since Brian O'Malley had died.

When Gracie arrived at the spot where the crowd had moved to hold up a train once more, she was recognized by some of the people. They egged her on, they later admitted to me with shame on their faces. They said they were just trying to stall the train until they got the signal from the men ahead that they had finished sabotaging a switch. But Gracie was incoherent and when she saw Stark she pulled out the pistol.

The crowd moved away then, but continued to taunt Stark. They accused him of being afraid of a woman, while others distracted the soldiers with rocks and insults. They pulled Stark down off the engine, then stepped away so he could see the gun. The captain in charge also saw it and yelled for the soldiers to protect Stark. But, as they moved in with bayonets, Stark raised his own gun. He was behind the soldiers, who didn't see his action. They said Gracie was screaming by then, the gun wavering in her hands, but Stark just took aim, cold-blooded steady aim. He surely would have killed her, but suddenly Whitbread leapt through the crowd, falling on Gracie and getting between her and the bullet.

The crowd came to their senses then at least, even if the

soldiers didn't. The people from Pullman, and a couple of weary policemen on the edges, commandeered a carriage and got us back to the clinic and Dr. Chapman. By then, Joe O'Malley had disappeared. Detective Whitbread was unconscious, but the doctor was hopeful he would survive. Gracie Foley also seemed to come to her senses then. She followed every direction the doctor gave her quietly and with great skill. She seemed to have awakened from a dream. I thought she would become hysterical back in the same clinic, the same room where we had brought poor Mooney, and where he had died. But she did not. She pulled herself together and helped the doctor, who judged it better to occupy her with commands and keep her with him as he shooed the rest of us out of the makeshift operating room that adjoined his office clinic.

I realized that I still had the burlap bag, with its frightening contents, clutched in my hands and decided to hide it behind a pile of empty boxes in a corner of the storeroom. Then I sat on a barrel and wept. It was a while later that I finally came out of the storeroom, locking it behind me. The young soldier at the door tried to avoid looking at me. He must have heard me weeping. I passed him quickly and went down to the hallway outside the clinic. There were half a dozen Pullman people waiting outside the frosted glass door of the operating room. On a table in the hallway there were the remains of a hasty meal that had been sent up from the grocery below—brown paper with crumbs of bread, and bottles of beer. They looked up at me, but said they were still waiting. There was a mere murmur that could be heard from the doctor and the two women he had helping him in addition to Gracie Foley.

I saw a pile of bloody clothes on the end of one of the wooden benches. They were Whitbread's clothes. Even his bowler hat had been retrieved from the scene and someone had placed it carefully on top of the hastily folded suit. His well worn, but polished, black shoes were on the bottom. I gathered the pile up and took it into the doctor's office. There was a heavy lump weighing down the middle. As soon as I carried it in and put it down on a table, I looked under the hat. It was the detective's long-barreled gun that weighed down the mass. It was lying on the bloodstained shirt they had removed. The shirt was torn through high on the sleeve by the left shoulder. I gulped back a sob, picturing again that moment when the shot rang out, with the acrid smell of the smoke lingering in the air afterwards. I pushed the pile away and sat in the doctor's armchair behind the desk in the corner.

The high windows were open in an attempt to let in some breeze. Outside, the sun was going down and dusk was descending, that dusk that lasts a long time in the summer months. But the air was hot and still.

I thought of Detective Whitbread and how I had first met him in his small office with a window looking onto a brick wall and a poster listing twenty maxims such as: "Never put off until tomorrow what can be done today," and "It is not enough to be honest and lazy." He had been so unexpectedly willing to work with a representative of the university and it was nothing to him that I was a woman. His enthusiasm for the project of collating the Bertillon measurements, that he had been collecting in shoeboxes from all over the city, was immense. He had a great love of the scientific method and a confidence in the ability to improve the condition of people he saw every day.

I soon found out that he did not spend much time in that office. He was hardly ever there when I was. He was always out on the streets of Chicago—sometimes in disguise—finding and arresting those who preyed on the weak. He was the one who was at the Harrison Street station when a murder happened at Hull House on Christmas Day. And he had no fear of going against political interests in the city if he thought they obscured the truth. Many times he had shown that he was incorruptible and indefatigable. He had mentored me in a brusque and efficient manner and I learned more than I ever could have imagined from him.

How could it have come to this, that so useful a man should be sacrificed in this insane occupation of the city by the troops of our own country? I dropped my head in my hands and entered a dream of bad thoughts. There was nothing good I could see coming in the future, nothing but a barreling downhill to disaster. I knew Raoul LeClerc was still out there with a stick of dynamite and that Detective Whitbread would want me to warn someone. But why? What would that do except to release more violence against those who least deserved it? I felt I wanted nothing to do with it any more. I didn't want to help either side. I could not bring myself to tell the army, and without Whitbread, I had no one I could trust.

The doctor came in at last, his arms full of bloody sheets. I helped him to stuff them into a hamper. They gave off the sickening smell of warm blood.

"I think he will live. He is weak from loss of blood. But I think he will live." He went to the table in the back and poured water into a porcelain basin and scrubbed his hands, neck and face. He was in shirtsleeves, with the sleeves rolled up and his suspenders over his shoulders. The ugly scars on his right arm had turned white and he favored that injured hand. The heat had made him tousled and sweat-stained. He turned away and grabbed a towel to dry his face and hands briskly. "What happened out there, Emily?" He stood toweling his hands, waiting for an answer.

I had to gulp back a sob and get control of myself. "It was Stark, again. Again! How can they let him go on like this?" I took a deep breath and told him the whole story, starting when Joe O'Malley had beckoned to me from the alley, through the scene at the brickyard, the race to the tracks, and the hectic scene bringing Whitbread back to the clinic. The only thing I didn't tell him about was the missing dynamite. Why burden him? What could he do? Besides, he already disliked LeClerc and the ARU. I could not bring myself to admit he was right. I still did not believe Raoul would really use that single stick of dynamite.

By the time I had finished, he was sitting behind his desk. His eyes never left my face.

"And the dynamite?"

"Hidden in the locked and guarded storeroom. No one will get to it. But if Colonel Turner knew about that there would be an immediate search and arrest of Raoul LeClerc. Yet, Leonard Stark is allowed to go out and kill people. He has even shot a policeman—he may have killed him—the very policeman who would eventually prove him a murderer. I am sure of it. But he is protected by the sheriff and the army. Will they never stop him? Does he just get to go on and on like this?" I was still on my feet in front of him, walking back and forth in my agitation. "We cannot allow this to go unpunished. He would never allow it—Detective Whitbread would not stand for such injustice. We cannot allow that man to go free. I won't allow it. I plan to go over to Colonel Turner and demand he do something. I was only waiting to hear from you how Whitbread is doing before I go." It was a test. If the army would do nothing about Stark, how could I tell them about Raoul and the last stick of dynamite? Why should I?

"I left Mrs. Foley with him. Seeing to him has calmed her down considerably. She seems to want to. I think it is best for both of them to let her care for him. Not that there is much to do, just make sure no fever takes hold, and wait for his body to heal enough to be able to eat and drink. He is not fit to move to the hospital and, in any case, they could do nothing more for him. I cannot say with any certainty whether or not he will live. We will know more tomorrow."

"How terrible for her if once again her vigil ends in death," I mumbled.

"Terrible for all of us if we lose him."

"I cannot bear it." I wiped my eyes and walked to the window. "And what to do about Raoul LeClerc and Fiona MacGregor? If we hadn't been called away by little Patrick and Lilly, I know

Whitbread would have pursued them. But how can we blame them for a crime that was averted, when that murderer Stark goes free for a crime actually carried out? I am determined—if the colonel will do something about Stark, then I will know he is worthy of trust and I will tell him all. But if, as I fear, he tells me there is nothing he can do about such a murderer, then he will learn nothing from me about what happened in the brick shed." I purposely kept my back to the room, looking out at the street where darkness was falling.

He sighed. "As long as no one was hurt, I suppose you must follow your conscience. I am not sure what good it would do to tell the military now." After that, the doctor was very quiet. Ominously so. I did not want to face him.

I struggled on. "I know it must pain you to learn that Miss MacGregor has been so unwise as to follow LeClerc. Joe O'Malley practically begged her to stay, but I fear she has fled with him. I do not know where. Since Detective Whitbread cannot pursue him, there is no telling how far away they may get. She is very foolish, but I can tell you that Mr. LeClerc can be very . . . engaging, when he wants to be, and Miss MacGregor is very young. She will regret it in the future, I know she will." I turned to see how he was taking it, but he was looking at me with a blank face. "Her illness no doubt clouded her judgment," I said, making excuses for the young woman. What a shock it must be for Stephen to learn what she had been doing with Raoul.

His eyes narrowed as he looked at me. I thought he suspected me of being insincere, but I was doing my best to understand. It seemed to me that Fiona MacGregor had captured his affections in a way that I had never done. And she had let him down, much as Raoul LeClerc had let me down. "Doctor, I am very sorry. I am sure it is a great disappointment to you that Miss MacGregor would act in such a manner."

He sat there squinting up at me in the lamp light. "I am disappointed in Miss MacGregor, but not, I think, in the way that you imagine. Emily, I must trust that you will never repeat what I am going to tell you. When Brian O'Malley was killed, Fiona MacGregor was already with child. She was with child when I first met her, here at the clinic."

"I did not know."

"No one knew. You have heard how Mrs. Foley was treated, even after she married the father of her child. No one knew and she was afraid to reveal her secret."

"But she told you."

"She came to me, to ask me . . . she wanted to find a way to stop the pregnancy, to rid herself of the child. Come, Emily, you are not so ignorant that you do not know there are methods, ways for a woman to rid herself of a child before it is born. Sit down. Of course, I would not consider such a thing. It is terribly dangerous to the woman, at least as dangerous as having the child."

I knew that. Not that it was in any way common in the society in which I grew up. There were always old wives' tales of methods to prevent a child from being born, but they were only rumors to me. On the West Side of Chicago, around Hull House, with so many children and so little to survive on, we had heard of women in dire circumstances who sought such treatments. Miss Addams and Mrs. Kelley took it in stride. They did not condone it, but they were not surprised.

The doctor continued, "I tried to help her. I tried to convince her to confide in her father, but she would not. I put her to work in the clinic, thinking that having her under my eyes I could counsel her. I thought I had convinced her not to seek to rid herself of the child. I am sure I had. Until Mr. LeClerc came along."

I thought of all the meetings I'd had with my committee that Fiona attended, and all the times that we had worked together in the storeroom, and handing out supplies. She had never told me and I had never suspected. "She confided in LeClerc, then? What did he do?"

"LeClerc has an answer for every problem, an easy answer.

Your wages are too low, join the ARU. They still won't raise them, strike. You have a child you do not want, get rid of it. LeClerc took her to someone in the city to end the pregnancy for her."

Raoul had done that—I could not believe it. "Surely he was only trying to help. It is true that it would be hard on a girl like her if it was discovered that she was with child and unmarried. It would ruin her."

"And this would not? They're butchers, the ones who will do this. God knows where she got the money, because it does not come cheap. He took her and had it done, but when they returned she started bleeding. That's when he brought her here. I was able to stop the bleeding, but it is likely that Fiona MacGregor will never be able to bear children again. It is a terrible price."

"Poor Fiona."

"And then you find her helping LeClerc make a bomb. How terrible the consequences of all this. Surely you cannot admire that man, Emily? You cannot excuse him."

I blushed. I had admired Raoul LeClerc once. "I do not, Doctor, I promise you, I do not. But they have been driven to this by the circumstances. Don't you see it? If Stark had not killed Brian O'Malley, he would have married Fiona and they would have had the child together. If Pullman had only supported the model town that he built, so that the people in it could live and thrive, none of this would have happened. Instead, he starves them and hires Pinkerton agents to provoke them further. If only he had continued the course that he started in building the town."

"You are wrong, Emily." He was shaking his head. "As Pullman himself has said, he did not build the town as an act of charity, he built it to make a profit. The very roots of this place are rotten with greed. And LeClerc came to build up the power of the ARU, not for any selfless reason. And MacGregor and the strikers want higher wages. You are the only one whose motives are pure, Emily. You and the other people at Hull House."

"And you, Doctor. Your motives are pure."

He stood up abruptly and turned away from me, fiddling with something on the bookcase behind him. "Not so, perhaps." He turned back to me. "In any case, not enough to remain any longer. I have asked Miss Addams to find someone else for the clinic. I leave next week for Woods Hole in Massachusetts. Your friend, Clara, is already there. There is a summer study program that has a place for me. They have been good enough to hold it open, but I must leave now if I want to accomplish anything this summer. I am leaving."

I was stunned and looked at him open mouthed. But I realized that with Fiona such a disappointment to him, it must be agony to remain. He studied my face as if memorizing it. "I am sorry to disappoint you, Emily. But there is little more I can do here. I can set broken bones to allow them to heal and I can stitch up wounds and help the patient to recover. But I cannot treat the root cause of these problems. They are beyond my help and continuing to watch them is beyond my endurance. There is nothing I can do to stop any of this."

"But there must be justice," I told him. "Stark must not be allowed to get away with all that he has done. Pullman cannot be allowed to win. It is not right that the government should take the side of the owners against the workingmen."

"But they already have, Emily."

"But we cannot stand by and let it happen, we cannot."

He sighed. "What do you plan to do about it?"

I stood up. "I am going to Colonel Turner. He needs to know what happened. The police are reporting to him now. That Stark could shoot a police detective and not have to pay for it is not possible. I am going to Colonel Turner and demand he do something."

"And if he does not?"

"He must."

The doctor began pulling down his shirt cuffs.

"You do not need to accompany me."

"It is the least I can do."

"It is not necessary."

He took his suit coat from the rack and put it on. It must have been warm in the summer evening. "Come." He held the door. I took a deep breath, felt for the heavy weight in my pocket, and marched out the door.

TWENTY-EIGHT

lectric lights illuminated the transformed billiard rooms in the Florence Hotel. Although darkness had fallen, we found Colonel Turner at work in his office, with men still milling about in the outer room. I demanded an interview and Dr. Chapman stayed at my elbow. Corporal Giles seemed a bit in awe of my apparent anger. But he quickly arranged for an interview with the colonel. This time Colonel Turner's coat was unbuttoned, and he was surrounded by maps laid out over his desk. He looked weary and annoyed.

"I heard about the incident. How is the detective, Doctor?"

"We'll know more in the morning. I've done what I can and he's resting at the clinic."

"Has Stark been arrested?" I asked.

"Miss Cabot, as I tried to explain before, it is not our brief to arrest transgressors. Our charge is to protect the property of the United States."

"And the Pullman Company and the railroads," I interrupted.

"Of the United States government, I say. And to ensure the flow of the United States mails. We do not arrest people. The police and sheriff's officers do that, my men merely support and protect them."

"This is how you protect them? A police detective is shot? How is that protecting them?" I demanded.

"Corporal, get Captain Saunders," he barked.

"Yes, sir."

Our corporal returned at double time with another officer.

"Saunders, you were in charge on the engine this afternoon. Dr. Chapman, and Miss Cabot here, say that the police detective,

Whitbread, was shot by one of our men. Tell them what happened."

"Sir, I am very sorry for this but it was a terrible accident. As you know, sir, we were faced by a mob that continued all along the railway line. It became a tedious exercise to remove obstacles placed on the track while saboteurs worked on blocking that further ahead of us. While we were at work, clearing overturned cars or fixing damaged switches, there were members of the crowd out ahead of us causing more obstructions." Colonel Turner moved some of the papers in front of him. He was impatient with the explanation. "At the same time a crowd was placed in front of us, so that when the obstruction was removed we still had to find a way to move the engine through the crowd without actually harming people, which we tried very hard to avoid."

"Yes, yes. But tell them about the shooting."

"We removed the overturned boxcar and were about to move. As usual, the cowardly men in the mob used the tactic of placing women and children in the front, making it even more difficult for us to try to move forward. Usually this lasts until they get some signal from those ahead that the sabotage work has been completed, then they melt away. But we were being cursed, that is the only way to describe it . . . sir, ma'am . . . we were being cursed by the women in the front of the crowd. Our men have been ordered not to reply, but the sheriff's men tend to respond. Mr. Stark . . . " He grimaced as if Stark were a thorn in his side, along with some, or all, of the other so-called deputies. "He and some of the other deputies were engaged in yelling back at the curses from the crowd. Then a particular woman rose up from the crowd and was out in the front, yelling at Stark. I could not hear exactly what was said."

"He shot her fiancé in front of her eyes—in front of my eyes—only three days ago," I interjected.

"I'm very sorry. I did not know that, miss."

"Go on, Captain," Turner erupted. His face was red from impatience and the heat of the summer night.

"Yes, sir. This woman was yelling back at Stark and suddenly I saw her raise a pistol. I ordered our men to move in to protect the deputy, but Stark fired. A man jumped in the middle just at that moment. We had no way of knowing that it was the policeman, sir. And Stark shot in self-defense. The woman held the gun in both hands and had it pointed at him."

"And then?" Colonel Turner demanded.

"We still had the train to protect. The crowd moved in immediately, sir. I could not see exactly what was going on. I had no idea it was the detective who was hit and the crowd quickly carried him off, for medical attention. We continued on with the train, sir. I am very sorry if we should have assisted the detective, but it was only after we stopped the train at Forty-Seventh Street for the night, and I returned here, that I learned it was the police detective that was injured."

"So, you can testify that Stark fired in self-defense?" Turner asked brusquely.

The captain was unhappy. "As I have told you, sir. These deputized sheriffs are a problem. They are coarse and unruly. They drink, although they hide it from us officers. Stark, in particular, refuses to follow orders and is provocative in the extreme, as are the others sent by Sheriff Arnold."

"Yes, yes, I have heard your complaints. But did he shoot in self-defense?"

"I have to say that he did, sir." Captain Saunders turned to me, his face full of regret. "Miss, the woman had a gun that she aimed at him. That he should shoot is only to be expected."

I was infuriated. "Do you mean to tell me you will do nothing? This man killed an innocent bystander, namely Mr. Mooney. Then he shot a police detective. And before that he killed a man and hung him up, with a sign saying he was a spy to try to put the blame on someone else. Then he conspired to plant a bomb in the factory, and you will still let him walk free and ride trains, carrying a gun to kill even more people? Because he is a deputy? You will let him continue?"

The captain was about to try to answer, but the colonel stepped out from behind his desk, with a hand up to restrain him. "Miss Cabot, this matter must be dealt with by the civil authorities *after* we have completed our work of securing the lines so that the U.S. mails may pass unobstructed. We are not here to deal with these matters. We can do nothing about this Stark. I have asked Sheriff Arnold to reassign him, but beyond that, *I can do nothing.* Do you hear me? *Nothing.* I cannot help you."

"I hear you, Colonel. I hear that you have no plan to stop this carnage or help these people. You will make trains run on their tracks and think you are done. But it will all be for naught. All of it." I turned on my heel and marched out. I had already known it was useless. The men in the outer billiard room looked uncomfortable as I passed through. They must have heard what was said, our voices were raised so high. I knew they would attempt to dismiss me as a hysterical female.

It was a relief to get out of the stuffy indoors to the wide porch. I let the screen door bang behind me. But I did not run down the steps and into the night, as I was sure the men inside pictured me doing. I moved, oh so quietly, to my left, to the empty wooden rocking chairs in the shadow of the porch and sat in one outside the open window of Colonel Turner's office. I was careful that the heavy weight of Detective Whitbread's pistol in the deep pocket of my skirt did not knock against the wooden slats of the chair.

I knew from spending some time on the wide porch on the north side of the Florence Hotel, outside the ladies' parlor, that the porch outside the billiard rooms had not been used since the military had taken over that part of the building. I also knew that I was hidden by the shadows. But I could hear what was said in Colonel Turner's office.

" . . . and keep that son of a bitch off the outside of any trains.

Stick him in the baggage car. If I hear that anyone has seen that so-and-so, or that he has been allowed to do any more yelling at the crowds, I'll have your scalp, do you understand?"

"Yes, sir. He's disliked by the men anyhow, sir, but then all of those deputies are. They're drunk half the time." Captain Saunders was trying to defend himself.

"Yes, well, next time shoot one of *them*, will you? Now get out." The captain left without further comment. He must have been happy to get out under from his commander's glaring stare. I could hear Turner move back behind his desk. "Doctor, I'm sorry to have upset the young lady. Of course, she's right. But my hands are tied. I have these confounded local politicians to deal with. That rascal, Stark, is protected by Arnold and there's nothing I can do about it. Whitbread would understand. I hope he comes through all right. He's a good man. Better than most of the local scum who've been assigned to us."

"I hope so, too, Colonel. We will know more tomorrow." There was a pause.

"Was there something more you wanted to say, Doctor?" The colonel sounded impatient.

"Only that—as a medical man—like you, I cannot control who I treat and what is real justice. I could have a man of highly questionable value, someone like Stark, brought to me to be treated and, as much as I disliked or disapproved or even abhorred the man, I would have to treat him."

"Yes."

"But, Colonel, at least in medicine, there is always some discretion. 'To do no harm' is absolutely my oath and my duty. But it can happen that without doing harm there are choices that must be made to do or not to do, to make extraordinary effort or to let nature take its course. I think you know what I mean."

There was silence then. I heard some papers being shuffled. Then more silence.

"In a battle, Doctor, it is often the case that more than one course of action may be possible, and more than one may be perfectly honorable, yet they still present a choice that must be made. I assume that is the type of situation you mean." He did not wait for a response. "Giles."

"Yes, sir." I heard the voice of our friend Corporal Giles.

"Find Stark and send him in to me."

"Yes, sir."

There was no conversation while they waited. Eventually I heard Stark come in. "You wanted me? Eh, sir? Colonel?"

"Mr. Stark, I understand you discharged your gun into a crowd of civilians this afternoon."

"There was a gun pointed at me. I've got witnesses. Your men saw it. There was a gun pointed at me."

"And are you aware that your bullet hit a Chicago police detective?"

"Well, no, sir. I'm sure I didn't know that. Well, that's a shame, sir. But there was that woman with a pistol pointed at us on the train. He must have been trying to stop her. You sure she didn't hit him?"

I felt my heart beat hard in my throat. That man was such a liar, such a cheat.

"That seems unlikely. However, Captain Saunders saw the pistol in the woman's hands and he says it was self-defense." I was looking out at the campground of soldiers, but I could imagine the smirk on Stark's face. "You won't be riding the trains any more. You are to go to the track south of here. The Diamond Special is due to go through soon after nine o'clock and we want to make sure there is no sabotage. You will walk the line between the switch at 117th Street and 130th Street."

"But I've already done my shift for the day."

"Stark, you're under my command per Sheriff Arnold's orders. You follow my orders and patrol that part of the line or, believe me, I will insist that you get relieved of your deputy star and your pay is stopped. Do you understand that?"

"All right, all right. I'm just sayin' . . . "

"I'm not interested in your back talk. Get down there now. If anything goes wrong with the track in that section, you will be out on your ear so fast you won't know what hit you. And another thing—I know some of you like to walk the west track beside the one used by the Diamond. Stay off all the tracks. You can look, you can inspect, but stay off the tracks."

"There's mud and bushes on the side, the track at least is level. A man could turn a foot, twist his ankle, break a leg even."

"I am not asking for your opinion, man. I'm telling you to stay off the track."

"That's just those railroad men thinking their precious . . . "

"No more. You don't question my statements. Get out there now and stay off the tracks or you won't get a cent of pay for your work. Understood?"

"Yes, sir, Colonel, sir." It was a mocking tribute. I could hear Stark shuffle out.

"I have done all I can for you, Doctor. There's nothing more I can do about that man."

"Yes, Colonel. Thank you anyway."

"I hope you can get Miss Cabot to see reason. And I hope the detective is all right. If there is anything I can get for you that would help him, let me know.

"Thank you. I'm afraid there's nothing else to be done. His constitution will have to do the rest."

"Well, that may not be so bad. From what I've seen of him he has the constitution of an ox."

"Yes. There's one other thing, Colonel. I will be leaving Pullman after this week."

"I'm sorry to hear that, Doctor. I understand you've been doing good work down here."

"Thank you. There is one thing you should know about. When the plot to blow up the clock tower was foiled, Detective

Whitbread discovered that there were a few sticks of dynamite that were not recovered. They have been found."

"Dynamite! Why wasn't I told about this? Where is it? Who had it and what were they planning?"

"The detective recovered the sticks before he was shot. They are in the storeroom at the relief station, under lock and key. One of your soldiers is guarding the door."

"The relief station. I suppose it was Miss Cabot who put them there? Do you have any idea how dangerous it is to have such material in the town? Who took it? Was it that ARU fellow they are all complaining about . . . what's his name . . . LeClerc is it?"

"You will have to ask Detective Whitbread, when he is recovered."

"Yes, I'll bet it was that LeClerc. He's quite the ladies' man from what I hear. They'll all go out of their way to protect him. But, if I find out he has been plotting to wreak havoc, I promise you he will hang. There will be no bombs while I am in charge here, Doctor, and no dynamite. Giles, send someone over to the relief station, right away. There's dynamite in the storeroom. I want it found and brought back double time. Take an armed escort. Dynamite! Not while I'm in charge. And bring that Miss Cabot back, too."

"No, Colonel, Miss Cabot knew nothing about it. I took the sticks from the men who had been with Whitbread. They've gone back to town now."

"Gone back to town. A likely story. If my men come back with the dynamite, I'll let it go, Doctor, but if there is any trouble, you can plan to stay here in Pullman until it is resolved. Giles, take the doctor with you and if you don't find that dynamite, bring him back and hold him. Do you understand?"

I felt the heat rising in my throat. I had to grit my teeth to keep from exclaiming. Now they would hold Stephen Chapman, but would allow Stark to roam free. And the doctor did not know that Raoul was still out there with a single stick of dynamite. What retribution would he bring down on all of our heads if he used it? How could I stop him?

I stopped rocking. No one had noticed me on the porch. There was never anyone there, so they did not expect to see anyone. Nonetheless, I held my breath as the doctor came out the door with Corporal Giles and they stopped at the top of the stairs. It occurred to me that if they did by any chance look around, and if they did spot me, I would have to change my plans. I felt the doctor's presence palpably myself and wondered that he did not sense me there, behind him. The corporal started down the steps, calling out for more of his men and the doctor to follow. But Stephen only stared into the darkness, as if looking for my retreating back, then ran down the stairs and out towards the town and the clinic, as if he had seen a trace of me.

Meanwhile, I rose quickly. I had seen Stark leave before him, heading south. I felt the heavy weight of the pistol in my pocket. I had to find Raoul LeClerc. But first I had to deal with Stark.

TWENTY-NINE

I t was easier than I ever would have expected to follow Stark. At first, he was heading south through the town of Pullman, past the Arcade, and the stables. He dallied. Perhaps he wanted to resist the colonel's order, or perhaps it was just to be ornery. The night was dark, without a moon. There was a slight breeze that caused the trees and bushes to sigh a little, rustling with their heavy load of summer greenery.

At the stables he went in to get a lantern to take with him. I could see him talking to a man inside, smoking a cigar with him. Eventually he came out, still smoking. I could follow the scent, even if I couldn't see him. When we got south of the town, he started to walk along the tracks. If I were seen, it would have been cause for remark, a woman walking alone there. Occasionally the yards of houses backed on to the tracks. They were small workers' houses, with fences to partition off the sound and dirt of the trains. Usually though, banks of gravel rose on both sides of the tracks. Four or five multiple lines ran parallel to each other, and every now and then there was a switch box.

There was no one to see me, and it turned out that, on the two occasions when there was another person on guard, I was warned by Stark himself. Meeting one of them was reason for him to stop and pass the time of day, maligning the military with curses and foul-mouthed jokes, so loud it was easy for me to slip by and get ahead of them while they were talking. I waited for him further south and followed after he passed again.

He paid no attention to the colonel's instruction to stay off the tracks. He walked along the outside track—which I assumed must be the extra one, not used by the Diamond Special, which was due to pass on its way to St. Louis. I stayed above the bank of gravel. It was harder walking, as there were unpruned and thorny bushes all along the way. I found it was all too easy to get to the edge and send a spurt of gravel flying down. One time Stark looked back when he heard that, but I expect he thought it was a rabbit or some other small animal.

I assumed that he had gotten to the part of the track he was to patrol when he stopped and used the end of his cigar to light his lantern. Before that, he had found his way by starlight. It was a clear night, even if there was no moon. He used the lantern to do a thorough examination now, as he walked along. I thought to myself that he was afraid of Colonel Turner. Afraid of what he might do if the Diamond Special was wrecked along Stark's part of the track. He was much more attentive to his task than he ever would have let other men know he would be. I followed him for a mile or more before I was confident that no one else could hear us. I was about to confront him when suddenly his lantern went out. He had shuttered it.

I stopped and heard what had caught his attention. There was the sound of scraping and digging. The track carried occasional echoes. Someone was up ahead. Suddenly the light flashed back on. I hurried as quietly as I could and found myself behind the silhouette of Stark, his gun drawn and pointed at Raoul LeClerc, who was crouched beside the tracks. Here several sets of tracks ran in parallel. Raoul was on the second set in. I realized this must be for the Diamond Special as there was the faint sound of a whistle off to the north of us. The train was coming and Raoul was placing the stick of dynamite under the track. He had a spool of fuse long enough to give him time to get away.

"Get away from there," Stark growled.

Raoul finished placing the stick and his face was devilish, in the harsh illumination of the lantern, as he edged away from it. I heard the shriek of a whistle in the distance and the irregular hum that comes from an approaching train.

"Hah, dynamite, is it?" Stark sounded pleased. "Well, isn't that something. The ARU is gonna blow us up. Guess the colonel won't like that a bit. Move away from it . . . over here . . . that's it. Guess I'll be a hero when that blows and I bring you in for it. Just bring that fuse over here a ways, like you was planning."

"No, you can't let it blow up," I said.

Stark pointed his gun at LeClerc, who was still crouched near the ground, but off the tracks now. "Oh, it's you is it," Stark said to me. "Guess you was helping him, wasn't you? Guess that'll teach the colonel about listening to complaints from ladies from the city, won't it. Oh, yes. That'll make me the one with the complaint this time."

"What are you doing?" I could hear the rumble of the train faint in the distance, but getting stronger. "You have to get the dynamite out of there." I started to move towards it, but there was a shot from Stark's gun and the dirt at my feet sprayed up in my face.

"You just stay where you are, missy." He wanted it to explode.

"The train is coming, you can't let it blow."

"Watch me."

"Raoul, how could you? This won't do anything except make Stark look good, don't you see? You'll destroy everything. You'll ruin the strike!"

The light from the train was a pinprick in the distance as the crouching man looked warily back and forth between me and the man with the gun. "It's over. Debs in jail, the army taking over. They won't even remember us without this."

"No." The ground began to shake with the approach of the train and the whistle shrieked much closer now, as the light came towards us.

"That's right, they'll remember," Stark sneered. If they remembered the explosion they would overlook his crimes. "Now, light it."

Raoul bent to do that, striking a match.

"No." I took a step forward, and Stark swung around to aim

at me, as Raoul scrambled up the gravel bank to get away. Stark swung back to fire towards him and began to follow. Just then a doubled-over figure slid down the side and rushed behind Stark as the light from the train grew larger and larger, blinding me for a minute. It was Joe O'Malley. He stamped out the flame of the fuse and jumped towards the dynamite to get it out from under the track. Raoul had gotten away, disappearing into the darkness.

"Nooo . . . you . . . " Stark slid back down the embankment to stop Joe, but I had Whitbread's heavy revolver out and cocked.

I yelled at him, "Stop or I'll . . . " but he turned and lunged towards me instead. His face was contorted with rage as he loomed up at me. I've never experienced such a wave of hatred coming straight at me. He was screaming like a banshee, looked like he would tear me limb from limb. I fired, but he kept coming, like something inhuman, screaming with rage at me. He hated me. I fired again, and again. When he was only one foot away from me, a round black spot appeared on his forehead, and all the muscles in his face suddenly contorted. He dropped to the ground, writhing for a moment, then was silent.

The screech of the train whistle, and merciless clacking of the wheels pounding towards us, reached me through a fog. Joe O'Malley, with the dynamite in one hand, pulled me up the embankment. Before we could reach the top, the train was rushing past down below, and gravel was spitting out at us. Joe pushed me face down, and covered me to shield me from the flying stone. As the train rumbled by in a powerful rush I kept twitching as I pictured Stark coming at me again, in the dark. Like a nightmare, it was inescapable.

Finally, the train was gone and Joe stood up. "Quick, there's another train." He pulled me up by the arm. I rose but suddenly my legs were gone, all sense of them gone, and they seemed to disappear from under me. He pulled and half-carried me over the top and just then there was another rumble of a huge powerful set of cars barreling through the night, only with no whistles or lights, like a ghost of the Diamond Special. Joe pulled me into a crouch and we looked down on it. "But Stark," I said. Suddenly I realized this ghost train was on the second set of tracks, where he had fallen. "Stark." I was appalled and started to get up, but Joe pulled me back down.

"No, come, we must get rid of this, we can't be found with it, don't you see?" He held up the dynamite with the fuse trailing from it. He slid down to the side of the track to retrieve Stark's lantern, then scampered back up and said, "Come."

I looked around but there was no sign of Raoul LeClerc. He had abandoned us without a second thought. I was stunned by the callousness of his actions. Meanwhile, Joe took me by the forearm and hurried me away into the night. Fortunately, he knew this area like the back of his hand. I kept imagining Stark's enraged face and when I would see it, I would run from it. I might have had a hard time keeping up with Joe O'Malley, but I was so determined to get away from that scene on the tracks—to escape the crazed look on Stark's face—that I ran and ran, pausing only when forced to by Joe, who was watchful. He did not want us to be seen. At last we were racing across the mud flats, but in the warm, dry weather they were not muddy, only dusty and cracked. We ran quickly and easily, the warm air rushing past us like a curtain disturbed by the wind. We ran past the huge brick shed and down to the brink of Lake Calumet where Joe propped me on a large rock, half leaning, half sitting. I found myself shaking.

Searching around, he picked up a smaller rock and tied the stick of dynamite to it. Then he took a step back and stretched his arm back for the throw. Incongruously, he reminded me of an athletic figure on a Greek vase. He hurled the rock out into the night and we heard it plop and splash as it landed. Then he doubled over to get his breath.

I was still shaking. "Stark," I said.

"He's gone. That second train is the one that's full of men with guns to protect the Diamond. It runs with no lights on the second track, it would have hit him but they wouldn't notice."

"Oh, God." I retched then. When I was done, he wet his handkerchief in the lake, then handed it to me to wipe my face. I was trembling.

"He killed Mooney," Joe reminded me. "He shot the detective and would have killed Gracie if he could. He would have killed you and me, right there. If the train was wrecked from the blown-up tracks he would have gotten away with it all."

I gulped air. "And Brian—he killed your brother."

Joe straightened up and stepped away from me. "No, not that. 'Twas I killed Brian."

THIRTY

I couldn't believe it, I wouldn't. "But I was sure Stark killed your brother. Brian must have found out he was a Pinkerton man. He was a traitor. He was working on the bomb plot. Surely your brother, Brian, found out and Stark killed him so he could not expose him as a spy and a traitor. He tried to make your brother look like the spy by hanging that sign on him. You told us about the bomb plot. You stopped it before Stark could make it explode. How could *you* have killed your brother?"

He stood in the light shed by the lantern, looking out at the glimmering waves on Lake Calumet. Then he hung his head as he began to speak. "It wasn't about the bomb plot. It was about Fiona. MacGregor and my da were best friends and we all grew up together. Fiona and Brian did love each other, but the difference in religion made it impossible for them to marry. We were used to harsh judgments from my father, and Brian would not cross him. Always one for the straight and narrow, our Brian. Da's death sealed his fate. He would never go against the command of our dead father, who had made him swear to it on his deathbed. He just wouldn't." He sighed. "But Fiona would not accept it. She loved Brian and she tried to make him see it, only he rejected her. She followed him around, like a dog, but she got only insults for her pain. She was such a beautiful young woman with a full heart. How could my sympathy not be moved by the sight of her? I didn't agree with my father's strictness that had driven away his own daughter, or the way my brother was bound by his rules, even after our father's death. So I comforted her."

He looked up, as if searching for my eyes in the dim light, and when I said nothing, he continued. "I always knew it was only in the disappointment of losing Brian that she had me. She never claimed to love me. She always loved Brian. But I was wild to have her, and wild to show her that, where Brian failed her, I could take care of her and love her. I seduced her and in her despair, she clung to me, even while she was whispering my brother's name in her dreams." He looked back out towards the lake. "It was enough for me. I wanted her. But then she found she was with child. I don't know what got into her. She must have known that in his heart my brother still yearned for her. I wanted to marry her. I wasn't like Brian, I was willing to do what was forbidden. But, then, I was the lowest of the low, a brick maker. Not a carpenter, like Brian. Not a metalworker and team leader like her father. There would be no money to live on. She wept and cursed her luck and she refused to marry me. She still had hopes of Brian even then."

He shook his head, continuing on as if he saw it all before him and I wasn't there at all. "She thought she could make him jealous. She knew how much he cared for her. She must have thought if he knew I was with her he would realize how much he wanted her for himself. She did not understand what a man like Brian would do in such a case. She had no idea. She was the one who let Brian discover that we would be in the brick shed together that day. I never thought she would do something so foolish. I think she bribed one of the children to tell him. She must have thought he would be angry enough to beat me up but jealous enough to take her into his arms and agree to marry her. I know Fiona. I know how she thinks. She couldn't be more wrong.

"He found us and he was mad with jealousy. He screamed. He called her whore and other terrible things. She cowered away from him. I stepped forward screaming back at him. I told him what I thought of him and our father. I blamed him for what happened to Gracie, for pushing Fiona away, for denying his heart. I told him he had no heart. He accused me of being a low-down seducer, told me never to come back to the house. He turned to

Fiona. I was afraid he would strike her. I yelled at him that I was leaving anyway and that I was taking Fiona with me because she was going to have my child."

In the dim light I could see tears streaming down Joe's face. I would have interrupted, but he was immersed in his story, as if he had to tell it to someone, and left me no chance to speak.

"He cursed her then and came at me." Joe flinched as if he were picturing it all in his mind. "We fought. We were brothers, we were always fighting, we grew up fighting each other, but this was different. I knew, if he could, he would kill me and I fought back just as hard—hating him for what he had done to me and Fiona and Gracie." Joe's hands were clenched, as if he would strike at something, but there was nothing out there in the darkness. He choked back a sob and turned to face me, his cheeks damp with tears. "Hating him like I did at that moment, I could see he was so much like our da. Still, I never meant to kill him. I never would have killed him. He never meant to kill me either, I know he didn't. But there was no time for thinking and there was only blind rage in that room and we fought and fought until he fell down against the corner of the workbench with a terrible crash. And then he didn't get up." Joe covered his face with his hands for a moment, then he took a breath and looked at me. "I tried to wake him, but he just lay there. I knew then I could never be forgiven. I killed my own brother. I killed him."

"Oh, Joe, how terrible. But why didn't you get help? Why didn't you tell someone? Why did you let him be found . . . like that?" I was thinking again of the body hanging from the rafters in the breeze of that brick shed. The body with the sign "SPY" around his neck. How could his own brother do that to him?

He wiped his tears with the back of his hand. "I would have gone for help, I would have turned myself in. How could I face Gracie and the little ones after what I'd done? But Fiona was hysterical. She yelled at me, she screamed and screamed. What about her? What about the child she was bearing? It was her idea to hang poor Brian's body and put the sign on him to make it seem he had been killed for spying for the company. I didn't want to do it. I tried to refuse, but she screamed at me, tore at my clothes and hair. She threatened to kill herself and the baby. She forced me to hang Brian's body, while she found a board and paint to make the sign. I was in tears. It was such a desecration, but she accused me of killing her as well as Brian. She said I ruined her, and I had to admit I had, so I did what she wanted.

"She pulled me away then and made me promise on the child in her womb that I would not do anything until Brian was found by others. She said her father was bringing visitors for lunch and she had to go and see to it, then she would return and pretend to find him and raise the alarm. She made me promise not to come until the shed was filled with others. So I did. For her, I pretended. For her and the unborn child, I let them all believe Brian was a spy." He shook his head. "As if he would ever do such a thing. But I had to do it to protect her. I had to."

It was a terrible, terrible story. I couldn't help wondering why Fiona had not married him. Were they waiting for things to blow over? Before I could think of a way to ask, he continued.

"She refused to marry me. After all that. She said it was a time worse than ever to be poor, that she would not bear a child, only to see it starve before her eyes. She avoided me. She wouldn't see me. I waited for her anger to subside. I thought I could protect her in the long run."

I wondered if he even knew that she had aborted the baby. He was so sad, I thought he must know. "But why didn't you tell the truth when she refused to marry you?"

"I promised her. I couldn't go back on that, I couldn't hurt her. I thought I could clear Brian's name by finding out who the real spy was. Then I heard Stark was looking for men to sign up and he was paying well. It was easy to make him believe I was desperate enough to do anything. I didn't know he was a

Pinkerton, but I got him to take me on for the bomb plot. But then I couldn't trust the police down here or the company to stop it. The company was behind it. I knew you and your brother could convince the detective to stop it. He wasn't in the pay of the company. At least Stark was exposed. But when I hid in the factory, I saw LeClerc take the sticks of dynamite. I followed him only to see Fiona come to him at his lodgings and stay with him.

"I thought she had refused to talk to me because of what had happened with Brian, but I could see it was because she had transferred her affections to LeClerc. I could see it all then. That was why she had tried to rouse jealousy in Brian. She had hoped to get him to marry her immediately, so when the baby came she could tell him it was his. I saw that now she was trying to do the same thing with LeClerc. Unlike me, he was a man her father admired. Most of the town admired him. She thought her child would never starve in front of her eyes with LeClerc as a father. But I knew he had the dynamite and I tried to warn her. I waylaid her the next day. I told her I understood if she was trying to give our child a better life by getting LeClerc to marry her, but I warned her about the dynamite. If he used it, he would go to jail for sure. She spurned me. She told me she would never ask a man like LeClerc to be the father of my child. He was going to help her get rid of it. She knew about the dynamite. She wanted him to use it. She wanted to help him blow up a train. She warned me that, if I told anyone, she would tell the police how I had killed my brother.

"You know the rest. I tried to stop them by telling you. But when the detective was shot and they got away with one of the sticks, I had to stop them myself. I couldn't find them, but I thought they would try for the Diamond Special. I saw you following Stark, so I thought you knew something. When I saw LeClerc planting the stick, I knew he was trying to destroy the track so the train would derail and it would be a disaster. I had to stop it. At least they couldn't make it seem the strikers had done it. He got away but at least he didn't leave that blame for all the others to shoulder."

"Stark wanted him to blow up the tracks."

"Yes, miss, and he would have killed you to make it happen. He would have killed us both. There's no blame in what you did."

I looked up at his tear-stained face flickering in the lantern light and realized that my whole world had changed from the minute I had pulled the trigger on Detective Whitbread's gun. It would never be the same again.

THIRTY-ONE

Emily, what happened? Come here, let me look at your face." Dr. Chapman was alarmed when I appeared in his office the next morning. I had awoken with a swollen face, my body stiff, and deeply bruised in some places. It was painful to walk. My head ached dully as if a huge pillow surrounded it and pressed against me. I was aware that the cuts on my cheeks, and the bruises around my eye, gave a hint at my injuries from the night before. But I had been careful to cover every other bruise that might give evidence against me. The previous night, Joe had taken me back to the Florence only after convincing me that no one must know about the dynamite on the tracks and the catastrophe so narrowly averted.

"I am all right, Doctor. I merely fell after I rushed from the colonel's office last night. I was angry, and in my anger I managed to trip and fall and injure myself. It was no more than I deserved for letting my temper get the best of me." It was difficult to tell him this outright lie, but I had promised Joe O'Malley, and I knew we had to hide the truth. Still, I felt a little sick, lying to Stephen. "How is Detective Whitbread?"

"He is much improved, Emily. Mrs. Foley stayed with him all night. I've only just sent her home on a wagon with one of her neighbors. She is still calm. Emily, I was so sorry you were unsuccessful in persuading Colonel Turner to do anything about Mr. Stark last night. I have to confess," he gently pressed my bruised cheek as he examined it, "I told them about the dynamite. Colonel Turner immediately sent men to retrieve it. They took it away when I let them into the storeroom. I'm sorry, Emily, but it was much too dangerous to keep it here, you must know that.

I tried to find out where you had gone. Turner can only do what he is allowed to do. He must abide by the rules, even if he does not always agree with them. You must believe that, in the end, Stark will be made to pay for his actions."

I flinched as the picture of Stark's enraged face lunging toward me appeared in my mind. The doctor apologized, thinking he had hurt me. I could not tell him. I was deeply ashamed and frightened by what I had done. I had killed a man. No matter what excuse I had, nothing could change that fact. And what had that death accomplished? Did the death of Stark end the strike? Did it make Pullman the perfect place for working men and women to live in peace and prosperity? Stark was dead and I was only too aware that I had awakened to a world as badly off as when he was alive. We had prevented the dynamite from making the situation even worse, but LeClerc had gotten clear away. How could that be right? I was too ashamed to tell the doctor that. Too afraid of how deeply disappointed he would be if he knew. As he gently felt my face with his long fingers, I wished I had never come to Pullman, that he had never met Fiona MacGregor and I had never met Raoul LeClerc, that we were back at Hull House where he had so kindly offered me his name to protect me from being alone in the world after my mother's death. What a fool I had been to deny him—because of pride. I thought he was feeling pity for me and not a romantic love such as I imagined it might be. And now I felt what a fool I had been. And now I had a secret I could never tell him. I had killed a man.

I pushed his hands away, unable to bear his touch. "I am all right. Can I see Detective Whitbread?"

"If he is awake, let me . . . "

There was a knock on the doorjamb. The door was open. Corporal Giles came in. "Excuse me, Doctor. Colonel Turner sent me to enquire after Detective Whitbread. How is he?"

"He is much improved, Corporal. I believe he will recover. He is in the next room."

"Would it be possible to see him, sir?"

The doctor frowned. "He is very weak. What is it about?"

"It's this, sir." The corporal took a bundle from under his arm and walked to the examining table, where he unwrapped it. It was Detective Whitbread's long-barreled pistol. I let out an exclamation. I had dropped it after shooting Stark. I never wanted to see it again. "You recognize it, miss? It's Detective Whitbread's, we believe. One of the policemen recognized it. It's a special issue, I guess, with this ivory handle. You'll want to know where it was found. It's that man Stark. He's dead. He was found this morning. He was sent to patrol part of the track last night. We keep men all along it for when the Diamond Special goes through. At first, we thought he was careless and got run down. We run a second train on the track beside the Special. It has no warning lights, it runs black and it's got armed men, so if the special gets ambushed they can protect it. We tell all the men to keep off the tracks, but that Stark, he wasn't one to listen. We thought it was his own fault.

"But then we found this, you see, near where he was hit, and when we looked more closely at him, we saw he was shot. He had his own gun, you know, so it's not that he couldn't defend himself. But we found this and they said it's the detective's. We think Stark must have had a gun battle with someone. But we don't know who. He wasn't much of a man, that Stark. So the colonel wanted me to return this to Detective Whitbread and let him know what happened to Stark." He looked down at the gun and wrapped it up again.

I saw the doctor look at the pile of Whitbread's clothes in the corner, but he didn't say anything. He had folded his arms and was thinking. "There's one thing, sir. There's no way Detective Whitbread could have recovered enough to have gone out last night, is there? We didn't think so, but the colonel wanted me to ask to be sure. There's some of the men are saying it's Whitbread who got Stark, you see." He cleared his throat. "There's some think he died and it was his ghost came back to get his man. That's what some of them are saying. The colonel wants to put a stop to it."

"Oh, if that's what you think, I assure you there is no way he could have gotten out of his bed last night. And I am happy to report he is not a ghost. He is very weak but I have every reason to believe now that he will be able to recover. Come, follow me. I'll show you," he said, as he walked out the door. We followed him to the corridor and into the next room.

Detective Whitbread was lying on a cot, breathing heavily. The air was warm, and smelled of sweat and blood. There was a small basin of water, covered with a cloth, on a table beside the bed and I could see the chair pushed away that must have been where Gracie sat all night, tending him.

"He was here all night. We never left him alone, someone was with him, and I was next door. I slept in my office."

Even though Stephen spoke softly, I saw Whitbread's eyes flutter. He cleared his throat and attempted to raise his head. The doctor stepped to his bedside. "Whitbread, you're in the clinic. You are very weak. Don't try to talk."

"Dr. Chapman. Miss Cabot." I stepped to the doctor's shoulder, anxious to see Whitbread's face and reassure myself he was going to recover.

"You were shot at the train siding yesterday," I reminded him.

"Indeed . . . Mrs. Foley. How is Mrs. Foley?"

"She's fine. You saved her. You took the bullet that was meant for her. She was here all night with you. She is fine."

"Very unhinged, going after Stark like that. Should not be left alone." He closed his eyes. It was too much of an effort for him to keep them open.

Dr. Chapman took his wrist and held it. He was checking the pulse. "She's calmed down. Seeing you shot seems to have cured her of her affliction. She tended you all night until I sent her home to the children this morning. She'll be back, I am sure, and you will see. She has regained her senses."

"Stark shot you," I hurried on. "It was Stark again. He was aiming at her."

"This will happen if you aim a gun at a man like that, it must be admitted," Whitbread offered dryly, his eyes still closed.

"Still, that man shot into the crowd again. Colonel Turner wouldn't do anything, but last night Stark was killed. He was hit by a train and he is dead."

"The corporal, here, has come to return your gun, Detective, and to ascertain that you were not there last night to push the man under the train. They're saying it was your ghost that did it," Dr. Chapman told him, releasing his hand.

Whitbread laughed then. It was a dry little cough of a laugh, but a laugh nonetheless. "I regret to say I was unable to pursue the man, although I do—or did, I should say—consider him a criminal. I am happy to report that whatever ghost may have been involved, mine is not yet available for such activities. That is no doubt due to your efforts, Doctor, for which I thank you."

"You are very welcome, but now you must rest. Corporal, Emily, we must leave Detective Whitbread to his sleep. If you please." He shooed us to the door, motioning the corporal to leave the detective's gun on the table at his side.

But Detective Whitbread called out for me. "Miss Cabot!"

I turned back. "About the other matter, Miss Cabot. Did you safely deliver the materials? What we found in the brick shed?"

I reached out to touch his shoulder. "Yes, that is all taken care of. All of it is out of harm's reach. You mustn't worry about it." With a sigh, he relaxed, closing his eyes again.

I followed the others to the door. As the corporal hurried away, the doctor turned to me with speculation in his eyes. He knew that Whitbread's pistol had been in the pile of his clothes the night before. He stared at my face as if counting every pore, every scratch, and every bruise from my supposed fall. I was tired. Perhaps he would see through me and discern the terrible thing I had done. I would never live it down. He shook his head.

But before he could begin to lecture or interrogate me, we heard someone climbing the stairs.

It was Gracie Foley, in her good, green taffeta dress with her dark green velvet-trimmed hat, complete with a jaunty feather, on her head. She wore leather gloves and carried a folded set of stiff parchment papers.

"Mrs. Foley, there is no need for you to return so soon. He is resting. You must be exhausted from your efforts last night," the doctor told her.

She looked back and forth between us. Her face was drawn and weary but determined, as ever. In that she reminded me of Whitbread.

"Joe has left. He has fled." I thought she searched my face in particular and I knew Joe must have told his sister what had happened the previous night. I steeled myself to hear her tell it to the doctor. But she had a different errand. "He left a confession. He wrote it out and he made me promise to give it to him." She nodded towards the door of Whitbread's room. "I must give it to him. I must do it this morning."

"What has he confessed?" I asked, before the surprised doctor could say anything.

She looked at me dully. "'Twas him who killed Brian. 'Twas Joe who killed our own brother. And last night he killed that man Stark, too. "

THIRTY-TWO

I was dumbfounded. The doctor was merely surprised. "It wasn't Stark who killed your brother Brian? We heard that Stark was killed last night—someone from the army was just here—but they didn't know who shot him. Was it really your brother Joe who killed Brian, not Stark? Why?" the doctor asked.

"Stark killed my Mooney," she said sorrowfully, "and he shot the policeman," she nodded at the door. "But he did not kill Brian. It was a bloody tragedy, but it was Joseph who done it. And he saw the detective jump in front of me to take the bullet. He feels he owes it to him to tell him the truth. Joe killed our brother Brian and he'll not have anyone else blamed for that, not even Stark who has enough bloodstains on his soul as will never wash away. Joe did it and he wants the detective to know." She took a step forward, but I jumped in between her and the door.

"Mrs. Foley, Gracie. You can't tell that to Detective Whitbread. He is my friend. He is a good man, a very good man. But he is upright in the extreme. If you tell him that your brother has done this, he will never be able to let it go. He will hunt him down. He will not rest until he catches him. You must see that it is wrong. After all your brother has done, it is Stark who was the most guilty and he is dead."

"I know what happened last night," she told me looking me in the eye and I knew her brother had told her that I was there. "I know that Stark is dead. But what is right, is right. He had to get it off his chest. It is a terrible thing to kill your own brother, Miss Cabot. A terrible thing."

Dr. Chapman had moved behind my shoulder. "In any case, Mrs. Foley, I must ask you to wait to reveal this information to

Detective Whitbread until he is recovered. Come away and think about it for awhile and let him rest."

But the detective had heard us. "Dr. Chapman, is that you? Is that Mrs. Foley? Dr. Chapman?"

The doctor frowned and shook his head. He looked at Gracie. "Miss Cabot is right, Mrs. Foley. If you tell Whitbread what you have told us, he will never forgive your brother. He will never let him alone."

"Dr. Chapman, I hear your voices . . . please."

The doctor opened the door. "Yes, yes, we are sorry to disturb you. Mrs. Foley has returned. But you must rest." Gracie swept past Stephen quickly, settling herself into the chair at Whitbread's bedside. She was a substantial woman, sturdy in every move, but the little green feather at the top of her hat trembled as she opened the sheaf of paper in her lap.

"I have come to bring you a confession."

"Really, Mrs. Foley, I must insist you put this off until later." The doctor tried to intervene but, meanwhile, Whitbread was raising himself on his elbows, trying to prop himself up. Gracie jumped up and shoved some pillows behind his back. As she carefully rearranged herself back in the chair, the doctor murmured, "Oh, really."

Detective Whitbread could barely raise his head on his neck for a few moments. He saw the papers she had placed in his hands and he looked across at her face. His eyes were rheumy with sleep, but I thought I saw a hint of amusement. And of respect. It occurred to me that Detective Whitbread really admired the Irish widow. She had some of his own implacability. It pierced my heart because I knew what was coming and what a rift it would make between them.

"Read it, if you would please," he told her.

She pursed her lips, but she took the pages, smoothing them out on her lap. I could see the carefully shaped, printed letters that were like the ones in the note I had received warning of the bomb in the clock tower. Her bosom rose with a deep breath and she read it out in a loud voice:

I, Joseph Liam O'Malley, of the Dens, Town of Pullman, do swear that, on the tenth of April, I killed my brother Brian O'Malley in the brickyard shed of the Pullman works. It was not planned but done in anger. I will regret it for the rest of my life and surely beyond. For Brian is dead and I can never pay for an act as terrible as killing your own brother.

I can never be forgiven by my family for this but know it came about, not from hatred, but from jealousy caused by love for his woman. I won't name her, for she has done all she can already and nothing I can say will harm her.

I also killed that traitor and murderer, Leonard Stark, with the gun of Detective Whitbread that I took from the clinic last night. He killed my sister's fiancé in cold blood and he tried to kill my sister. I took the gun, followed him, and we fought. He fired his gun first, but I killed him. It is as the Lord wills that he is gone to his deserts and I am sure he burns in Hell where I will someday meet him.

I was stunned. Joe was claiming the death of Stark for himself. He had gone to great lengths to make me promise not to report what had happened the night before. Now I understood. I thought he only wanted to prevent information about the dynamite from ruining the reputation of the strikers in Pullman, but he had planned this all along.

Tears welled up in my eyes as I listened to Gracie read the rest of the letter. He told the story of Fiona and Brian, as he had told it to me the night before, only he said nothing about the fact that she was carrying his child. He told of the awful fight with his brother, and how he had fallen and hit his head and how Joe had disguised the murder by hanging the body with the sign. He didn't mention Fiona's part in that. He did put some blame on his father, and Fiona's father, for preventing the young people from marrying in the first place. Finally he described taking Detective Whitbread's pistol, while people were milling around the clinic after the shooting, and following Stark along the track until he confronted him and they both shot, but Stark missed, and Joe hit his target.

Gracie's voice wavered a little as she read the end of the letter:

I'm confessing to Detective Whitbread to thank him for saving my sister Gracie O'Malley Foley. I hope she will take care of our younger brother and sister, Patrick and Lilly. I will never contact them again. They are innocent and I ask them to pray for me and for Brian and for our da. Except for shooting Leonard Stark, I regret what I did and I will to the end of my days.

Joseph Liam O'Malley

When she finished reading, Gracie took out a handkerchief and wiped her eyes.

"Do you know where he's gone?" I asked. I was concerned. "He wouldn't do anything to harm himself? He wouldn't take his own life, would he?"

"No, no. 'Tis forbidden by the Church. Although he'd no great fondness for the Church—as he says—he would be hard put to go against such a teaching. No, I don't think he would do it. Though I know I'll not be hearing from him again. It was a tearful goodbye. I've a thought he will have gone back to Ireland. It's a sorry place and such a one that would allow him a might of suffering if he's repenting his sins."

Detective Whitbread snorted. "Gone west, more likely. A man can get lost out there and there's plenty of company for those who want to be forgotten. He's gone west."

"You don't know that," Gracie objected.

"I do. We'll have to put out a warrant."

"Not now, you won't," the doctor said, stepping over to remove the pillows behind Whitbread's head. "He needs to rest now. We must leave him."

He looked too ill and tired to object but, just as we were about to leave, the door flew open. It was my brother, Alden.

"Have you heard? They arrested Debs and the heads of the unions. They put them in jail. All the trade unions and fraternities he was trying to get to join the strike have refused. Some of the railroad unions are going back to work, too. They've done it. They've broken the strike."

THIRTY-THREE

H e should be at home in bed." Dr. Chapman shook his head as we watched from a distance. The big, open brickyard shed where so many horrible things had happened was behind us, the wind from the lake whipping through, drying the bricks. We were standing, watching as a wagon was being loaded with all the meager belongings left of the O'Malley's. The doctor had rushed over when he heard, worried about the strain on Detective Whitbread, but we were unnecessary. All the neighbors were helping Gracie and the children load the wagon, while Detective Whitbread sat on the high seat in his bowler hat and woolen suit, holding the reins. "I sent him home yesterday. Apparently he only left because he wanted to tell his landlady that he would be bringing the pack of them."

"He's marrying Gracie and taking in the children, too," I said. It still amazed me.

"I'm not sure he'd take her without the children. And I'm not sure how two such strong-willed people will inhabit the same dwelling. It certainly won't be quiet."

Even from as far away as we were, we could hear Gracie calling out orders. "I'm still so surprised," I told him. "I never thought of Detective Whitbread marrying."

"Why? Because he is so single-minded in his job? It won't change him."

"Nothing can change him."

"Exactly. You should not be surprised. He saw the great injustice of what happened to Gracie Foley and he admired her for not submitting to it, for fighting it, no matter how hopeless the struggle. It is what he would do."

"He is right to admire her. She will do everything she can to take care of him. And she can see how someone so independent needs taking care of. She could see what he needed."

"Indeed. I expect them to be very happy. Or, at least as happy as any couple may be and happier than most. Mrs. Foley, soon to be Mrs. Whitbread, has known much sorrow. It will make any happiness that much sweeter to taste, I think."

I remembered how her first husband had beaten her, and I recalled Mooney, the dapper little man who brought her flowers. "I hope she is happy. Detective Whitbread is a good man."

"He is." We stood watching for a few more minutes. It was about a week after Whitbread was shot and Stark was killed. I had come to the uneasy conclusion that I must let Joe O'Malley's false confession stand. To tell the truth would require explaining about the dynamite and to do that would only harm the remaining strikers. I had many sleepless nights over it, but I could not believe that my stepping forward would do anything but harm, as Joe had feared. Reluctantly, I kept silent.

"You have delayed your departure for Woods Hole." Dr. Chapman had stayed to care for Detective Whitbread. He had not left on the following Monday, as he had threatened. "Will you be leaving now?" In the sudden calm, as after a storm, that followed the breaking of the strike, I was fearful of what it would be like not to see the doctor every day. I had become so accustomed to his presence.

"Soon enough." He was still staring off towards the wagon. The children were being helped into the back, and they were waving goodbye to neighbors, as they prepared to take off. Gracie climbed to the high seat beside Whitbread and took the reins from his hands.

"Doctor, I am so grateful that you have given your time here during this awful strike. I know it was not a happy time for you, and only your very great generosity has been responsible for keeping you here, when you could have been doing your research at Woods Hole. I hope it has not been too disappointing." That word reminded me of our earlier conversation about Fiona MacGregor and I could see him stiffen as if it reminded him, too. It was an unfortunate choice. I hurried on to cover it. "I am so glad you were here, though. For myself I do not know how I could have survived this, if you were not here, and I thank you. We all thank you. You are the kindest, most dependable of men."

He shook himself, then, and turned to face me. "Emily. I once asked you to be my wife and you refused me. I know you believe the offer was made from pity and that is somehow insufficient. A wild enthusiasm or easy intimacy, such as you might find with someone like Mr. LeClerc, appears more like affection to you."

I felt my eyes fill with tears and struggled to keep them from falling. Raoul LeClerc had been such a mistake. I had been so misled by him. But it was my own mistake, my own stupidity and naïveté that had tricked me. He was what he was.

"But there is something I must tell you, Emily. I know you think some great generosity on my part brought me down here to care for these people. You are wrong. I am not that fiercely generous. You somehow came to believe I cared for Miss MacGregor and was disappointed in her actions in running away with Mr. LeClerc, as she seems to have done. You were very wrong about that, all wrong.

"The only reason I came down here and remained all this time was for you, Emily. It was care for you that brought me, concern that you would bruise your heart on the hopes and failures of the people you were trying to help. I wanted to watch out for you. When I saw you attending to LeClerc and admiring him, it was all I could do to keep from lecturing you. But it is not the sort of thing you learn from a lecture. And you are not a child for me to teach. You are a woman for whom I care very deeply—more deeply than I have ever cared for anyone in my life. If you cannot believe in the strength of my affections, then I will never mention them again. But then you must expect me to avoid you at all cost, as it would be too painful for me."

The tears would not be restrained and I could feel them on my cheeks. I felt myself trembling. At last, this was what I wanted, I could see it now. But how could I accept him after what I had done? How could I ever tell him what I had done? I gulped for breath and started to turn away, but he took me by the shoulders and turned me to face him. "What is it? What is wrong?" I shook my head, unable to answer, I felt choked with tears I could not shed. "Emily, Emily." He was shaking his head at me. "It's Stark, isn't it? Joe O'Malley didn't shoot him, did he?"

He held my arms so I had to look him straight in the eye. I could not avoid it. "He said he had been at the clinic and took the gun, but he was never in the clinic. It was you, wasn't it? You took the gun. What happened? Tell me, Emily, tell me."

Before I could answer, I found myself sobbing in his arms. It was such a relief that someone knew. We embraced on that windswept expanse of mud flats and I told him what had happened. He made me see that, while my actions were foolish, there was nothing else I could have done, once Stark attacked me. In the end, I felt more at ease in my heart than I had since the death of my father.

Collapsed in his arms, with the warmth of him encircling me, comforting me, I felt at home. A thrill ran through me. Never had I thought to feel like this. I pushed back and looked up into his kindly face and felt so sad. He looked exasperated. I hiccupped in the most awkward manner. "Knowing what I've done," I blurted out, "you couldn't possibly marry me now."

"Oh, Emily." He lifted my chin with his hand and planted a firm kiss on my lips. I felt his other hand on my shoulder blades pressing me to him. The instinct to resist lasted less than a second before I responded eagerly, wrapping my arms around his neck. I hung on to him, as if he were a life raft in a troubled sea, not wanting the embrace to end. He kissed my neck and hugged me to him. "I will marry you, Emily Cabot. I must, you know." He pulled back, not letting me out of his arms but wiping a few tears from my blubbering face and brushing aside a lock of hair. "We will manage, Emily, I promise you. If Whitbread can sweep away all obstacles, surely we can deal with this. I won't let you lose your place at the university, my dear, you'll see."

I stopped him with a hungry kiss. It was a few more minutes before I asked him breathlessly, "What about Woods Hole?"

"You'll come. Surely you want to come."

"Woods Hole . . . I suppose we could stop in Boston." The world was reeling. I leaned against him, watching the Dens settle back to normal after the departure of the O'Malley clan.

He handed me a white linen handkerchief and I could feel his heart beating in his chest. "It will be all right, Emily. You'll see."

I knew logically there would be heartache and problems, but at last I did not care. It was the beginning, rather than the end, of our personal tribulations, but we would weather many storms together.

EPILOGUE

The strike fell apart. The trade unions had not joined the strike, the ARU leaders continued to be held in jail, and the railroad union workers began to negotiate a return to their jobs. There were rumors that the Pullman factory would soon reopen, but jobs would be offered only at the original pay scale, and those who had been blacklisted would not be rehired. It was bitter to know the same conditions would ruin the viability of the pretty town. There were others, besides the O'Malleys, who were leaving. Something had broken.

Governor Altgeld and Mayor Hopkins demanded an investigation and, later that summer, members of a congressional committee came and listened to endless testimony. But these things take time. It was another year before the General Managers' Association was banned and companies were forbidden to do the kind of joint price-fixing and wage-fixing that they had participated in. It was another ten years before a battle through the courts—that I continued to be involved in—resulted in the decision that the Pullman Company must give up its real estate holdings and sell the houses to the workers instead of renting them.

Even before that, George Pullman died. So hated was he, and so afraid of what people thought of him, that his casket was encased in a wall of concrete to avoid the kind of desecration that he fully expected to be his due, from the people he had wronged in his life. It was a sad end for a man who had the potential to be much loved by his workers. But, even when planning his own burial, he thought there was "nothing to arbitrate." I wondered how far that statement got him in the afterlife, if he pronounced it so finally there. But, at the time of that declaration, the strike was only just coming to a sorry end.

 C3

The reporting of my brother Alden, Nellie Bly, and others forced the government to act, so the congressional committee was eventually able to make some reforms. Miss Addams published a thoughtful essay, comparing George Pullman to King Lear. She concluded that philanthropy would not succeed if it was imposed as if by a king on his subjects. Change comes only with the consent of those who must change—a perfected social order, like that of the planned factory town, cannot be forced upon people. I never heard anything of Raoul LeClerc again. I think he must have gone on to do more agitating, but I have no knowledge of it. Joe O'Malley was good to his word and was never seen in Chicago again. Gracie managed to keep her husband too occupied to allow him to go off in search of her brother, even if he was a murderer. He complained sometimes, but she was ever ready with an argument. He had much to do in his police job in Chicago. Fiona MacGregor I heard of only many years later. She became a prostitute and rose in her profession to the post of madam. It was said that she was wily and her tricks had gotten her ahead of others. They told me she was feared and mistrusted.

I don't suppose she ever contacted her father again. Poor Mr. MacGregor not only lost his child, but was blacklisted as one of the strike leaders. I tried to help him to fight it, but any attempts at legal action only made matters worse. He was forced out of his house and drifted around doing part-time work—always trying to have his condition righted. Several times I saw him at Hull House—he would arrive and carry me off to a corner to tell me, once again, the long and sorry tale of how he had been unfairly treated. I always spared the time to listen for as long as he wanted to talk. For, when it was all told, and even he was spent with the telling, it was still true that he was treated very unfairly. But there was nothing I could do.

HISTORICAL NOTE

R eading the original articles in the *Chicago Tribune,* and some of the later testimony in the report of the congressional investigation, gives a wonderful feel for what people were thinking during the action. There is also a contemporary account, *The Pullman Strike* by William H. Carwardine, a minister in the town, that paints a vivid picture of conditions.

Another important source of information for me was *Touring Pullman; a Study in Company Paternalism,* by the Illinois Labor History Society. This walking guide, which is still available at the Pullman Visitor's Center, gives useful details on the geography of the town at the time of the strike. In particular I learned of the existence of the brickyard, and the brickyard cottages known as the Dens.

The Pullman Strike; the Story of a Unique Experiment and of a Great Labor Upheaval, by Almont Lindsey, was helpful in getting a full picture of what was going on in Chicago, Washington, and the rest of the nation as the ramifications of the strike and boycott spread. There are many other publications and websites about the strike. Over the course of time, I consulted a number of them. I was also able to visit the thriving neighborhood of Pullman as it exists today. The Pullman Visitor Center houses a video presentation and exhibits about the history of the town. I was also able to attend the annual tea at the Florence Hotel and a number of the annual Fall and Christmas house tours of the Historic Pullman Foundation. It is a great place to visit.

Death at Pullman, like the other volumes in the Emily Cabot mystery series, includes a mixture of real and fictional characters. It's always a tricky decision to choose which real characters to include and how to portray them. Real people in this book include

George Pullman, Eugene V. Debs, George W. Howard, Jennie Curtis, and Nellie Bly, as well as Jane Addams. In many places I have quoted or paraphrased things said by these real people that were printed in newspapers or in the compilation of the findings of the congressional hearings published after the strike. In particular, the words of Pullman and Debs at the beginning of the book are from such sources, and the speech of Jennie Curtis is from her own accounts, which are included in the hearings and may be found on various web sites about the strike. What Debs says during his visit to Pullman is drawn from the article "They May Go Hungry", *Chicago Daily Tribune,* May 15, 1894. The words of his speech are quoted from the article "Can Stand a Siege", *Chicago Daily Tribune,* May 16, 1894. The description of how the system was set up at the relief station, and the stories of some of the people of the town, were drawn from "Hunger In Its Wake", *Chicago Daily Tribune*, June 4, 1894.

On the other hand, the dialogue of Jane Addams is imagined, except where I paraphrase a few of her thoughts from her 1896 speech, *The Modern Lear,* which she published as an essay in 1912. She compared George Pullman to King Lear and the workers to Lear's daughters. While Hull House did contribute to the relief effort in Pullman, and Jane Addams did participate in an early attempt at reconciliation, the two face-to-face confrontations with George Pullman are entirely fictitious.

I have to thank Tracy, wife of Centuries & Sleuths bookseller Augie Aleksy, for pointing out that the famous woman reporter, Nellie Bly, came to Chicago to investigate the strike. I consulted Brooke Kroeger's biography *Nellie Bly: Daredevil, Reporter, Feminist,* and found that Nellie did indeed come to Chicago, at first skeptical about the strikers, but extremely sympathetic to their cause by the time she left.

Emily Cabot, her friends, and family are all fictional characters. The O'Malley and MacGregor families of Pullman are also entirely made up, as is the labor agitator, Raoul LeClerc.

Any other Pullman employees, such as William Jennings, are also fictional. The General Managers did have a headquarters in the Rookery building, but the specific characters portrayed are fictional. A Colonel Turner was in charge of the troops, but the character as he appears in this book, along with the other soldiers, is fictionalized. Leonard Stark is also fictional. There was an incident in which a sheriff's deputy shot a bystander. It was recorded in the article "Two Are Shot Down", *Chicago Daily Tribune,* July 7, 1894, but served merely as a suggestion for the events and characters of my story. There was also a report that a plot to bomb a railroad shop was discovered, but, again, that only served as the inspiration for my fictional incident.

The events of the Pullman Strike were extremely dramatic and provided both suspense and conflict as a background for this story. As with the other volumes in the series, I hope this book will remind people of the rich history of Chicago and the people who suffered and struggled to make the world a better place for us to live in, and who are often forgotten. While the outcome of the strike was disappointing—or encouraging, depending on your point of view—it did lead to reforms that made some of the actions that the General Managers had taken illegal, and eventually forced the Pullman Company to leave the real estate business. I found the fact that the federal army occupied a part of a major American city rather an eye-opener, and I know that is not something that any of us thinks would be desirable. But it is important to remember that it *did* happen in the past, and *could* happen again.

CPSIA information can be obtained
at www.ICGtesting.com
Printed in the USA
LVHW092302150219
607775LV00001B/11/P